LAST DAYS
of the
TIGER

Pat Mullan

LAST DAYS of the TIGER

By Pat Mullan

An ATHRY HOUSE book

Copyright © 2014 Pat Mullan

ISBN-13: 978-0615434049
ISBN-10: 0615434045

Cover design by BEAUTeBOOK
*Original photography by Daniel Clauzier at Wikimedia
and Daniele Zedda and rpavich at Flickr*

The *buzz* about *LAST DAYS of the TIGER*

*Here are some of the most recent reviews for Pat Mullan's latest thriller, **LAST DAYS of the TIGER**, (you can read the opening chapter - titled 'Tribunal' - in the anthology **DUBLIN NOIR**, out in the US from **Akashic Books**, and in the UK and Ireland from **Brandon Books**):*

"Pat Mullan's latest, **LAST DAYS of the TIGER**, is a razor blade down the spine. So fast-paced, expect whiplash. This is Irish noir with a hero whom you'll want at your back in any gunfight. Grab a copy and clear your schedule!" **James Rollins, New York Times best-selling author of BLACK ORDER.**

"A high-powered legal thriller chocked full of betrayal, deceit, corruption, and murder. Mullan is Ireland's answer to John Grisham, with a smattering of Ross MacDonald thrown in. **LAST DAYS of the TIGER** will make your head spin." **JA Konrath, author of RUSTY NAIL.**

"Pat Mullan is a natural born storyteller with a gripping, engaging style. He may just be the next big thing in Irish crime fiction." **Jason Starr, author of LIGHTS OUT.**

"**LAST DAYS of the TIGER** bristles with ingenuity, and a plot to kill for ... this is a thriller of such high caliber that it transcends all genres ... has all the Irish gifts: dizzy narrative, sly humor, and marvelous readability. It rocks! **Ken Bruen, Shamus and Macavity Award winning author of THE GUARDS.**

"**LAST DAYS of the TIGER** is a tight, intelligent thriller. Author Pat Mullan blends political intrigue and murder with a unique Irish flavor that goes down smooth. His hero, Ed Burke, is striking – almost an anti-hero in some respects. To unravel the deception and save himself, Burke must test old friendships, and determine who to trust in an Ireland changed by the Celtic Tiger. Mullan writes suspense with an edge reminiscent of Bob Ludlum. An author to watch." **Cerri Ellis, Mostly Mystery Reviews.**

For my brother, Sean, who *'walks and talks'* us through the mist and shows us the sunshine.

LAST DAYS of the TIGER   Pat Mullan

All that is necessary for the triumph of evil is that good men do nothing.

Edmund Burke (1729 · 1797) *Irish orator, philosopher, & politician*

LAST DAYS of the TIGER   Pat Mullan

LAST DAYS
of the
TIGER

LAST DAYS of the TIGER   Pat Mullan

1

Dublin, 8:00 am

There's a buzz about the place. Sure as hell wasn't here when I left twenty years ago. He remembered Dublin as the pits then. Dark, priest-ridden, can't do culture, living on government handouts and money from the emigrants. A god-forsaken hole of a place. For himself anyway. Edmund Burke. *Yeah, that's me. My old man had delusions. Thought if he named me after the great Irish statesman that the name would overcome the bad genes and the lousy upbringing.* Willie Burke had been a failure, failed at every no-risk job he ever attempted, and the old man had ended his days earning a mere pittance as a salesman in a tailoring shop that had seen its best days in the last century. Mass on Sunday was the highlight of his mother's week, a timid woman from the west of Ireland who'd never felt at home in the big city. An only child, Edmund had been conceived as his mother's biological clock was about to stop ticking. She'd been forty-two when she had him.

All these things flooded his mind as he jumped into the taxi at Dublin airport and told the driver to take him to Ballsbridge. He'd survived. Succeeded

10

because his father's failure terrified him. Got into Trinity, earned a law degree, headed for England, stayed a year in a boring clerk job in a London legal firm as resident Paddy. Luck intervened. His mother's uncle in Boston sponsored him to the States. Decided that he'd go by sea instead of air. Took a 28,000 ton liner out of Liverpool. Gave him a sense of being a pilgrim setting out for the New World.

Now he was back. Why? Money, that's why. Well, one of the reasons. He was running away again. But that's another story. Taking a year off from his New York law firm. Had about enough of his mob clients. As well as his ex who wanted to rob him blind. Oh yeah, he'd stashed away a few dollars but still hadn't made that million. Maybe Dublin's the place to be these days. Everybody's here. All these faces in Dublin on a Tuesday and you see them again in New York or L.A. at the weekend. Aidan Quinn. Gabriel Byrne. Liam Neeson. Colin Farrell. Michael Flatley now a household name with Riverdance conquering the world. And Michael O'Leary and Ryanair conquering the skies. The priests are scarce on the ground these days. Divorce is legal. The Bishop of Galway has a love child with an American lover and the President of Ireland has crossed the religious divide to take communion in a Protestant cathedral. The IRA is about to call it quits and the border separating the Republic from Northern Ireland is gradually becoming an imaginary line. Money talks. And money goes where it's well treated.

Money! That's really why I'm here, he reminded himself. *Not here to feel sentimental. Still, the old city looks good, he thought. New roads, new houses, construction cranes everywhere. Plenty of Mercs and*

11

BMWs.   They're not taking the Liverpool boat anymore.   No!   They're in investment banking, working for McKinsey and Microsoft.   Turning Ireland into the largest exporter of computer software outside of the United States.

At Ballsbridge Burke paid the taxi fare and walked up the Shelbourne Road. Dublin 4. The most sought after neighbourhood in Dublin. Bright skies and the early morning briskness countered his lack of sleep. Old stately homes lined the streets. Surrounded by sturdy stone walls, they exuded wealth and power. As a kid this would have been an alien place to him. *Still is*, he thought, as he reached a modern four-storey apartment block in Ballsbridge Gardens. He already had a key, mailed to him in New York before he'd left. Once inside, he realized that he could be anywhere. Luxury that would be right at home on Fifth Avenue. He dropped his bags, started the coffee machine, and minutes later sat in the large Jacuzzi bathtub watching the bubbles welcome him to Dublin.

2

Refreshed and dressed he arrived at Lillie's Bordello at six. The most elite club in Dublin. Had he been here a few nights ago, after the Irish Film and Television Awards, he could have joined Pierce Brosnan and James Nesbitt as they sang Danny Boy at the piano in the VIP room.

This was Murphy's idea. Drop him into the deep end. Meet who's who in Dublin society. Hit the ground running! That's always been Murphy's modus operandi. Murphy was his old law school buddy at Trinity and the reason he'd returned to Dublin. Murphy had built a successful legal business, rich from tribunal money and litigation. Now with more business than he could handle, he'd developed distrust for his partners.

It didn't take much persuasion to tempt Ed Burke back to Dublin. His mob clients were a little annoyed at the moment. One with a bullet behind his ear in a ditch in Westchester. Another behind bars on a federal indictment for corruption.

Jesus Christ! I really could be in New York or LA! The same confidence. The same body movements. Damn it. Even the accents are mid-Atlantic. All the right people at tonight's reception for a noble cause. Charity. Aid for Africa. Medicine for Chernobyl. Sexy stuff. Good publicity for the rich and powerful.

He felt a finger trace its way up his spine, lingered to enjoy, then turned slowly and came face to face with her.

13

"Edmund", she said, moving to within inches of him. The only person, other than his mother, who'd called him Edmund.

Just then Murphy arrived with drinks. "Ah, a reunion, you two...OK! OK!" He protested their stares, handed Burke his drink, and moved on. But the spell had been broken.

"Pia, it's been a long time", said Ed, looking at the woman who had broken his heart. Days and nights of endless lovemaking when they both attended Trinity. Summers in Donegal. Running naked into the sea on the Fanad beach at midnight. Dark, Latin beauty, born in Barcelona, Irish father, Spanish mother. Something Irish flashing through, the same way you'd see the Irish in Anthony Quinn's Mexican face.

"Twenty years, Edmund. You're looking well. If I'd known you were going to be such a success ..." she let the sentence hang in the air as she thought he hadn't aged a day. Trim and erect at six feet with a classic Irish face, fair but tinged with a darker hue, probably from his west of Ireland mother. A few grey hairs only added lustre. And the confidence! *He was always so confident*, she thought, *I can imagine him in the courtroom.*

Ed wanted to hold her, kiss her, take her to that Fanad beach again. His mind spoke to him, *Oh Pia, I loved you so much. And you broke my heart when you left me for that geek, David Manning. Now he's the Minister for Trade and Industry and Tánaiste too, second only to the Taoiseach in the government. Being touted as a future Taoiseach. Speak of the devil.* The man himself approached. *Still the tall, lanky geek I remember. Wearing glasses now and the hair's thinning out.*

"Ed, I see you're back. Good. We need your talent here. Building a great country these days."

14

"Well, I'm looking forward to it, Tánaiste. Had things looked like this twenty years ago I might never have left."

"Well, you're back. That's what matters."

Looking at his wife, he said, "Pia, you and Ed are old friends. Introduce him around. New blood he should meet here." And, with that, he was gone. Working the audience. Consolidating his mandate.

Pia and Ed's fixation was interrupted again by a tall, good looking, sandy haired man who said:

"Pia, aren't you going to introduce me?"

She turned around and looked into the eyes of Tom Flanagan. Tom, who had told her long ago if she couldn't return his love, then he'd be there for her as a friend and confidant at any time. He knew about Pia and Ed Burke and the past. Pia had told him all of that.

"Oh Tom, I didn't know you'd be here", she said, holding his hand between hers and kissing him warmly on the cheek.

"Tom, this is Ed Burke, an old friend. Just back from New York," and looking at Ed, "and Ed, this is Tom Flanagan, a very dear friend."

"Ed, good to meet you. Are you visiting?"

"No, Tom. I'm back. Giving Dublin another try. Who knows, maybe I'll stay this time. Are you the same Tom Flanagan that's giving Michael O'Leary a hard time these days?"

Flanagan's head went back in hearty laughter, "Oh, you've been reading the tabloids. They'd love to create a big drama out of all of this. O'Leary makes good headlines. Always shooting off his mouth. I don't see myself as a warm-up act for him."

"But *FlanAir* has grabbed a share of his market. That's sure to light a fire under him. You're warming him up alright!"

15

"Enough about me, Ed. What are you doing in Dublin?", knowing well that Burke was in the legal profession.

"I'm a lawyer. Joined the firm of an old law school friend. Plenty of tribunal business these days."

"Too much of it. But I suppose we're finally flushing the system of all the gombeen men and their brown paper bag hand-outs. This country has grown up and can no longer be run by people who use it to feather their own nests. The 'nod and wink' people have got to go. So good luck. Make sure you're defending the right people."

Then looking at Pia, he said, "I'm off to Brussels tomorrow. Probably be gone four or five days" and, leaning over, he kissed her and slipped a key into her hand.

"Good to meet you, Ed. I'm sure we'll be seeing more of each other. If you need anything, let me know."

Pia had the key to Tom Flanagan's apartment and they met there the next evening. A bottle of Armagnac, two crystal glasses, and a welcome note awaited them in front of the fireplace.

Ed Burke knew that it was a mistake. But he was addicted. Always had been. In the days that followed he and Pia threw caution to the wind. They were inseparable and indiscrete. Glued together in cosy corners in the best pubs and clubs, unabashedly naked in private saunas. It seemed their passion had only been fuelled by the passing of time.

3

Three weeks after his arrival Ed Burke found himself 'in at the deep end', defending Dan Mortimer, one of Dublin's elite, against a class action suit brought by a rabble of welfare dependent inner city denizens. As Murphy had said, "Good way to announce your presence to the world. This is a case you can't lose. And making an ally out of Mortimer will seal your career. Besides it'll be great PR for our firm." A good quarter of the construction cranes criss-crossing the Dublin skyline bore the Mortimer name in huge capital letters. The new dockland development had Mortimer stamped all over it. But this case had aroused the emotions of the people. The class action suit claimed that Mortimer had illegally acquired derelict inner city land that should have been used for the community and had then used his influence to have it rezoned for commercial purposes. Site development had commenced, excessive noise polluted the air, and cracks had appeared in the foundation of adjacent houses. The suit also claimed that Mortimer had used aggressive tactics to persuade local homeowners to sell and leave so that he could demolish their homes and make way for further commercial usage. Two hungry young lawyers represented the claimants. *Like me twenty years ago,* thought Burke, *idealistic and naïve.* They could not support their case with solid evidence. They promised to produce a witness who would testify that Mortimer had made illegal payments to someone in government to get the land rezoned. But the witness did not show up in court. The judge gave them a second chance. Produce the witness within one week. Otherwise the court finds the claim unsubstantiated.

A late evening wind blew the rain into Burke's face as he stood on the corner awaiting the taxi he'd ordered. It had been a long day in court and he felt uneasy about the whole business. New York was different. There he knew the good guys from the bad guys. Everything was direct. In your face. Here nothing resembled that. Too much grey, too little black and white. This country thrived on ambivalence.

An elderly man approached him. Something familiar searched his brain for a memory, a connection.

"Hello, Eddie."

The 'Eddie' completed the circuit in his brain. He hadn't been called Eddie since he was a little boy. Marty, Marty Rainey. Age now hid the vitality he remembered. Marty had been almost a surrogate father. Often there for him when his own father was down in the pub in the evening.

"Marty! Is it you?"

" 'Tis indeed. Not as supple as you remember. But the old head still works."

"Marty, it's great seeing you again!"

"Eddie, I need to talk to you. It's life or death for me."

Saying it so matter-of-factly took the surprise out of it. The taxi pulled up, saving Ed from looking lost. He insisted on taking Marty home. As the taxi pulled out into rush hour traffic, Marty said:

"I'm your witness."

For a moment Ed Burke was mystified. Then it struck him that Marty's telling him that he's the missing witness at the trial. Ed gripped Marty's arm and looked at him. Marty continued:

"I couldn't show up. They threatened me. Told me that I'd wind up in the Liffey. They meant it, Eddie. I suppose I'm a coward."

"Who threatened you?"

"Thugs! That's who. You don't think they'd do their own dirty work, do you? No, they hired a bunch of thugs who don't give a shite. They'd kill me as easily as look at me."

"Who ordered it?"

"Come on, you know who. You're defending one of them in court. I suppose you're gettin' well paid for that. But you've forgotten where you came from, Eddie."

"Damn it Marty! Don't fucking lecture me! If you're telling me the truth, then you were the bagman for these bastards for years! Selling your own people down the drain!"

"You're right.   I was stupid. Gambling, bookies, the horses. I owed too much and they paid it off. But, believe me, Eddie, I never thought they'd turn our own people out of their homes. I didn't know. Now I want to get them. The bastards. They destroyed me and I want to destroy them."

He reached inside his coat and pulled out a large bulky envelope.

"Everything's in here.   All the evidence. Record of payoffs, who, where, and when.   Bank account statements showing how the money was laundered. There's enough here to start a dozen tribunals. It'll destroy Mortimer and it'll bring down the Tanaiste. He's a corrupt bastard! The word

19

around is that you're pretty close with his missus. Watch yourself!"

Ed Burke sat in silence holding the envelope as though it was a bomb. Which, in a sense, it was. Before he could gather his thoughts, the taxi stopped outside Marty's front door in Harold's Cross. Marty gripped his hand, said "Do the right thing, Eddie", and left.

And Ed Burke did the right thing. He met next day with Murphy and told him that he could not defend Mortimer, told him about Marty Rainey's evidence, told him that they'd have to meet with the judge and turn this evidence over to the court. Murphy reluctantly agreed and insisted that Burke secure the envelope with the firm for safekeeping until they could take it to court. Burke considered this to be sensible advice.

That evening, he waited until everyone had left the office. Then he copied every document in Marty's envelope. He replaced the originals with the copies and lodged the envelope in the firm's safe. He slid the originals into a new envelope and put it in his briefcase. Tomorrow he would take it to his safe deposit box at his bank. Burke did not trust the system. Anyone in the Attorney General's office could be a supporter of the Tánaiste. It would be easy for one or more incriminating document to disappear. So he'd wait. When the evidence got that far and they needed the originals, he'd be glad to provide them.

4

Two nights later, the jarring ringing of his phone brought Ed Burke out of a deep slumber. He growled:

"Yeah?"

"Ed Burke? Is this Ed Burke?"

"What do you want? Do you know what time it is?"

"This is the emergency call service. We have an alert on Martin Rainey. We think he has fallen in his home and can't get up. He needs help. Can you go there now?"

"But I'm not on any alert system!"

"You're on it, Mr. Burke. Mr. Rainey insisted that we call you if he needed help."

Ed Burke decided that he had no choice. Marty Rainey wouldn't have put him on the alert list without a good reason. He confirmed Marty's address with the emergency service, dressed, and called a taxi.

At 3am with no traffic on the streets, the taxi reached Harold's Cross in fifteen minutes and dropped Burke at the end of Marty's street. A neat row of red brick houses wound in an arc ahead of him; houses that cost a few thousand only fifteen years ago now ran into hundreds of thousands. A cat scurried across the street in front of him, breaking the silence of the night.

He found number 27 and rang the doorbell. No answer. He rang it again, holding down the buzzer. Still no answer. Now he stood contemplating what he should do. He knew that he must get inside. Further down the street he saw a break in the pattern of the houses and what seemed to be a large commercial doorway. Counting the houses he reached it and got lucky. A smaller door stood closed but unlocked. He took out his flashlight, opened the door and passed through a dry stone wall, to find himself in an open grassy space at the rear of the houses. Counting back he reached Marty's house. The dry stone wall at the back provided a natural foothold. He climbed up. Marty's house, probably his kitchen, had been extended and took up the small backyard. Its flat roof backed up against the wall. Burke simply stepped onto it, reached up and leveraged himself onto a ledge outside the window on the second floor. His luck held. The window stood slightly ajar. He squeezed inside, shone his flashlight around, and saw that he stood on a landing at the head of the stairs.

Calling out Marty's name, he inched his way down the stairs to the living room. He found the light switch and turned it on. He saw the blood first. Pooled around Marty's head where he lay on his side in the middle of the room. A huge open gash crossed his forehead. Burke knelt down and took his pulse. No sign of life. He turned him over to try CPR and that's when he knew that this had been no accident. Marty's throat had been cut.

Burke waited till the ambulance and the Guards arrived and sealed off the house. As it was a crime scene, Marty would stay right where he lay until the State Pathologist arrived. The Guards took a statement from Burke and he left.

Burke made it back to his apartment by 4.30 AM. Too wired to sleep, he headed for the whiskey. Half a bottle later, he sank into a deep stupor.

5

Ed Burke arrived at the church as the requiem mass was beginning. Marty Rainey's coffin sat at the head of the centre aisle in front of the altar. Ed walked up the side aisle and took a seat midway up, near enough yet apart from the first three rows where Marty's close relatives were seated. *Close relatives, that's a joke,* thought Ed, *I'll bet none of them came to visit him when he was alive; now they're only here to be seen and maybe to hope that Marty left them some money...*

"*Marty, I'm sorry,*" Ed said to himself, "*I shouldn't be thinking like this.*"

Ed Burke reflected that he now only attended church for funerals and weddings. He found it hard to believe that heaven waited for the good and hell for the bad. On the plane over he'd been reading Richard Dawkins' *The GOD Delusion* and he thought that the quotation from Einstein described himself quite well: *I am a deeply religious non-believer.*

Ed's reflections were interrupted. People left their seats and started walking up the centre aisle towards the priest who had was now waiting, at the foot of the altar, to administer the Holy Communion. He looked at the people as they returned to their seats, young, old, some threadbare, some in the best of clothes, all sombre and unsmiling in their attitude of reverence. And he felt lucky. Lucky to have escaped. The mass was over before he realized it. The four pallbearers lifted Marty's coffin onto their shoulders and carried it down the aisle to the waiting hearse outside. Marty's relatives followed and then the rest of the mourners. Ed waited at the edge of his pew as they passed. He didn't notice the red-eyed young man glance in recognition as he passed.

It rained, it poured relentlessly as they buried Marty. People stood in clusters under umbrellas at the graveside as the coffin was lowered into the grave and the priest recited the final prayers. Ed stood apart, in a raincoat with a hood over his head that permitted him a narrow vision of these last ceremonial moments. Nobody knew him here but he was here for Marty. That sufficed.

Suddenly it was over. A life was gone. The people huddled against the rain as they left. Ed turned and bumped into someone. He looked the person in the face and apologised. A young man, oddly familiar to him. It seemed that the young man knew him but didn't speak, just kept moving. And then it hit him. *Denis! Denis Rainey!* Marty's nephew. A kid of thirteen or fourteen when Ed had left Dublin for the States. Must be in his mid-thirties now. And Ed remembered the young boy who loved Marty, and Marty as the uncle who could relate to his autistic young nephew. That's it, remembered Ed; Denis suffered from an autistic spectrum disorder. He was an Asperger. In the minute or two that it took Ed to recall this, Denis had disappeared. Ed looked but couldn't find him.

A missed opportunity, he thought, *I would have really liked to talk to him.*

6

Pia! Pia! Ed Burke agonized about what to do. In days the scandal would break. The Tánaiste's career would crash. In public. And Pia would crash too. Every tabloid would exploit the story. Exploit her!

Thoughts bounced wildly around his head: *I've got to do something. Got to protect her. But how? I could leave again. Go back to the States. Take her with me. Start a new life with her. Agh, wishful thinking! It's too late for us. Pia won't leave Dublin. It's the centre of her world. The entire world comes to Dublin now. So what's the incentive to leave? Why should I leave again? Got to brave this thing out.*

Still Pia must be warned. He must tell her what's coming. Get her to leave the Tánaiste. Get out first. Make the first move. Yes, that's what she must do. And he'd help her. Once he had decided, Burke took action. Called her mobile. She picked up immediately.

"Edmund, it's only nine AM"

"Let's run away together. Now."

"Oh, how I wish."

"Look, it's Friday. I'm off today. Let's go somewhere. Get away from it all. Can you break all your social commitments?"

"Yes! Yes! Yes!"

"OK, great! I'll make the arrangements. Pick you up by noon."

7

Too many days like this, thought David Manning, noting that it was ten after nine in the evening as his driver dropped him at the front gate of his home in Howth, *but it goes with the job.* Solar powered lights illuminated his way up to the front door. *Have to go green, take care of the environment, prevent global warming, set an example as Tánaiste.* Pia's constant harping about the environment invaded his consciousness. He turned the key in the door, entered the hallway and hung his coat in the cloakroom. An energy saving light in the chandelier that hung from the cathedral ceiling above shed just enough light to let him make his way through to the drawing room. Not a sound anywhere. No sign of his beautiful wife greeting him with cocktails and a huge kiss. The way it used to be in the beginning. Now she spent her days elsewhere. Usually in somebody else's bed.

"*Oh, Pia, where are you?*" He yelled to no-one, "*Out screwing your old lover? Is that where you are? You and Burke in some cosy bolthole. Fucking each other's brains out, aren't you? Think I don't know. Or you don't give a shite. That's it, isn't it? Well, it's my house and my money, darling, and there'll be no divorce for you! Not a fucking penny, do you hear me?*"

He threw his jacket on the couch, left his briefcase on the coffee table, walked through to the bar and fixed himself a whiskey. Then he went out through the French doors to the deck where he sank into the cushions of one of the large deck chairs and looked out to sea.

26

Sipping his drink, he let his mind wander: Always wandering to my mother. Those little pictures in my head. Her laughter, her smell, her skin, her touch. Only five years old and I still remember. Waiting and waiting and waiting for her outside the shops. Said she'd be back in a minute. But she never came back. They said I'd been abandoned. But what did they know. Then the orphanage. A prison, a place of abuse and torture, run by a bunch of sadistic nuns and a priest who came around once a week to fondle me. How I hated it and hated them. The two years there seemed forever. Until the Mannings rescued me when I was seven. Hugh Manning, a farmer. Some farmer! Twenty acres of poor land in Roscommon, not enough to support them. So he worked as a labourer at every odd job he could find. And Mary, his wife, who couldn't have kids and couldn't find a baby to adopt. Hell no, all the unwed mothers' babies were given to the nuns to be shipped to places like Australia, never to be seen again. Sweep it under the carpet. No scandals in Holy Ireland! So Mary Manning settled for a seven year-old orphan. My son, she called me. And she promised that I wouldn't have to slave on a poor farm for a living. No, I would get an education. They scrimped and saved every penny so that, at eleven, she could send me off to boarding school.

"Damn!" Manning awoke from his reverie as the glass slipped out of his hand and hit the wooden deck at his feet, spilling the remaining half of his whiskey. He went back to the kitchen, got a fresh one, and returned. And started where he'd left off.

Boarding school! Another prison. Run by priests. Sadists worse than the nuns. Beat us all with leather straps, even if we simply ran across their precious lawn after a ball. Scraps for food while they dined on the best. But I promised myself that

27

I'd show them. And I did, didn't I? Well, they haven't seen anything yet!

He shook himself out of his reverie, finished his drink, took his briefcase from the coffee table and walked down the hallway to his office. Might as well stay ahead of the game, he mused, as he took a sheaf of documents out of his briefcase and sat down at his desk to work on them.

The next evening Murphy met Tánaiste David Manning in Buswells Bar, where all the members of the Dail went for their regular tipple. Manning asked, "What'll it be, the usual?" and ordered two Jamesons with water chasers.

No preamble for Manning, he went right for the jugular, "If he brings me down, you go too"

Murphy said nothing.

"Did you hear me? You go too"

"Goddamit, he's my friend. Isn't there any other way. We could persuade him to lay off"

"Persuade, my ass! Do you realize he's been fucking Pia since he got back."

"I hate to say it but ..."

"Yeah, do you think I'm dumb? I know she's been screwing the world for the past five years. Well, it's over! She won't be making a fool of me anymore"

"What do you mean?"

"Killing two birds with one stone. That's what I mean!"

"Jesus! You're crazy! I want no part of it."

"In for a penny, in for a pound! You knew that! Do you really want to lose the mansion in Howth, the little hideaway in Shady Lane in the Bahamas where you entertain your Caribbean beauties, your yacht and your membership in the Royal Cork ... Fuck no, you don't want to lose any of it.   And you don't want a tribunal looking into everything while you rot your arse in Mountjoy !"

Murphy shut up and gulped down his Jameson.   Just as quickly another, a double, appeared in front of him. He had to admit to himself that there was no way out.   Ed Burke was an investment that he couldn't afford.

8

Burke chose well. *Get the hell out of Dublin,* the first command he issued to himself. *Go west young man,* said Horace Greeley in America. And that's what Burke did. Go west to Galway. He knew exactly where. *St.Cleran's.* Once the Galway home of film director John Huston. Been turned into a most exclusive guesthouse by another famous Irish American, Merv Griffin. Just the place for them, away from their Dublin 4 crowd. Time to tell Pia, time to hold her, time to decide.

After they'd checked in, Ed ordered a beer for himself and a cider for Pia. Looking around, he said, "John Huston must have loved this place. I think Angelica lived here when she was a little girl."

Ed had always been a movie fanatic. When he was eleven or twelve, he used to save every penny to pay for his weekly trip to the cinema. Always American movies.

"Ah, so getting me out here was a ruse. You only wanted to spend the weekend in John Huston's home!"

Ed smiled, reached across and held her hand.

"What's the matter? There's something wrong, isn't there?"

"Yes, I'm afraid so. That's really the reason I brought you here. Get you away from Dublin right now."

Pia squeezed Ed's hand, encouraging him to continue.

"You know I've been defending a very close friend of your husband's in this Barton Tribunal. Mortimer, the developer.   Defending him against charges that he had property rezoned for his own commercial use, evicting people from their homes, among other things. There were charges that he paid off ministers in this government to have the land rezoned.   Charges levelled right at the Tánaiste. It's his ministry and under his watch.   But no-one could get any evidence to help them make any of these charges stick. Until an old friend of mine showed up one evening."

Ed finished his beer and Pia said, "You never told me any of this. Of course I never really asked you what you were doing. I've been so happy being with you these last few weeks."

"I know. But I have to tell you now. That's why we're here.   That old friend *was* Marty Rainey. He was murdered a few days ago!"

"Oh, my god! How? Why?"

"I've jumped ahead of myself.   Marty was supposed to be a witness at the tribunal. A witness against Mortimer. But he'd been threatened and had been afraid to turn up.   He had a lot of important documents.   Pretty incriminating against Mortimer. And others. Maybe even the Tánaiste."

"What happened to the documents?"

"I have them. Put them in the company safe. Murphy'll turn them over to the tribunal."

"But Marty ..."

"I found his body. In his own home. His throat had been cut. It wasn't any robbery or random act of violence. Believe me. It was an execution. I believe whoever did it was looking for Marty's documents. This will all hit the papers in the next couple of days."

"And you think that David ..."

"I don't think it! I'm sure of it. This will point a finger directly at him. He's going to be in a hot seat. And you'll be there with him. That's why I wanted to get you out of there. Get you away before this all blows up in your face."

"I wish I could stay away."

"Listen, it's your choice to make, you know that, don't you? You know what I feel about it."

They talked about the scandal that would break in the days ahead and teased out all their options, all their choices. And Pia agreed to leave the Tánaiste as soon as they returned to Dublin. Brave out the turbulence ahead. They retired early, Pia reminding him that they had run away together.

Much later they noticed the bottle of Chablis, sitting invitingly in a crystal cooler. Into their second glass, Ed began to feel drowsy, a drugged feeling, and saw that Pia had already closed her eyes and had sunk into the pillow beside him. Moments later, he followed her.

9

Ed Burke's eyes hurt. Bad. His head hurt too. Worse. He tried to open his eyes. Couldn't. Sunlight grilled him through the open blinds. Eyes closed, fighting to stay awake, he slid out of bed, stood up, and felt his way to the window. Gripping the curtains, he yanked them closed and then risked opening his eyes. They still hurt but he could see. Turning around, he stopped, halfway between the window and the bed. Pia lay there, naked, one leg dangling on the floor, a trickle of blood from her lips forming a small red pond between her breasts.

Shocked, he stood impaled to the floor. His head throbbed and his heart thumped. He moved, unsteadily, towards the bed and knelt down beside her. Her right arm hung over the edge of the bed. He reached for it, tenderly, knowing that the life had left her. Yet he still felt for a pulse, hoping against hope.

Finally he released her wrist and sank onto the floor. His anguish seemed too much to bear. He rolled over into a foetal position and squeezed his head between his arms, wrapping his hands over his ears, shutting out the world, shutting out the reality that Pia was dead. He howled like a wounded animal. Then the tears came, an unstoppable flow. He suppressed the sounds of his own crying until it

33

became impossible and he cried loudly and inconsolably.

He blamed himself for taking Pia away, to this safe place where they killed her. His infatuation had turned to love in recent days and he had hoped that there might have been a future for them. Now, in the darkness of his soul, he didn't even see a future for himself.

He stayed that way for a long time. Until the shock and sorrow turned to anger. Until his mind emerged from its drugged state.

Drugged! We were drugged! The wine! And they murdered Pia. They're making it look like I killed her. They? No fucking they! Only one person did this, only one person responsible! Manning! I'll get him if it's the last thing I do! I'll get him!

Anger dragged him out of his stupor. Rising to his knees, he gripped the bedside table and pushed himself back on his feet.

Then he reached for the phone.

10

Steam from the mug of hot tea carried the aroma up Jack Clooney's nose. Cupping the mug in his hands he sipped slowly, staring out of the window into the middle distance. Daydreaming, seeing himself out on the golf course. Soon, soon, he told himself. Only six months until he retired. Crime was down, corruption off the front pages, the IRA retiring just like himself. Next six months should be a breeze.

The phone's harsh ring jarred Garda Commissioner Jack Clooney out of his daydream. Reluctantly he put down the mug and answered:

"Clooney"

"Commissioner, Tim Quigley. I had to call"

"Hello, Tim. What's the problem?"

Garda Superintendent Tim Quigley commanded the west. A strong independent leader, Jack Clooney considered him the front runner for his own job when he retired. Tim only called if it was important.

"We've got a situation in Galway. Felt I should warn you. The Tánaiste's wife, Pia, has been murdered. Dead in bed in St.Cleran's. She was here with a lawyer, Ed Burke. He's defending Mortimer in that Dublin case. We're holding him for questioning. This will hit the news. RTE have a team on the way already."

"Jesus Christ! The Tánaiste will be all over us on this one!"

"Yes, that puts us right in the hot seat."

"This Ed Burke. Did he kill her?"

35

"We don't know. We're questioning him now. I'll keep you updated."

"I knew her, you know. Pia. A looker. And you know what the dogs on the street were saying, don't you?"

"Everybody knows. They only had to read the society pages in the papers."

"I expect I'll hear from the Tánaiste soon enough. Keep me informed on this one, Tim. I'll probably have to call a press conference. Damn it. I hate that."

Commissioner Clooney gulped down the last of his tea, almost cold now. *Next six months should be a breeze.* Funny how the world can change with one phone call. What did Robbie Burns say;... *the best laid plans of mice and men ...*

11

"Good evening. This is the RTE six o'clock news. Our top story is the murder of Tánaiste David Manning's wife in Galway. Our reporter, Charlie Crowe, is at the scene. We will now take you to Charlie for his report."

The picture changes from the news desk to an aerial shot of St. Cleran's, the stately Galway mansion where the murder took place. The camera zooms in on the house itself, finally settling on a cluster of people gathered outside the main gates. Onlookers held back by the police crowd reporters from various news agencies. Finally the camera seeks out the familiar face of Charlie Crowe.

"We're standing outside the entrance to St. Cleran's. Once the Galway home of director John Huston, this is now a very exclusive guest house, part of the hotel empire owned by the American entertainer Merv Griffin. And this is where Mrs. Manning was found dead at seven this morning. We do not yet know the cause of death. But we have been informed that she did not die from natural causes. Sources at St. Cleran's have told us that she'd booked in here yesterday, accompanied by a man we now know to be Ed Burke."

RTE News anchor:

"Charlie, what do we know about Ed Burke?"

Charlie Crowe:

"Ed Burke is a solicitor.   Returned recently from America. He's been defending Mortimer in that high profile Dublin rezoning case. I've been informed that he and Pia were old friends, going back to their days together at Trinity."

RTE news anchor:

"Where is Mr. Burke now?"

Charlie Crowe:

"The Gardaí have detained Mr. Burke for questioning. No charges have been made against him at this time."

RTE news anchor:

"Thank you, Charlie. We will return to Charlie for an update later in the programme. Now to other news of the day."

12

Sergeant O'Rourke was a solid man. Square shouldered, square jawed, and square minded too. Only accustomed to dealing with local crime, brawls outside pubs, land disputes between farmers, feuds in the travelling community, traffic accidents, he found himself in completely unfamiliar territory. So he approached Ed Burke with some trepidation.

Burke sat wrapped in the hotel bathrobe. With a curt nod and an awkward greeting, the sergeant pulled a chair in front of Burke and sat down.

"Mr. Burke, I'm Sergeant Tom O'Rourke. Can you tell me, in your own words, what happened here?"

Ed Burke seemed distant, drugged. In shock, he still felt drugged from the wine. But he had clearly heard and understood the sergeant. Took a while to compose himself and answer. The sergeant, a patient man, waited.

"Sergeant, I don't know what happened here."

He took a long gulp of his hot tea and continued.

"Somebody drugged us and then killed Pia."

"And who did this, Mr. Burke?"

"I don't know!"

Sergeant O'Rourke knew that he would get nothing more from Ed Burke. Advising him that he would be taking him to the station for further questions, he waited until Burke got dressed. Then he guided him, under the curious gaze of the staff, out the front door of St. Cleran's and into his car.

Fifteen minutes later Ed Burke found himself in a room at the local Garda station, facing two members of the Special Branch. The Sergeant had briefed them and they picked up where he had left off. One of them did the talking.

"If someone killed Pia, why didn't they kill you too?"

"Don't you think I've asked myself that?"
The detective didn't answer. Just waited for Burke to continue.

"It's a set-up! They wanted to make it look like I killed her!"

"And did you?"

"Goddamnit, I loved her! I brought her here to protect her."

"Protect her?"

"From the media. The madness."

"What do you mean?"

"Her husband is corrupt. I have enough to send him to Mountjoy for life. It'll hit the headlines in the next few days. I wanted to take Pia away from it all."

"Those are serious charges. I hope you can back them up, sir."

"Oh, I can back them up with hard evidence. It's already in a very safe place."

"Are you suggesting that the Tánaiste had his own wife killed? And set you up, as you say, to take the blame?"

"That's exactly what I'm saying!"

"Come on, Mr.Burke. This is all a little far-fetched. You really don't expect us to believe all this, do you?"

"No, I don't. But you'll be arresting David Manning very soon. That I guarantee!"

"And why would he set you up?"

"To get me out of the way."

"Then he must know that you have this evidence on him, mustn't he?"

Burke had to admit the logic of that. But it didn't fit. Manning did not know that old Marty had given him anything. He couldn't ... unless ... yes, yes, that's it! The bastards who killed Marty tortured him before they killed him. And Marty had confessed. Told them he'd given me the evidence. Probably laughed in their faces. Marty would have done that. That had to be it!

"You're right! He knows! Marty Rainey, a key witness to the Barton Tribunal was murdered last week. He gave me the evidence that I have. They must know that. I believe that's why they murdered Marty!"

"But why would the Tánaiste have his own wife killed?"

Again Burke had to consider the implication in their observation. Still in shock from Pia's death, pure emotion and gut feel had taken over. Now he reached into that orderly mind of his for more answers.

"Because power has gone to his head. Their marriage was a sham. Pia led her own life these past few years. With no discretion. I'm sure he was planning to end it all. What an opportunity! No divorce, no sharing of communal property. No drawn out legal battle over assets. He couldn't be sure that Pia wouldn't have done that. And who knows what a trawl through his assets would have uncovered? The millions he's illegally stashed away in the Caymans? This was the perfect solution for him. Kill her! Kill me too? No! That would have been a missed

41

opportunity. Set me up instead. Have me arrested for her murder! Even if it didn't stick, it'd have taken me off the Tribunal. Prevent me from sinking his friend Mortimer. This would destroy my credibility, my reputation, my career. Finish me in the legal profession in Ireland. Why kill me and miss a golden opportunity like that?"

Ed Burke leaned forward, crossed his arms on the table and cushioned his head on them. He had a severe headache and waves of nausea swept over him. Felt like a hangover from a three-day binge. Many years since he had one of those. Must be whatever they put in the wine.

The two Special Branch detectives wrapped it up and left the room. Within fifteen minutes another person entered the room. Alone. Burke looked up to see a tall, good looking, well groomed, 'spit shined', senior Garda officer.

"Mr.Burke, I'm Superintendent Quigley. We have started forensic testing in St.Cleran's. The State Pathologist is examining Pia's body. I expect those matters to be completed in the next few hours. I have assigned a special investigation team. You must know that this case will become the number one priority for the Minister of Justice. The Taoiseach will insist on immediate progress. I am advising you now, Mr.Burke, that you are still a suspect. We will be following up on the allegations you have made against the Tánaiste. And we will give you the rest of this week to turn over the evidence you claim to have. I'd advise you to seek legal representation. As a lawyer, I'm sure you don't need me to tell you that."

Ed Burke nodded. Garda Superintendent Quigley concluded.

"We are releasing you now, Mr.Burke. But we want you to remain available. Do not leave our jurisdiction. Keep us informed of your whereabouts at all times."

With that, he left the room.

Ed Burke found himself in a quandary. He couldn't go back to Dublin and he didn't want to stay in Galway. He needed time to think. To mourn the death of Pia. And to fight back. To plan his revenge. To get Manning and his murderous henchmen.

The shock had anaesthetized him. But it was wearing off and now the pain was coming back. He could feel the tears trickle down his cheeks and he made a promise to himself, and to Pia. *He won't get away with it! If it's the last thing I do, I'll get him! I'll get the bastard!*

Shit, he thought, *I'm beginning to sound like one of my New York mafia clients. I need to lie low for a while. Where? Christ! Where else? Connemara! Of course!*

13

Commissioner Jack Clooney had been right. It didn't take long for the Tánaiste to call. Manning's voice played well, a mixture of loss, sadness, and anger. Too well played, thought the Commissioner.

"I want him charged!"

"If he did it, he'll face justice. I promise you that, Tánaiste."

"*If* he did it! What do you mean '*if he did it*'!"

"We need proof to charge him, to hold him."

"Proof! Didn't Pia die in his bed? What more proof do you need?"

Jack Clooney could see that this Ping-Pong was heading nowhere. So he tried deflecting it.

"We're questioning Burke now. The State Pathologist is examining your wife's body. We have preserved the scene and our forensic people are on it as we speak. Believe me, Tánaiste, I intend to bring your wife's killer to justice. I promise you that."

"Burke is clever. He knows the law and he'll try to weasel out of this. Don't let him get away with that, Commissioner."

"Tánaiste, I promise you. Nobody's going to 'weasel' out of this."

The call ended almost as abruptly as it had begun. Brief and brutal. Two words that described the Tánaiste's call, thought Jack Clooney. He walked over to his golf clubs, stacked in the corner against the wall, picked out a driver, went around his desk to the middle of his office, and practised some swings. Always loosened him up. Broke the tension, helped him think.

And his thoughts troubled him. The Tánaiste's call seemed staged. More of a campaign voice than that of a grieving husband. And more focus on getting Burke than on getting his wife's killer. A vendetta against Burke? Wants to pin Pia's murder on Burke, no matter what. Jack Clooney just didn't buy it. And when he didn't buy it, he knew from experience that something stank ...

He put away the golf club, picked up the phone, and called Tim Quigley in Galway.

14

Burke got the keys to the family cottage from his cousin in Galway, rented a car, and headed west into Connemara.

The cottage overlooking the beach in Claddaghduff hadn't changed in twenty years. That last summer before he went to America. Oh, the inside had been modernized. New kitchen, microwave, oil fired central heating. But the rest remained the same. Even the thatched roof. Few of those left in Ireland. The cottage had been in his mother's family for ages. When he was a little boy, he remembered coming here in the summer time with his mother and father. A cheap holiday that let his mother escape her hated Dublin. How she loved it here. Totally at home. She became a changed woman after a week. A spring to her step, a glow in her cheeks, a sparkle in her eyes. His father hated it here. Hated the isolation, the barren Connemara landscape, the people. Couldn't wait to get back to his Dublin. But Ed always had a good time. Running on the beach, taking riding lessons on the Connemara ponies, learning to swim. It had been a playground for him. A vast playground with no people. He imagined that he was a great Irish King and ruled as far as he could see ...

These memories flooded Ed Burke's mind, almost driving away the pain of Pia's death. He had built a peat fire in the stone fireplace when he arrived. Now the flames cast flickering shadows on the walls and the smell of the peat smoke only intensified the memories.

He stood near the stone wall and watched the sun set over Omey Island.

Next morning the sun woke him. The 16-foot tide was out when he walked on to the beach. A flat half-mile expanse of sand, covered during high tide, interrupted by a few rock clusters, now connected Omey Island to the mainland at Claddaghduff. An island filled with standing stones and stone circles dating from the earliest of times, it had been the home of St. Feichin, who had built an abbey there around the seventh century and lived the ascetic life of a religious hermit.

The bright blue sky and the gentle breeze in the air made him feel that this must be one of the earth's very special places. He set out to walk the short stretch of strand to Omey. He could see the island's Ollabrendan Graveyard outlined in the distance. It rested on an ancient monastic site of St. Brendan the Navigator whom the Irish believe crossed the Atlantic in the sixth century and discovered America. *Just like me*, mused Ed, *but I did it in comfort in the twentieth century and the discovery was personal.* Time to visit and pay his respects.

Soon the sandy beach ended and he climbed the rough grassy slopes of Omey Island until he reached the wall that surrounded the small graveyard. Walking slowly and reverently along the outside of the wall he read the names on the gravestones: Lacey, O'Connor, Clancy, O'Toole, Coyne, McDonagh and Davis until he reached King, his own great-grandfather's grave. He stood now, not in prayer because he didn't believe, but in memory. Memories of his mother bringing him here and passing along the family stories about the Kings, his great grandfather Cathal, or Charlie, who'd stayed in Ireland when his brothers and sisters had fled to the four corners of the earth, the most intriguing tale of Willie King who had gone to Salt Lake City. One letter two years after he arrived there was the last the family had heard of him. *Maybe he was shot in a gunfight, or maybe I have a whole bunch of Mormon relatives now*, Ed speculated to himself. Taking one last look at Cathal King's grave, he turned and started to walk back across the sand to Claddaghduff.

Still devastated by Pia's murder, he determined to let her go this morning. Here, on this beach, his mind seemed to rise above his human existence, making Pia one with even the grains of sand. A good place to say goodbye. Burke wasn't a religious person. He'd shed himself of that. But here, this morning, he felt a spiritual connection.

Picking up a shell from time to time, he examined it and pocketed it or threw it away. At the first cluster of rocks, he stood and looked out to sea and back at the horizon on all sides. New cottages dotted the Connemara landscape, banishing forever the isolation of this place. *Yes, I'm afraid the world has discovered Connemara,* he thought.

15

Detective Tom Buckley faced a crisis. He was a member of the Garda team investigating Marty Rainey's murder. They'd found spots of blood on Marty's coat that weren't his own. DNA results were run against the Justice Department's data base of criminals and usual suspects. A formality that seldom produced results. But this time they hit the jackpot. Perfect match. Johnny Fox. Small time thug, connected to the Martin gang, one of Dublin's notorious criminal gangs. Record as long as your arm. Drug dealing, hijacking, counterfeiting, assault and battery. But never murder. This crime would have been a new departure for him, a step up, a promotion. Buckley remembered Johnny Fox. Didn't think he had the talent to be a hit man. *Fucked it up this time, Johnny, haven't you*, thought Buckley, with a feeling of glee. Couldn't wait to bring the little shit in for questioning. But Johnny Fox was nowhere. He'd gone missing. They did find out that he'd been working in New York, illegally, a year ago. They suspected he'd returned there. Flown the coup till the heat died down. The investigating team reckoned that Fox was sure he'd left nothing behind that would point to him.

They had planned to talk with Ed Burke. He'd found Marty's body. Burke was never considered a suspect. But they felt that he might have some crucial information that he was unaware of. And then the Tanaiste's wife was murdered. And Burke was all over the front pages. The tabloids even suggested that he had killed her.

So Tom Buckley found himself in a dilemma. As far as he was concerned, the whole thing smelled rotten! He knew Ed Burke, had grown up with him on the same street, knew the family, he'd played football with Ed after school. Hadn't seen him in years but he knew something bad was going down.

Buckley hated the Tánaiste. Had always thought he was a cold, ambitious prick. And for good reason. Buckley's mother and father had downsized to a small comfortable home. Quiet street, old neighbourhood, crime-free, good bus connections into town. They were so happy. Until the Tanaiste had the neighbourhood condemned and rezoned for commercial use. Mortimer came in, bought the houses for prices well below market, and then demolished them. That killed his parents. His father died of a heart attack in the middle of it. His mother spent her last days, alone, in a joyless nursing home with old people who sat around every day, slack-jawed, motionless, and dead-eyed

Why would Ed Burke be at the scene of two murders in the space of a week? And he'd been Mortimer's lawyer in the tribunal. *Should I stay out or get involved,* he asked himself. Getting involved would put him in jeopardy. After two sleepless nights, he'd made his decision. He'd talk with Ed Burke. But first he had to find him. It wasn't difficult to get the phone number of Ed's cousin in Galway. He called him immediately.

Ed Burke had poured himself a generous slug of Bushmills and was about to prop his feet up in front of the fireplace when his phone rang.

"Hello, Emmett, what's up?" he asked, recognizing his cousin's voice and knowing that Emmett Joyce wouldn't call only to chat.

"Just had a call from a fellow from your old neighbourhood. When you were a kid. Tom Buckley. He's in the Gardaí, a detective in Dublin. Do you remember him?"

"Tom Buckley? Tom Buckley?", Ed repeated, jogging his memory banks, "yeah, yeah, little red haired kid. Used to play football with me. Haven't seen him since. What does he want?"

"He wants to talk to you. Claims that it's not official. That nobody in the Gardaí know he's doing this. Says he's got important information for you. Wanted to know where you were. I wouldn't tell him. Told him you'd have to make your own decision on it."

"I don't know about this. What do you think? Do you trust him?"

"Trust! How would I know? But he did sound sincere. That's all I can say. I only promised to call you."

"OK. Give him my phone number. Tell him to call me."

Two days later Tom Buckley and Ed Burke came face to face in E.J.King's pub in Clifden. A bustling place, frequented by locals and tourists, it was a bar where the well known could drink alongside the unknown without the slightest hassle.

They'd talked by phone and Tom Buckley had convinced Ed Burke of his sincerity. And of his discretion. And of the risk he was taking.

They wouldn't have recognized each other if they'd met on the street. The years had moulded different people out of the two fresh faces they remembered. Nevertheless they knew. A little easier for Tom because Ed's face had been on the front pages. Tom still had his red hair, sparser and receding now, but still distinctive. And Ed still retained that air of curiosity that set him apart from others.

At the end of a long firm handshake, Ed ordered a pint of Carlsberg for himself and a pint of Guinness for Tom. They retreated to the farthest corner of the pub. It was late morning and there were few people in the pub. Only a couple of local businessmen, in conspiratorial conversation, over their morning coffees at the bar.

Tom Buckley talked about his parents, focusing on their last years and what had been done to them. His hatred for David Manning simmered inside. One day he felt it would boil over. And he sensed this was the day.

"I don't know why you were defending Mortimer. But that's your business. I'll give you the benefit of the doubt. You've been away for the last twenty years. You didn't know all this."

"I'm a lawyer. I don't always defend nice people. You'll have to accept that."

"Whatever, Ed. I'm not here to debate that. I know you wouldn't have killed Pia. Something I know deep inside. But you found Marty Rainey's body. That bothered me. Don't you think it's odd to be at two murders in one week?"

"No, I don't think it's odd. I think it makes perfect sense."

"What do you mean?"

"I'm going to tell you something. For your ears only."

"I'm listening. This conversation, this meeting, never happened as far as I'm concerned."

"Marty Rainey was the missing witness. The one who failed to show up at the tribunal. He had evidence that would have proved Mortimer guilty. It would have put him behind bars for a long time."

"So that's what got him killed?"

"Exactly!"

"And where's this evidence now?"

"It's in a safe place. Right now it may even be on the desk of the Minister of Justice or the Attorney General. Can't be too long before the shit hits the fan. That's why I took Pia away from there. Keep her out of the media glare ... at least until the initial shock wore off."

"So what happened?"

"I think they killed her and planned to have me arrested for her murder. I've told your people that but they think I'm crazy."

Buckley's Guinness had sat almost untouched. Now he reached for it and sipped slowly, taking time to absorb everything. Finally he set the pint down, cleared his throat, and said.

"If the shit is about to hit the fan, you may not need to know what I was going to tell you!"

"Don't make that choice. You know I didn't kill Pia. And you want to get Manning. So give me all the ammunition you can. I'll need it all. Believe me."

"You're right. OK. We know who killed Marty Rainey. We can't find him. If we could bring him in, maybe we could get him to talk. Get him to tell us who hired him. Maybe, just maybe, we'd get lucky, and the trail would lead us to Mortimer, or Manning, or both. I know, I know. It's a long shot. But we'd like to find the little shit."

"And you're going to tell me who it is."

"Johnny Fox. That's his name. A small time gangster. Into everything. But never murder. This is a step up for him. And we think he's skipped town. Left the country."

"Where?"

"Back to New York. He's spent a couple of years over there, working illegally. Got lots of contacts, places to go, I suppose. We figure he's left town till this blows over. I'm sure he thinks there's nothing to tie him to the Rainey killing. But I'll bet he didn't want to be around when we started to ask questions. Reckon we'd pull in every bad egg in town and ask them to account for their whereabouts on the night Marty Rainey died."

"Johnny Fox. Can you tell me everything about him. What he looks like. What contacts he might have in New York. Anything."

"OK. That's what I'm going to do. That's why I came to see you. I figured that if we couldn't get to him, maybe you could. Maybe you could use your own methods of persuasion on him. I don't care how we get Manning. Or who does it!"

16

When he got back to the cottage Ed Burke picked up his mobile phone and called Murphy in Dublin.

"Ed, where are you? You're all over the front pages here. They're saying you killed Pia. What the hell happened?"

"That's bullshit! I didn't kill her!"

"I know that. But nobody else does. The Tánaiste's telling the world that he thinks you killed his wife."

"The bastard! He set me up! Made it look like I'd done it."

"You know what you're saying?"

"I'm saying that he had Pia killed. That's what I'm saying!"

"That's crazy!"

"No, no, think about it. I believe he and Mortimer killed old Marty. They threatened him. That's why he never testified at the tribunal. They knew that Marty had contacted me. They were watching him. So they decided to take him out. Now, suppose, just suppose, that they tortured him into telling them that he'd given me the evidence."

"Jesus!   Your imagination is running away with you. That's wild speculation. They'd never resort to murder. Marty was probably killed by a drug addict who thought he had money under the bed. You know what crime is like in Dublin these days."

"Now, Murph, come on! You know better than that!"

"Well, then, tell me this. If they thought you had evidence against them, wouldn't it have been foolish of them to have framed you for Pia's murder? Surely that would make you use the evidence you have against them. The whole thing would have backfired. So, you see, it doesn't make sense. Think about it."

Ed Burke thought about it. His steely legal mind had failed him. The drugs, Pia's murder, the trauma, he blamed it all.

"Murph, the evidence. Where is it?"

"You told me you had it. I asked you to put it in the firm's safe. Remember?"

"I put it in the safe that same evening."

"There's no evidence in our safe. Maybe you only thought you put it there."

"Jesus Christ! What are you saying? That I'm getting senile or some fucking thing! I put that envelope in your safe. And you're telling me that it's not there! Is that what you're telling me?"

"That's right. It's not there."

"No, no, no! It didn't disappear into fucking thin air! What happened to it?"

"Ed, you never put it there."

Ed Burke couldn't believe this conversation. He took the phone away from his ear and looked out at the water lapping against the beach. Then it hit him!

"Murph, they've got you in their pocket too, haven't they? That's it, isn't it? You're lying to me. You've sold me down the drain!"

"Ed, Ed, you've lost it! Listen to me. Where are you? I'll come and get you."

But Ed Burke had hung up. Murphy was one of them. Why hadn't he realized that before? Murphy couldn't have built his business without being in the club! His business had prospered on the nod and the wink, and money in brown paper envelopes. Murphy had destroyed the evidence. Damn it! That's when Manning had decided to kill Pia and take him out too. He'd say that my accusations were a feeble attempt to avoid a murder charge. He'd promote me as a raving lunatic.

But they were only copies, Burke reminded himself, *they didn't examine them very well before they destroyed them. They underestimated me and I'll make them pay!*

17

Before Ed Burke left his cottage in Connemara he booked an Aer Lingus flight to New York, leaving Dublin Airport at noon.

Five hours later he dropped his rental car off and checked into his apartment in Ballsbridge. He had one very important matter to attend to before leaving for New York. He found the copies of Marty's evidence he'd stashed at the bottom of the closet. He browsed through it, and selected one page. Then he addressed an envelope to Sean Coyne at *The Irish Daily News,* inserted the page, and put a local stamp on the upper right hand corner. Finally, in bold capitals, he wrote *Strictly Confidential* across the top of the envelope. He planned to drop it in the mail on his way to the airport next day.

By noon next day he had passed through the boarding gate at Dublin Airport. Seven hours later he landed at Kennedy Airport in bright afternoon sunshine. He hadn't told the Gardaí that he was leaving the jurisdiction. He was sure they would not have approved.

Two hours after landing and fighting his way through traffic he turned the key in the door to his apartment. He'd kept his apartment on the upper west side. It had been his best investment. Better than the market. He'd lost his shirt there when the dot.com bubble had burst. He hadn't rented it. The mortgage was paid off and he had the monthly maintenance charges automatically debited to his New York account. And his cleaning lady still dropped in from time to time. To keep the dust down.

It was exactly 5 pm New York time, 10 pm Dublin time. He told his internal clock to forget that. It's only 5 pm. Plenty of day left yet. He stashed his suitcase in the bedroom, took a shower, changed into some casual clothes and headed across town to Murphy's on Second Avenue. A pint and shepherd's pie would do fine. And maybe he'd get a lead on Johnny Fox. Tom Buckley had said that Fox might be working as a bartender in one of the out-of-the-way Irish gin-mills that weren't too scrupulous about who they hired, or what they paid.

A damned fine shepherd's pie and two pints of Carlsberg later, Burke watched the place fill up with regulars and business types downing a last pint while they waited for the rush hour traffic to disappear before they headed home to Westchester, or Connecticut, or Long Island.

Half an hour later he spotted the man he wanted to speak to. Mike Kane. Just off the boat from Ireland thirty years ago, he'd leveraged a slave job in a First Avenue pub into the ownership of six bustling Manhattan pubs. He'd sold out two years ago for millions and he didn't know what to do with himself. Spent his evenings from pub to pub, with a group of hangers-on who were only into it for free booze. Mike always picked up the tab. But Mike was no fool. He knew that. He didn't care. As long as he was the centre of attention. He didn't realize that he'd miss being centre stage. In his own establishments he was on stage every night, like an impresario, like a talk-show host. Every night was show-time, every night like the opening of a Broadway show. Yeah, he'd really been in show-business, he reckoned. The pubs were sets to facilitate his nightly performances.

And he was still performing. He had three hangers-on with him tonight as he entered the bar, laughing out loud as usual. Nodding to the bartender:

"Set up a tab for me"

Just then he spotted Ed Burke and pushed his way down the bar.

"Ed! How the fuck are you? Where you been, babe? I've missed your ugly face around town. Somebody told me you'd gone back to the auld sod. That can't be right, can it? I told them no. Told them all you were probably in Vegas, shacked up with some high-flyin' bimbo. Was I right – or was I right?"

"Mike, great seeing you. Can I buy you a drink?"

"Buy me a drink! Are you nuts? You can never buy me anything ever. You saved me from that bitch. Don't you remember? Sued me for half a mill for sexual harassment. While she was putting out for every married customer, male and female, in my establishment. You skinned her alive, didn't you? So, no, the drinks are on me ···· Joe, Joe, another Carlsberg for Ed, and give me a Paddy ..."

He squeezed in beside Ed.

"Was I right?"

"No. I wasn't in Vegas. I was back in Dublin. Doing some business over there. But I'm in a bit of trouble. I need your help. Can we talk?"

"Anything for you, Ed. Let's go back in the corner, away from this throng at the bar.

They took their drinks to a table in the back. Ed reckoned that he'd tell Mike all that he needed to know. Not everything. Only enough to fill him in and bring him on board. Mike had no love for the police or the law in any land. He'd had to pay many of them to protect his business over the years. He regarded them as being rotten to the core. And he believed they were even worse in Ireland. So Ed was not concerned about Mike keeping his mouth shut.

"This Johnny Fox. Tell me what he looks like. And anything else."

Ed told Mike everything he'd been told by Tom Buckley.

"Leave it with me. I'll nose around. Without alerting a soul. Trust me. Meet me back here same time tomorrow. If your man's in town, I'll find him."

Next evening, at 7:30, Mike Kane walked into Murphy's. Alone this time. Ed Burke waited at the back table. He'd disobeyed Mike and had a Paddy on the table for him. An hour later, Ed left with the information he needed. Johnny Fox was indeed in town. Well, almost. He was working in *Hangin'Jacks*, a bar in a real tough neighbourhood in the Bronx.

18

Ed Burke found *Hangin'Jacks* about nine next evening. No point in getting there too early. Might as well wait till they had some customers. Wasn't easy finding the place. Looked like a condemned building from the outside, with graffiti on every inch of the gable wall, even new graffiti covered the old because they'd run out of blank wall space. The front looked grim. Paint flaking front door, with a black glass window on either side, very little light shining through. And not much light inside either. Dim and smoke filled. A few regulars at the bar, a TV showing some football game with the sound muted. *Good,* thought Ed, *I can't stand TVs in pubs, let's hope they leave it muted.*

He had no trouble finding Johnny Fox. He was the bartender. Ed pulled out a stool at the end of the bar closest to the door. In case he needed to make a quick exit. Although the customers didn't look very threatening. A lacklustre bunch, silent drinkers drowning their sorrows.

Two hours later he sat sipping his third Carlsberg. Johnny Fox was known here as 'Gerry'. He'd tried and failed to strike up a conversation with him. 'Gerry' was a man of few words and wanted to remain unknown. At eleven another bartender appeared, chatted briefly with 'Gerry' who then left through a door behind the bar, and reappeared a minute later, head down, hands in pockets, straight out the front door. Ed threw some change on the bar and went after him.

It was dark outside and the street lamp had been broken by vandals. He looked left and right and saw what looked like Johnny Fox's small hunched image almost disappearing into the dark night of the south Bronx. Now or never, Burke reckoned. He ran after him. Not the sound of another soul on the street and Fox, startled, stopped and looked back. Burke, within shouting distance, yelled:

"Gerry, Gerry, wait up!"

He could see Fox hesitate, then turn and run. But Burke, running faster, soon caught up with him. Fox, out of breath, stopped and wheezed.

"What'ya want, man? I don't know you."

"No, you don't Gerry. Or should I say Johnny? Johnny Fox?"

Fox now looked frightened. He tried to make a break for it. But Burke blocked him and they stood there, staring at each other. Then Fox moved back and shoved his right hand inside his jacket. Not taking any chances, Burke jumped him and pinned him up against the old brick walled building behind them. Fox squirmed and kicked Burke in the shins. But Ed Burke was larger and stronger. He put Fox in a neck hold with his left arm and forced Fox's right arm painfully up his back. Fox screamed. Nobody heard. Burke forced him to his knees and found the gun in an inner pocket. He took it out.

"The game's up, Johnny."

"Who the hell are you?"

"Name's Ed Burke. I'm a lawyer. I flew in from Dublin. They want you over there, Johnny."

"For what? I'm clean. They have nothin' on me. The fecking guards. They never get off my case!"

"Don't bullshit me, Johnny. You thought you got away with it, didn't you?"

"Get away with what? What're you talkin' about?"

"Marty Rainey"

At the mention of Marty Rainey's name, Johnny Fox went into a kind of convulsion, choking and coughing. He spluttered:

"You crushed my neck, you fuck!"

"Now you know what it feels like to hang, Johnny. Lucky for you, they don't have the death penalty in Ireland. But there's even worse. You'll spend the rest of your days in one of their best prisons. Then again, maybe you'll get lucky. Become a 'pretty boy' for one of those old grizzlies. You'll really be fucked then, won't you Johnny?"

"They've got nothin' on me. I dunno what they're talkin' about."

Fox had gotten a grip on himself and now tried to brazen it out.

"Oh, they've got you alright, Johnny. Didn't think you'd left a trace behind, did you? Well, you screwed up this time. Must've cut yourself or something because they found a couple of drops of your blood on old Marty's coat."

"That's a crock! That could be anybody's blood."

"No, Johnny. You've heard of DNA , haven't you? They matched the DNA to your blood. They've turned it all over to the DPP. You can expect a warrant for your arrest any day. They know you're here, Johnny. After 9/11 the Americans aren't too happy about murderers coming here. Being Irish won't help you any more. They're gonna lock you up in Rikers – now that's a nice place – till the Gardaí come over and take you back. Then it's life without parole for you, Johnny. Like I said, you'll be fucked. Know what I mean, Johnny?"

"But I didn't do it. I didn't kill Rainey. You gotta believe me. I didn't kill him."

"You were there. You killed him."

"I only roughed him up. I never cut his throat."

"Oh, so some imaginary buddy of yours did it."

"He's not imaginary. Brendan isn't ... ... "

He stopped in mid-sentence, realizing that he'd blurted out the name of his accomplice.

"Brendan, is it? I'm sure the Gardaí will be able to find him, Johnny."

"Fuck you, you bastard!"

"You see, it doesn't matter if you sliced Marty's throat or not. They'll find you just as guilty. You won't be able to blame your buddy and get away with this. There's no way out, Johnny."

Burke still held Johnny Fox in a disabling grip. Now he said:

"Johnny, I'm going to make you an offer. I'm going to let you stand up. You can run if you like. They'll get you. But if you listen to me, I can offer you a deal. What have you got to lose?"

At that Burke let go. Fox crouched for a while and then gradually stood up and faced Burke.

"OK, what's the deal?"

"Simple. You tell me who hired you to kill Marty Rainey and I'll cut a deal for you with the Minister of Justice."

"No shit! You want me to sign my own death warrant."

"Listen to me again, Johnny. I can get you a deal. You tell us everything you know. We'll get you into the witness protection programme. New name, new identity. New life somewhere. Maybe Australia,

Canada. Leave your past behind, Johnny. Personally I'd like to see you suffer for killing Marty Rainey. I'd like to see you behind bars for the rest of your life. But I want the people who hired you even more than I want you. So I'm willing to trade you for them. And I think I can get the Minister of Justice to agree"

"In your fucking dreams!"

"No. They've cut deals like this before. How do you think they solved the Veronica Guerin murder?"

Johnny Fox shut up and stood, hands in pockets, looking at the ground.

"Johnny, I'm keeping your gun. You won't need it. The cops will pick you up soon. You'll be extradited to Ireland. There's no way out. You can't run. And you can't hide. You can only cut a deal. I'll arrange it. Here's my card. That's my Dublin number. I'll be in New York for the rest of the week. I've written the number on the back. I'm going to let you go now, Johnny. I'll see you in Dublin. If you have anything you'd like to tell me before I leave, you know how to reach me."

With that, Burke walked away. At the next block he looked back. Johnny Fox still stood where he'd left him. Cornered. Nowhere to go.

19

Next morning Ed Burke walked down Fifth Avenue, past the Sherry Netherland on his left and Central Park on his right until he reached his ex-wife's new residence. Mordy Stein's penthouse. A self-made multimillionaire, with interests in everything from transportation to textiles, Mordy'd be the partner to give her the lifestyle she craved. *No*, contemplated Burke, *I don't miss Sue but I sure as hell miss my son.*

The doorman greeted Burke and, in answer to his question, held the doors open and pointed inside. Kevin saw him immediately, sprang to his feet, dashed across the foyer, and jumped into his dad's arms.

"Dad, dad!"

"Kevin, God I missed you!"

They stood there in one huge tight hug until Ed released his son and eased him to the floor. He looked different, more grown-up.

"Dad, what's the matter?"

"You look different, that's all. More grown-up."

"Well, I'm ten and a half now, Dad. I'll soon be eleven you know."

"Kevin, I keep forgetting that you're not a kid any more."

"Oh, Dad!" laughed Kevin, taking a mock punch at his father's midriff.

Ed held him firmly around the shoulders and marched him out the door. The doorman was already flagging down a taxi for them. A yellow cab pulled into the curb almost immediately and the doorman held the cab door open for them. Ed slipped a fiver into his hand.

"Where to, folks?"

"Chelsea Piers" replied Ed and turned to Kevin.

"Thought we'd go bowling, maybe get some pizza for lunch. How about that?"

"Yeah, Dad, that's great!"

The cab connected with the street that bisected the park and exited further west. Then they crossed eighth, ninth, and tenth avenues until they entered the highway and turned south. Traffic was light in late morning so they reached Chelsea Piers in about fifteen minutes.

Kevin loved to bowl. Ed remembered him trying to lift the heavy ball when he was a toddler, toppling over, and almost rolling down the lane with the ball.

"Dad, what's so funny?"

"I was remembering the time you rolled down the lane with the ball. How old were you? Three? Four? Do you remember that?"

"I think so," laughed Kevin, "but I think you remember it better than me."

They got their shoes, a lane, two cokes, and Kevin was in heaven. Bowling with his dad. They tossed a coin and Ed went first. He knew when the ball left his hand that it wasn't right. Five pins stood standing. Tried again. Two still left. Kevin was up next. The fingers of his right hand seemed moulded to the ball. Cupping it gently with his left, he strode out and bowled. Didn't hesitate. Didn't think about it. The pins fell and he turned, triumphantly, towards his dad and yelled:

"Strike!"

And that's the way it went. Later, over piping hot pizza, Kevin said:

"That was fantastic!"

"Hey, you whipped me, Kev. You were fantastic. I wasn't."

"Oh, Dad, come on. You had an off day. Don't tell me you didn't enjoy it because you didn't win."

"Just joking, Kev. That's all."

Ed waited until Kevin had polished off two huge slices of pepperoni and then ventured:

"How's school doin'?"

"Aw, it's OK."

"And everything else? Are you OK? How's your mom?"

Ed lumped all these questions together, almost in a hurry to get them over with. He felt awkward and uncomfortable. But he still wanted his son to know that he was there for him. Even if he felt that he'd let him down in some way because he and his mom had split up.

"We're all fine," said Kevin, and then got to what he wanted to know about.

"Dad, are you going back to live in Ireland again?"

"Yes, son. I am. I've got business to take care of there. And it is my country. Just like America is yours."

Kevin gulped down the last of his coke and, almost inaudibly, said:

"I wish you were closer. So I could see you more often."

"Kev, I know, I know. Me too. But I'll be back as often as I can. Maybe you can come over for the summer. Stay with your cousins. Would you like that?"

"Do you mean I could? Do you really mean that?"

"Absolutely! You were only five when you were last there. So you probably don't remember much. But you'd love it. Ask your mom. OK? If it's alright with her, I'll make the arrangements."

They didn't say much in the taxi on the way home. Content to sit close together, absorbing each other's warmth. Ed knew that the loss of his son was almost too high a price. But he and Sue could no longer live together. And he'd never have started a custody battle for Kevin. But he promised himself that Kevin would never lose his dad. He'd always be there for him. He glanced at Kevin and saw the happiness in his son's face. Yes, he wished he didn't have to leave him again. But he'd be brave. No tears, no weakness. He wanted Kevin's respect. Not his pity.

20

The Irish Daily News,
Dublin,
Friday morning, 10:30 am

Sean Coyne glanced at himself in the mirror in the men's room and said out loud:

"You look like shit! Started the weekend too early! You'll never fucking learn!"

He hadn't heard the door open so the next voice bounced through his skull, louder than normal.

"Well, you'd better do something about it. The old man's looking for you. Where the hell've you been? No, no, don't tell me. Not that bimbo again! Why don't you wise up, Sean?"

Coyne turned around to see his friend, Paddy Roche, standing there, zipper open, holding it, halfway to the urinal.

"For Christ's sake, Paddy. Use it or put it away."

Paddy Roche, oblivious, turned to the urinal, and said:

"There's a stack of mail on your desk," and anticipating Sean's question, "and I don't know what

71

McDevitt wants.   That you'll have to find out yourself."

Five minutes later, hair combed, freshener in the eyes, Sean Coyne negotiated the people, desks, and obstacles of the *The Irish Daily News* newsroom and headed directly for the coffee machine, which stood in the corner close to that good looking summer intern's desk. Journalism at UCD. But he could never remember her name.

She smiled at him as he said, "Give me an IV. Hook it up to the coffee machine and let it flow!"

Downing one huge cup, he filled a second and made it to the stack of mail on his desk. Figured he'd browse through it before he faced McDevitt. Mostly junk mail. The usual crap. Keeping the post office in business. Half way through the pile, he reached a large brown envelope, addressed in a neat pen to him, with 'confidential, in large block letters across the top. Can't be junk, I'd better open it, he judged.

He sliced it open at the end and found one large document. A statement of investment accounts managed by Gerry Donley, the Dublin wunderkind, the Irish Warren Buffet. Offshore placements. Ansbacher in the Caymans, Isle of Man, Zurich, elsewhere. Millions! And the names. The rich and famous too! There, near the top of the list, the name Manning. Could be the Tánaiste himself!

He swore as the hot coffee dripped through his trousers onto his thigh and he realized that his hand shook. So he sat back, took a number of deep breaths and made himself relax. He put the document back in the brown envelope and held it, just like a bomb. Which he felt it was. A bomb. And somebody has chosen me to be the bomber, he thought.

McDevitt didn't even look up as Sean Coyne entered; only growled,

"Where the hell you been Coyne? Just 'cause you're a star around here doesn't mean you can come and go as you please."

"I'm sorry, boss!"

"Look, Sean, I don't care what you do in your personal life. That's your business. But once it begins to affect your work here, then I do care. Do you understand?"

"Yeah, I know, I know. What do you need?"

"It's too late now. I sent McTaggart. He's not you but he'll have to do. Homicide, down by the docks."

Coyne said nothing, stood holding the brown envelope, twitching a little. Sam McDevitt's burly look was topped by an ungainly mop of white hair that seemed to be in constant battle with itself, as indeed McDevitt seemed to be with himself.

McDevitt, looking at him, finally gave in and said, "Do you want to say something?"

Sean Coyne got a grip on himself, crossed the distance to McDevitt's desk and handed him the brown envelope.

"I think you should take a look at this."

McDevitt opened it, took out the document, leaned back in his swivel chair and began to read. A couple of minutes later he looked up,

"Where did you get this?"

"It was on my desk when I came in today. Came in the post. A regular stamp. Not registered or anything. And I have no idea who sent it. But it's 'Page One', isn't it? This is the biggest story in months, years. It could bring down the government."

"Easy, easy, Sean. How do we know this isn't a fake?"

"Oh, come on, it looks good to me. Besides, I believe it. We all believe this stuff's been going on, don't we?"

"Even if you're right, I have to be sure. I can't publish this and expose the paper to libel. We'd lose millions. And our reputation. And you and I would be forced to resign!"

Sean Coyne had no quick response. From high elation he now felt low. Ready to scream this at the world from the front page, he had sobered in more ways than one.

"And we can't even ask Donley."

Coyne knew that. Gerry Donley had dropped dead of a heart attack on the golf course at the K Club six months ago.

"So you're not going to publish it then, are you?"

"I didn't say that."

McDevitt got up and walked around his office, circling Coyne, then stopping and coming face-to-face with him.

"I want to publish this. I'd love to break this cabal of corrupt bastards who think the Celtic Tiger belongs in their own private zoo!"

Red-faced, he headed back to his desk, plopped into his chair, reached for the document again and waved it in the air.

"But I must be certain this is not a fake. Look what happened to Dan Rather and CBS in the States. They broadcast that memo about Bush. The one that said he faked his time in the National Guard. Turned out the memo was the fake. They hadn't done their homework. Rather resigned. CBS won't recover for a long time."

He put the document down on his desk and finished the thought in his head.

"Suppose there really had been something fishy about Bush's National Guard service. Just suppose. The Rather fiasco put the kibosh on that, didn't it? I want the best experts to examine this document. Get them for me!"

Coyne was back in McDevitt's office four days later.

"I've had your document examined by experts. Hasn't been messed with, they say. They have ways to detect that. I've also had legal take a look at it."

Sean Coyne felt like jumping up and down in McDevitt's office. But he restrained himself. Raised his fist in a clenched salute instead and growled:

"Yeah! Yeah!"

"Listen, when this hits the street, the shit will hit the fan! Do you understand?"

"Yeah, boss. Sure do!"

"You'll be tempted to talk about it. Don't! Not even in the pub. Especially not in the pub! I know how a couple of pints can loosen you up. Do not do it! Keep your mouth zipped on this one. Refer all questions to me."

"But we can't hide."

"We're not going to hide. We're going to do this like the professionals we are. As soon as the weekend edition hits the street, I'll set up an interview with RTE. And I'll agree to appear on next week's *Prime Time* program with Kate O'Donnell. Believe me, we are not going to hide."

"But the Tánaiste ..."

"The Tánaiste, the Taoiseach, yeah, I know. They'll all be all over me. What do you want me to do? Ask their permission to publish? This is a free country. A free press. We're a democracy, not a dictatorship. It's our responsibility to keep it that way."

"This is war ..."

"Fine! That's what you wanted, isn't it? You can't get cold feet now!"

"I'm not getting ..."

"Sean, I know that. But I want you in the background. These people fight dirty. And there's dirty laundry in your closet. They'll dig it up and smear you all over the place. They'll try to divert attention. Destroy your credibility."

21

Ed Burke's New York to Dublin flight landed on time at 7.30 am. With only a briefcase and carry-on bag he bypassed baggage claim and made it to the taxi rank in less that fifteen minutes. He beat the morning rush hour traffic and, thirty minutes later, the taxi dropped him in Ballsbridge.

He dashed into Tommy's Shop on the corner for some milk, eggs, fresh croissants, and the morning newspaper. Picking up *The Irish Daily News* the headline catches his attention:

IT'S A SMEAR, SAYS TANAISTE.

Reading on he discovers that his document has made the weekend edition.

"Tommy, you wouldn't still have a copy of the weekend *News*, would you?"

"Ah, Ed, are you kidding? That paper flew out of here like it had wings. But you're one lucky sod. One of my regulars went away for the weekend and forgot to cancel his copy. It's here."

He reached down behind the counter, "Do you want it?"

"Tommy, fantastic! I sure do."

Loaded down with his carry-on bag dangling over his shoulder and briefcase in his left hand, and his groceries and paper in his right hand, Ed Burke picked the key out of his apartment door with his teeth and used his shoulder to push it open. Kicking the door closed behind him, he dropped his bags, sat down and spread the weekend edition of *The Irish Daily News* out on the coffee table. The headline proclaimed:

THERE'S SOMETHING ROTTEN IN THIS STATE

No punches pulled there. Better than his hopes. They've not only published, they've gone on the offensive. He scanned the opening paragraph:

We have recently obtained a document showing how large sums of money were secretly moved off-shore to the Cayman islands. Our experts have verified the accuracy of this document....

The red light on his phone blinked at him. He put down the paper and leaned over, continuing to read, while he picked up the phone, entered his password and accessed his messages. Only one, from Tom Buckley: "Ed, call me when you get in. It's very important."

He pressed the dial button and, after three rings, Buckley's familiar voice answered, "Hello, Tom Buckley."

"Tom, Ed. Just got in from New York. Found Johnny Fox. Let's meet and I'll fill you in. So what's so important?"

"I have good news for you. Well, I hope you'll think it's good."

"OK, tell me."

"The results are in on Pia's autopsy. Won't be public knowledge for a couple of days. Pays to be on the homicide team at a time like this. But I thought you should know that it clears you."

There was a long pause on the line. Ed didn't reply and Tom spoke again, "Are you listening? Did you hear what I said?"

"I'm listening."

"Alright, here's what I know.   Pia was suffocated.   With a pillow.   Apparently she wasn't drugged very heavily and she woke in the middle of it. They found abrasions around her mouth, pressure marks. And injuries to her tongue and the inside of her mouth as well. That's what caused the bleeding. So, there's no doubt. She was murdered. But not by you!"

"How do they know that?"

"DNA! They found a couple of hairs on the pillow and they've compared the DNA to you and to all the staff at St. Cleran's. No match. So they're pretty sure they're the killer's. But they don't know who ... "

"That is good news. It'll get the Gardaí off my back .   And maybe those few hairs will wind up strangling the Tánaiste!"

"Pia's body will be released to him later this week."

"Yeah, that's perverse, isn't it?"

"Ed, please be careful. The fact that you're off the hook for Pia's murder doesn't get you out of danger. Anybody who'd kill Pia and Marty Rainey won't think twice about bumping you off. And if you're suspicions are right, then you're a threat to them. Do you understand?"

"No need to tell me that.   I believe they're corrupt and dangerous men. And they are a threat to this nation."

"You can't use this until it's public. You'll undermine me if you do."

"I know that. I'm in your debt. This gives me a head start."

Off the phone, Ed continued to read the newspaper article which ended with the Tánaiste threatening to take legal action against the paper and calling for the Editor to reveal his sources. No-one believed the paper when they said that the source was anonymous.

Oh, yes. Watch this space. Read the next edition! Ed Burke said to himself. *The next edition? Yes, I need to claim that space again!* With that thought dominant, he gulped down the rest of his coffee and left.

Twenty minutes later, he entered the safe deposit vault at his bank and, after he'd retrieved his deposit box, sat in a private cubicle and opened it. It contained only one item, Marty Rainey's document package. He opened it, took out the documents and carefully leafed through them. Finally, he selected two and enclosed them in an envelope he'd pre-stamped and pre-addressed to Sean Coyne at *The Irish Daily News,* with 'confidential' neatly printed in large block letters across the top.

22

Johnny Fox was arrested by the NYPD, brought before a judge on foot of an Irish extradition warrant on a charge of murder. He was remanded in custody in the Tombs, pending his extradition to Ireland. The court offered him legal representation but he refused.

Worthless, he reasoned. *Might satisfy the Yanks' sense of justice but it'd only delay things. They'd still send him back to Dublin.   Besides, Mountjoy was a lot better than this hell hole. No, he decided he'd contact Ed Burke. Go for that witness protection deal he'd promised. Yeah, that's the way to go. No way was he goin' to let them hang him out to dry on this one.*

Allowed one phone call to his lawyer, Fox called Edmund Burke. Tried the New York number but he was no longer there. The answering machine referred him to the Dublin number. 7pm New York time would be midnight in Dublin. He decided to call Dublin anyway. But, as he expected, he was greeted by another answering machine. This time he left a message: *This is Johnny Fox. They got me. The*

*Guards are coming over to take me back. I want to do
that deal you talked about. OK?*

Ed Burke filled his coffee mug for the third time
before he felt awake enough to check his phone
messages:

*"You have three new messages. First message
received yesterday at three thirty-two pm ...."*

Some telephone sales person with another
telephone sales pitch. *Seems like there's a new
entrant into the market every day*, he mused. Second
call came from the same sales person two hours later.
Sure are a persistent bunch, Burke said out loud. The
third call, at 12.04 am, brought him fully awake:

"This is Johnny Fox. They got me ..."

"No shit, Johnny. Didn't I tell you?" shouted
Burke to no-one, and then reflected, *OK, maybe we'll
get somewhere at last. If Fox talks. Got to get him a
deal ...*

Minister of Justice Brian Cosgrave looked across his
desk at Ed Burke.
    "If I didn't know you from law school, you
wouldn't be sitting there today."
    "I know that. And I know that I'm a hot topic
today. But, believe me, you won't regret having seen
me."
    "You said it was about this Johnny Fox. The
man we're extraditing from New York for the murder
of Martin Rainey."

"That's right. But he's a nobody. A hired hand. I thought you'd want to get the real murderer. The person who hired Fox and his accomplice."

"What're you trying to tell me?"

"OK, cards on the table. I've talked to Johnny Fox. He wants me to represent him. I want him to tell us who hired him. But he won't talk unless he gets a deal."

"A deal? What kind of a deal?"

"Immunity. The witness protection programme. A new name, a new identity."

"Ed, this is not the US of A. You're in the wrong country. We've only done one or two of these deals in the entire history of the state."

"I know. But we have done them. When the stakes were big enough."

"And you're telling me that the stakes are big enough this time."

"I'd say that these are the biggest stakes ever. Our entire democracy is at stake this time. Can you think of anything bigger than that?"

"Don't beat about the bush! Spell it out for me!"

Ed Burke began with the Mortimer tribunal, the murder of Marty Rainey, the missing documents, the killing of Pia, and finally his confrontation with Johnny Fox. He refused to tell the Justice Minister how he found out about Johnny Fox, only saying that he was no stranger to Dublin even after an absence of twenty years and that he had his sources.

"So you believe that Mortimer ordered the hit on Marty Rainey. To shut him up."

"I'm certain of it."

"I find it hard to believe that a man in his position would resort to such mob violence."

"Suspend your disbelief for a minute. Let's say I'm right. If I am, this country is in real danger. And I'm scared because I don't believe it stops with Mortimer."

"Oh, you mean your wild accusations against the Tánaiste. You actually suggested that he had his wife murdered. The Commissioner keeps me fully informed. That's one of the reasons that I had a debate with myself about whether or not to see you today."

"The Commissioner knows I didn't kill Pia. And you know that too. So who did it? You tell me."

"I don't speculate on these matters. We all know that Pia led a pretty open lifestyle. You weren't her only lover. Who knows what a jealous and jilted lover might have done."

"No, I don't believe that. Pia's death was an opportunity. It was me they wanted. Take me out of the game at any price. If they couldn't get me for murder, they'd destroy my reputation instead. Leave the smear out there. Make sure the public thinks I'm guilty."

"OK, I'll suspend my disbelief for another minute. When you say you don't believe this stops with Mortimer, what do you believe?"

"I believe that Mortimer and Manning are guilty. Of corruption, of undermining this state. And of murder! And the scary thing is, it may not end with them. Suppose their strings are being pulled by someone even higher?"

"Ed ... enough! Now your imagination is truly running wild!"

"But suppose even a little of what I believe is true. Even that little is too much corruption to cover up. Don't we owe it to the people of this country to find out?"

Justice Minister Brian Cosgrave finally agreed that they did owe it to the people to find out. He told Ed to advise his client, Johnny Fox, that the State was prepared to offer him witness protection for full disclosure of all information and his willingness to testify at any and all ensuing trials.

23

PRIME TIME
RTE Television

Kate O'Donnell opens the program:

"Tonight we ask the question posed in Hamlet: *Is there something rotten in the state of Denmark?*

In recent weeks we've had the sensational murder of Pia Manning, wife of the Tánaiste; the revelation in the *Irish Daily News* of the millions illegally lodged in the Ansbacher accounts in the Cayman Islands; the murder of Martin Rainey, a key witness in the Barton Tribunal, and the publication of documents concerning land rezoning in inner city Dublin.

We will be asking if all of these matters are linked and if these murders are coincidental or are indeed more sinister.

Tonight we have received denials from Government and Justice Department sources that there is any connection between the murders of the Tánaiste's wife, Martin Rainey, and the mysterious publication of secret documents that must have been intended for the Barton Tribunal. Judge Barton is furious about these disclosures and claims that it is undermining the work of the tribunal.

We examine all this against a backdrop of apathy among the public and we ask if Ireland is ambivalent over the work of the Barton Tribunal.

But, first, a report from Charlie Crowe."

Charlie Crowe:

"Thank you, Kate. Firstly, let me say that the cast of characters in all of this would do justice to a Robert Ludlum thriller: the high profile wife of the second most powerful man in the government, the financial movers and shakers who are riding high in the current favourable economic climate, a venerable judge, a high-powered lawyer with a historic name, recently returned from the United States, and an old man who knew too much.

In recent weeks a series of seemingly unrelated events have been reported in the national press. It began with the brutal murder of Martin Rainey during a break-in at his home in Harold's Cross in Dublin. Initially this was dismissed as a statistic in the rising rate of crime in the capital. However, Mr, Rainey was the key witness who failed to appear to testify against Mr. Dan Mortimer at the Barton Tribunal. It is understood that Mr. Rainey was in possession of material that would have been very relevant to the case. Indeed, it was just days after Martin Rainey's murder that the *News* acquired anonymously the documents they published.   Could they have been Rainey's ?

Next we had the tragic murder of the Tánaiste's wife at St. Cleran's in Galway. She had been in the company of Mr. Edmund Burke, a lawyer who had recently been defending Mr. Dan Mortimer against a class action suit over land rezoning. Mr. Burke has not been detained and it is understood that he is not a suspect in this murder. He only recently returned from the United States where he'd been practicing law for a number of years in New York.

Incidentally, Mr. Burke is also linked to the Martin Rainey murder.   Mr. Rainey had been a childhood family friend and it was indeed Mr. Burke who had found the body of Mr. Rainey and called the Gardaí.   Mr. Burke may indeed be very important to all of this.

Kate, it seems that no-one is available to talk with me on any of these matters.   Mr. Burke has disappeared.   Sean Coyne, the investigative reporter from the *Irish Daily News*, under whose by-line the documents made page one at that paper, has been unavailable. I suspect that his editor has asked him to keep a low profile because Sean Coyne has always been available and cooperative in the past.

It appears there's mystery surrounding these events.   One that I have been unable to crack. However, the one common theme linking all of these events is the revelations of the Barton Tribunal."

Kate O'Donnell:

"When our best reporter Charlie Crowe finds doors   closed,   it   only   deepens   the   suspicion surrounding these mysterious murders.   We asked the Tánaiste to appear on the programme this evening but he declined. He is still in mourning over his wife's death and is refusing all public appearances at this time. The Minister of Justice had prior engagements and was also unable to appear. Mr, Sam McDevitt, the Managing Editor of the *Irish Daily News* has agreed to appear on our programme this evening and we are indebted to him for that."

"Good evening, Mr. McDevitt. Thank you for being here this evening. May I ask why you decided to accept our invitation?"

"Kate, I'm a professional. We're not hiding from the public at the *News"*

"Do you think it was professional to publish those documents?"

Sam McDevitt's face turned red with anger and his mop of white hair seemed to stand on his head as though it had been the target of an electrical charge.

"Professional! This country's being governed by a bunch of corrupt bast ---"

"Mr. McDevitt, I have to ask you to refrain from ---"

"I'm sorry but I think it's time we came out in the open in this country. Take a stand! We have to fight these people!"

"And you think you're justified in publishing those documents?"

"Absolutely! I am a firm believer in the freedom of the Press. Believe me, we had those documents examined by experts before we published. They are authentic. We would not have published them otherwise. Don't you think the public has a right to know?"

89

"Our programme is all about the public's right to know. That's exactly why you are here. But do you not think that you should have turned those documents over to Judge Barton. He says that, by publishing them, you are undermining the work of the tribunal."

"With all due respect to Judge Barton, what has his tribunal accomplished? Nothing! How many years have passed and how many millions have we spent on this tribunal? Has a single person been convicted of anything? Name me one person who's been jailed, who's had to resign in disgrace. No-one! Can't you see why the public are apathetic? "

"Mr. McDevitt, who gave you those documents?"

"We don't know."

"But you must have your suspicions?"

"No. They arrived anonymously in the mail. We had the envelope thoroughly examined. It's untraceable. Maybe we should be thanking whoever did it. Instead of going on a witch hunt. It's about time that we opened these matters up to the public. Let them get a good whiff of the corruption in the country."

"Where are these documents now?"

"Oh, we've turned them over to Judge Barton. Let's see if his wonderful tribunal can earn the legal fees it's costing. Let's see if he can get these tax cheats indicted. And convicted. Or will these powerful people go scot-free?"

"Thank you, Mr. McDevitt. I'd like to invite you back at a later time. We fully intend to do a more comprehensive programme on all of these matters."

Kate O'Donnell turned to face the camera and her national audience:

"These are indeed the most serious of matters and we will be putting the resources of this programme into uncovering the mystery that Charlie Crowe has spoken about. We have seen, in recent days, the argument between the government and the tribunal over the estimated costs of these tribunal proceedings. Some government sources estimate it at €1 billion. Are we getting our money's worth? Or are many lawyers becoming wealthy at taxpayer's expense? We intend to explore all of these matters in the coming weeks.

24

Pia looked asleep.

An American corpse. That's what Pia is, thought Flanagan. *It's not enough that we're surrounded by McDonalds and Pizza Hut and Starbucks. Now our dead have to look better dead than alive. Just like theirs. The Tánaiste came back with more than his graduate degree from the Harvard B School. Sucked up the finer points of the American Funeral Home culture as well. Surprised he hasn't sold the photo rights to VIP magazine. Now there would be a first. Society corpse. Could start a whole new trend. Fuck it, listen to me. I came to say goodbye to Pia and this prick has me ranting and raving. Forgive me, Pia.*

Held in Tánaiste David Manning's palatial home in Howth, Pia was laid out in the drawing room beneath the huge bay windows that looked out over Dublin Bay. But the cosy, intimate feel of a good Irish wake was absent. Refreshments were provided by a catering company hired for the occasion. Dark-suited assistants of the funeral director guided people in and out of the house. Mourners were more appropriately dressed for a theatre opening or a business conference. This robbed the wake of its spontaneity and close personal touch. This was just another formal event where attendance was required of the rich, the famous, and the powerful.

Tom Flanagan had not come to pay his respects or offer condolences to the Tánaiste. As far as he was concerned this wake was a charade.

But business was business and he'd go through the motions like many others in attendance. The Tánaiste, in his role as Minister for Trade and Industry, controlled the future direction of the Irish airports and Flanagan still hoped to encourage him to wrest control away from the moribund and conservative State agency that ran them. The health of *FlanAir* depended on it.

Lingering over Pia's peaceful face, he reached out and placed his right hand briefly over hers. Saying a silent goodbye, he left the drawing room and crossed to the main reception room where people clustered in threes and fours while the caterers hovered with trays of tea, and the Tánaiste received condolences.

Seeing Tom Flanagan, he approached him and said, "Good of you to come, Tom."

"Pia was a special person and a good friend. I came to say goodbye."

"I'm sure she knows, Tom. Thank you."

"Such a tragedy. I still can't believe it."

"Neither can any of us. But, rest assured, she will be avenged. I will get her killer."

"Tánaiste, I hadn't intended to talk about this. It doesn't seem right tonight. Not at this time. Not now."

"I know. I understand how you feel. But I think about nothing else these days. But you're right. Another time.   Tonight we're all here to say goodbye, just like yourself."

Lying bastard, thought Flanagan, as he shook the Tánaiste's hand in a civil act that Manning could interpret as personal condolence if he wished.

As he turned to leave, the Tánaiste gripped his elbow and leant close to say, "When the funeral is over, we must get together on the airport issue. Life must go on and we have to make decisions."

Flanagan nodded and, as he made a quick exit, thought: *a cold calculating bastard too. Pia barely cold and he's ready to move on, right here at the wake.*

25

Judge Andrew Barton was livid with anger. He felt that *The Irish Daily News*, in publishing documents relative to the individuals under investigation by the Barton Tribunal, was undermining the tribunal. He had requested the court to impose a permanent ban on the publication of such documents. The tribunal claimed that the publication of such documents affected due process and interfered with the constitutional rights of the participants. He had obtained a temporary injunction from the court.

Barton's anger was nothing compared to McDevitt's. He went berserk when told that he couldn't publish. Sean Coyne ducked as he flung papers across the room.

"This is shite! Denial of freedom of the press. Undermining the tribunal, my arse! If they did their feckin' job instead of lining the pockets of the lawyers, we wouldn't have to publish any documents because these people would be locked up now!"

"So we can't publish these two last documents we got," said Sean Coyne,

"Hold on! Are you going to take this lying down? Well, are you?"

"But the courts ..."

"I'll say it again! This ruling is shite! We've lodged an immediate appeal with the High Court. Go ahead and get that front page completed. We're going to get this overruled!"

The High Court, energised by the topic, moved it up the list for early consideration. They met one week later and overturned the decision. Mr. Justice Reilly remarked that the tribunal had taken a sledgehammer to kill a fly when what they needed was an instrument of precision that would protect that deserving of protection while preserving the freedom of the press. He rejected blanket secrecy saying that it was too crude a response to the delicate balancing of free speech, due process, and the confidential rights of those appearing before the tribunal.

McDevitt was ecstatic. Sean Coyne thought that a miracle had happened as McDevitt reached down into the bottom drawer of his desk and pulled out two glasses and the bottle of Jamesons. He only did that at Christmas.

Pouring two nips of the whiskey, he offered one to Sean, saying, "Cause for celebration. Free speech wins! Freedom of the press wins!"

"I thought it was Christmas!"

"It is! Can you think of a better gift than this?" And he raised his glass and dunked the remainder of the whiskey down his throat, "You got that front page ready to go?"

"I sure do!"

"Right! Here's the headline: *Victory for Freedom of the Press!* I want this out on the evening edition!"

26

The Beetle parked his Lexus directly opposite the front entrance to Finnstown Country House Hotel in Lucan. Sitting amid forty-five acres, eight miles west of Dublin's City Centre, it promoted its old-world charm as a 'home away from home'. Discreet, quiet, close yet far enough away. *A damn good place to meet*, thought *The Beetle* as he closed his car door and headed for the hotel entrance. A big hulking man, ungainly in his movements, one would have mistaken him for a farmer in town for the day. But Joe McGinnis, otherwise known as *The Beetle*, was estimated to be the most successful major criminal in Dublin since *The General*. Some said that he had always had more power and influence than *The General*.

He strode, unchallenged, through reception towards the bedrooms. Stopping at the number he'd been given, he knocked three times as arranged. Tánaiste David Manning opened the door, ushered him into the room, and closed it behind him.

"Right on time, Joe."

"I don't believe in being late. It's a thing with me."

"Well, at least we have that in common."

"Oh, we have a lot more than that in common, Tánaiste."

The Tánaiste didn't reply, walked instead over to the bureau and reached for a bottle of Black Bush, "Whiskey?"

"Too early in the day for me. But don't let me stop you."

"I won't."

As the Tánaiste poured himself a generous measure, straight up, *The Beetle* strolled to the window and looked out at the tranquil view of lawns and shrubs and said, "Lovely but boring."

"Joe, that's sad. This is what it's all about."

"Life you mean? The big enchilada? The gold at the end of the rainbow?"

"Many people can't wait to spend two weeks a year in a place like this."

"People, people ... naw, give me the hustle and bustle of the city. That's my world. You can keep all of this fresh air and green shite!" And turning around, he said, "You didn't bring me here to talk about this. What's up?"

"You've been reading the papers?"

"You mean all this shite about off-shore accounts. See they're hinting that a major figure in the government is involved. Now, that wouldn't be you, would it?"

"Don't fuck around, Joe! You know damn well they mean me! You didn't take care of it."

"What the fuck do you mean? Are you saying I'm responsible?"

"Damn right! You had one simple job to do. Take care of Rainey. "

"We did, damn it! And we didn't find a thing! Told you he was either bluffing or had hidden the stuff where nobody'd ever find it."

"Well, it wasn't hidden. I'm certain he gave it to that lawyer friend of his. Burke."

"But we fixed Burke's ass for good. He's the prime suspect in your wife's killing."

"Not prime enough. The Gardaí didn't charge him. He's wandering around out there. And I believe he's got Rainey's stuff and he's the 'anonymous source' who's releasing it to the media."

"So what do you want me to do?"

"Dead simple!   Find where he stashed Rainey's documents and bring them to me. Even if you have to trash half of Dublin to do it!"

"And if we find them?"

"Not if! When!"

"OK, when we find them. What then?"

"Kill him!"

27

They threw Johnny Fox into an overcrowded holding cell when he reached Mountjoy. Ten others, black, white, Irish, foreign, young, old, sat on ugly green couches that lined the wall. Fox grabbed a dirty duvet from a man on the floor, sleeping in a stupor, who crawled over on his stomach and continued to sleep. Fox squeezed into a corner and pulled the duvet over his head. Nobody bothered him.

Twenty-four hours later they moved him to his own cell. No words were spoken.

That same afternoon Ed Burke was back in Justice Minister Brian Cosgrave's office, agitated, holding a document in his hands.

"Fox is valuable. I don't want anything to happen to him in Mountjoy."

"Happen to him? He's behind bars. That's a whole lot safer than the Bronx!"

"Come on, you know Mountjoy is a mess. Here, look at this report from the Irish Prison Chaplains. You've probably seen this before but I haven't. It scares me and it sure doesn't make me feel at ease."

Burke handed the document to Cosgrave and proceeded to read from another copy in his hand.

The 2005 Annual Report from the Irish Prison Chaplains unreservedly criticised Mountjoy Prison: 'Huge sums of money continue to be spent on the Mountjoy complex in spite of the fact that it is to be demolished and replaced.   Able-bodied, intelligent and capable people walk aimlessly around prison yards, or lie in bed for over 17 out of every 24 hours. It has become a dumping ground for the mentally ill and those struggling to cope with it through homelessness, addictions, or vulnerability.   Large numbers of people with psychiatric illnesses are left languishing in the prison. We must yet again this year note our serious concerns regarding the continued use, in some situations, of padded cells as punishment. This is now contrary to the policy of the State and should not be allowed to continue.'

       "I'd like to get Fox out of there as soon as possible. When are you going to talk with him?   Cut the deal?"

       "Look, we're moving on it. Something like this must be done right. It's in the hands of the Attorney General. And I expect approval."

       "Does he know the urgency?"

       "He knows.   He's the best legal mind in the country. And he moves with care."

       "He's got to move on it now. Waiting may cost us. Fox is scared. He could change his mind."

       "As soon as we have the Attorney General's approval, we'll move. Fast!"

       "Well, at least move Fox to a safe place now. Don't wait. If he's going into the Witness Protection Program he's a valuable asset.   And we need to protect him.   Anything could happen to him at Mountjoy. He could get in a fight. Someone could stick a knife in him. Any damn thing could happen to him."

"OK, OK! I'll get him out within the next five days. With the Attorney General's approval. That's the best we'll get. And that's damn good!"

28

"Fox's in Mountjoy. You know that, Tom." Tom Buckley really didn't need this briefing from Ed Burke. He'd kept himself well informed since that day in Clifden when he told Ed about Fox.

"Yea, I know. But I'm concerned. Is he safe there?"

"No, he's not. But I've got a promise from the Minister of Justice to get him out of there in the next five days. That's the best I can do."

"Didn't he agree to put him in the witness protection programme? What's he waiting for?"

"He's waiting for the Attorney General's approval. These things seem to take forever."

"What if he doesn't get the approval?"

"He assures me that he will. And that he'll have it in the next five days. Seems pretty confident about it. So I can only take him at his word. That's all I can do."

"If we lose Fox we've got nothing. Nothing!"

"I know that, goddamit! Oh, I'm sorry man, I shouldn't yell at you."

"Forget it!"

"No, you're right. If we lose Fox, that's it."

"He will testify, won't he?"

"That's what he says. I've convinced him that he's a dead man walking. He believes that. He knows these people. When I grabbed him in New

York, he was at his wits end. Scared, Tom, really scared."

"Good. What do you think he knows?"

"He knows who did the Rainey job with him. And he knows who hired him. He'll testify to that."

"And you think whoever hired him will lead us to Mortimer. Maybe even to the Tánaiste!"

"That's the only card we can play at this point. It's high stakes but I'm betting on it."

"Well, we better make sure that Fox stays alive!"

They were in Ed's apartment. It was late evening and Tom was off duty. So they decided that they both needed to relax. Ed opened a bottle of *Lagavulin* and reached for two glasses.

29

The phone was ringing off the hook as Burke turned the key in his apartment door. He made it seconds before his answering machine.

"Burke."

"Ed, Brian Cosgrave. Have you heard the news?"

"What news? What's happening?"

"It's Johnny Fox. He's dead. Found hanging in his cell. You were right. We should have moved sooner."

"What happened?"

"Suicide!"

"Jesus Christ! Suicide! I don't believe it!"

"Well, believe it!   They found him hanging from one of his bed sheets this morning. He did it sometime during the night."

"Why? Why would he kill himself? This just doesn't make any sense."

"Suicide seldom makes any sense.   I'm meeting with the Assistant Governor at Mountjoy in an hour. I want you there."

"Oh, I'll be there alright."

James Rice, the Assistant Governor of Mountjoy, greeted them in his office. Lean, sharp, agile and youthful, he looked more like a University student than the Assistant Governor of a prison.

"The Governor would have been here himself if he could.   But he's attending a conference in Strasbourg on the EU penal system."

Brian Cosgrave introduced Ed Burke and said, " We're very concerned about the Johnny Fox suicide. Fox had knowledge that we planned to use in a major indictment.   Ed had convinced Fox that this was his only way out, convinced him that he was *a dead man walking*. And convinced us to offer him the Witness Protection Programme."

"I know, I know.   We were prepared to transfer him today to a safe house. This has been a total shock."

Ed Burke asked, "Why do you insist that it was suicide?"

"There's no way it could have been anything else. Nobody got near Fox since we locked him in his cell.   My officers tell me that he was very very nervous."

"Yeah, he looked twitchy.   But that didn't mean that he was going to kill himself. That's just the way he looked. I'm still asking 'why'.   Why would he have killed himself? We had a good deal waiting for him.   A way out.   Change of name. Relocation to a new country, a new life.   He knew that. He was sitting on the best deal of his life. And he knew that he was a dead man without it."

"Maybe he didn't trust you.   Maybe he was afraid.   We're trying to see if he had any history of mental illness, depression.   The Gardaí are hunting through his medical history.   But, let me tell you, we're depressed. We consider it a huge failure when one of our inmates kills himself. We've made a lot of progress here in Mountjoy.   In 1999 we had 6 suicides, last year 2, and Fox is the only one this year. Maybe we'd have had a zero suicide year if it hadn't been for him."

"So you should be as sceptical as I am. If this isn't a suicide, you'll still have a shot at your zero suicide year," persisted Burke.

"But if it's murder, that's worse. That would mean that Fox was killed by one of our own officers. They are the only ones with access to him. No, I can't believe that. It's just not possible."

"So, other than checking Johnny Fox's medical history, you're doing nothing."

"No, no! We're performing an autopsy. And forensics are examining the body."

Justice Minister Brian Cosgrave had left the questions to Ed Burke. Now he stepped in and said, "Thank you, James. You've been very frank. If forensics turn up something, you'll let us know."

"Absolutely! Whatever the outcome, I'll let you know."

In the car on the way back to the Justice Minister's office, Cosgrave and Burke took stock of the matter.

"Fox was our only hope," said Ed.

"You're right. Without his testimony we have nothing on Mortimer. The tribunal is treading water and Mortimer will be celebrating when he learns of Fox's death."

"I don't believe it was suicide. I believe that Mortimer already knows that Fox is dead."

"You mean you believe ... "

"Yes, I believe they killed Johnny Fox. That's exactly what I believe. Let's hope forensics spots something."

"But it won't matter. If Fox was murdered, you won't be able to prove that they did it anyway. The result is the same. We lose. They win!"

30

Five floors up in the bleak block of flats in Ballymun, now scheduled for demolition, Brendan Tucker looked out the window at the grey skies and the steady downpour. He smiled to himself and started to hum the Eddie Rabbit song, *I Love a Rainy Day.* It promised to be a good day for him. He had a job, well paid in advance. And he had the promise of action, of danger, of life on the edge. Maybe he'd feel alive again today.

Suited up in his leather boots and riding gear, he picked up the gun and slipped it into the inner zip pocket of his leather jacket. Satisfied, he locked the door to the flat and started down the stairs. The lift had been broken for months.

Passing the graffiti decorated walls on the ground floor, he crossed the rubbish strewn green at the rear of the flats and reached the lane on the other side where he had a key to one of the small storage lock-ups.

Inside he reached for the helmet, fixed it on his head, kick-started his motorcycle, listened to the engine purr, slid into gear, pulled out of the lock-up, closed it behind him, and eased down the lane.

He had his orders. He knew what to do. Driving onto the rain drenched road, he edged his bike through the clogged-up traffic and headed for Ballsbridge. He'd start with Burke's apartment.

At exactly eleven every Wednesday morning, Martha Cooke pulled her van into the kerb beside her sister Eileen's house.   She never needed to ring the doorbell. Eileen was always waiting at the door with her buckets, her mops, sponges, cloths, and cleaning liquids. Martha often thought that *WellClean*, their small cleaning business, structured Eileen's day in a way that her genes could not. She already had two cups of coffee sitting in the holders on the car's dashboard, courtesy *Supermac's* local drive-thru. They had a tight schedule, starting with Edmund Burke's Ballsbridge apartment at eleven-thirty.

Sean Coyne sat in his car outside Ed Burke's apartment. He'd been there for over an hour, waiting for Burke to appear. Ever since he began receiving the anonymous packages with the documents about the money laundering, he'd teased his mind – and his best investigative skills – to try and identify the sender. He wanted the source. He had brainstormed it with McDevitt.   When it came down to it, there weren't very many possibilities. Marty Rainey'd been murdered and Rainey had been due to testify before the Barton Tribunal. Burke had found the body and maybe he'd found what the killers were after. And who had a better motive? So Ed Burke had moved rapidly to the top of his short list.

He wanted to get Burke alone and find out if he *was* the *'deep throat'* who'd been feeding him the documents he'd been publishing. Coyne was fed up being used. He wanted in on the game. He was never any good at playing on the sidelines. He didn't mind waiting. He considered this to be a stakeout. As crime reporter for *The News*, stakeouts were his specialty. In fact the Gardaí could always count on Coyne appearing out of nowhere when one of their stakeouts saw action. He saw the leather-clad biker arrive and enter the building. *Odd, certainly not a resident, probably delivering something, hell – here I go with my wild speculation*, he thought, *profiling the natives and getting it all wrong.*   Twenty minutes later, the biker had not returned when a small white van, *WellClean* on the side, pulled up and two young ladies got out. They opened the back of the van, took out their cleaning equipment and walked quickly into the building.   *Yeah, don't see that in my neighbourhood,* Coyne contemplated, *we clean our own filthy toilet bowls!*

Once inside Ed Burke's apartment, Brendan Tucker looked for the expected: bookshelves, closets, bureaus, chests of drawers, desk, etc... and was immediately taken aback by the sparseness.   Modern and minimalist.   An apartment for a transient.

Tucker accepted the challenge, believing that Burke must have stashed the stuff somewhere.   He started in the kitchen, pulling out every cabinet drawer, tipping the contents on the floor, looking behind the drawers into the inside cavities.   Moving to the bathroom, he pried the medicine cabinet off the wall, leaving large gaps in the plaster, just in case it might have been hiding a wall safe.   In the living room, he tore up the couch, ripped holes in the cushions and left the stuffing in clumps everywhere.

Leaving the bedroom until last, he pulled all the clothes out of the closet, searched the pockets, ripped open the lining, and then threw them on the floor. Taking down the suitcase from the closet shelf, he opened it.   Finding it empty and still not satisfied, he cut the lining open and slashed through the outside leaving the inner spine exposed. Nothing! Standing in the middle of the room, he started moving toward the bed when he heard the front door open and the sound of women's voices...the door to the bedroom stood ajar and he could see enough. Two cleaning women. Good looking too. "Fuck, now what ?" he said under his breath as Eileen Cooke pushed open the bedroom door, saw him and with mouth open and eyes wide and frightened, dropped her bucket and cleaning stuff at her feet. Tucker pulled out his gun, pointed it at her and told her not to move. But Eileen Cooke's fear and terror overcame her. She lived with an irrational fear of being raped and now she believed that this man in black leather was going to rape her. She screamed and screamed. Tucker grabbed her and closed his left hand over her mouth. But she bit him and squirmed away as her sister came through the door swinging a mop at him. He shot her and she crumpled to the floor. Eileen ran screaming towards the front door of the apartment.

Outside two things happened at once. A taxi dropped Ed Burke off as the woman's screams rang out from the building. Sean Coyne ran into the building followed closely by Burke. Coyne bypassed the elevator and took the stairs. The screams were now muffled as he pushed open the door onto the second floor. Just in time to see the biker drag one of the screaming cleaning ladies towards the elevator. Coyne yelled and ran towards the man. He saw the gun fire and felt the sharp pain. But he kept going as the elevator doors opened and Tucker backed right into Ed Burke. Burke hit him hard and he fell. Eileen Cooke crawled away, whimpering now. Burke kicked him again and again until he couldn't move. Coyne felt faint and sat down facing the open elevator, a steady stream of blood dripping down his right arm onto the floor.

31

"You look like shit", said Sean Coyne, right arm bandaged to the wrist and suspended in a sling with face pale and drawn, as he gingerly sat down opposite Ed Burke, "mind you, I don't look too good meself!"

"You're right, you don't", said Burke, "but you're luckier that Martha Cooke. We don't know if she'll make it or not."

"You should have kicked the bastard to death. Pricks like that don't deserve to live!"

"Yeah, I know how you feel. I really do. But we can't play Clint Eastwood."

"Clint Eastwood!   Even better – Charlie Bronson. Take them out!   Our courts are filled with bleeding heart judges.   Bleeding for bastards like this.   Never for their victims.   Talk about justice. He'll get five to ten and walk after three. Three years! Do you think that's good enough? You're a solicitor. You defend shites like this, don't you?"

"Tucker is nobody. Just a street thug. It's not him we want. I thought you knew that. Why the hell are you publishing my documents? Don't you want the real villain? Sure you do!"

"And you think Tucker can hand him to us?"

"No, I don't. But he can tell us who hired him to kill Marty Rainey.   To kill Marty for the documents you've been happy to put on Page One and make a name for yourself!"

"Come on, that's crap!   You were the person who wanted me to put those documents on Page One."

"OK, you're right. Let's call it quits. We need each other."

"Precisely! And that's why I was hanging out at your apartment waiting for you. And why I'm sitting here tonight all fucked up.   I wanted confirmation that you were my source. And I wanted to cut a deal with you."

"What kind of a deal?"

"A partnership. Me on the inside, you on the outside. I think we'd make a great team."

Ed Burke took his time to digest that.

Sean Coyne didn't wait for him, "I want to get David Manning as much as you do. And I can get information that you can't. Listen, it may not be strictly legit but we need to bend the law a little to nail Manning and his corrupt cronies, don't we?"

So Burke accepted Coyne's proposal. It made sense.   Coyne was a good investigative reporter. Burke had to lie low and Coyne could go places where he couldn't.

Martha Cooke died that morning. She had never regained consciousness.   Making his way to her wake, the memories flooded over Ed.   Their little chats on those mornings she and her sister'd catch him before he left.   Her disarming smile, her surprising knowledge of the day's events, her ability to chat as she continued to dust, to mop. Her pride in her work. Never subservient, she possessed a quiet dignity.   Ed felt that part of him had died with her and the words of John Donne came to mind, *No man is an island. Everyman's death diminishes me.*

Martha was being waked at her sister's house in Dundrum. The house was crowded when Burke arrived and he squeezed past the people standing in the hallway behind the front door. Eileen saw him and he went to her, took her by the hand, and, looking into her red-rimmed sleepless eyes, offered his condolences in words that seemed woefully inadequate. Then he hugged her until her sobs subsided. She held him by the hand and led him into the front sitting room, the best room in the house, where Martha lay in her coffin surrounded by sympathy and mass cards. Eileen left him there.

He stood looking at Martha, at her colourless, lifeless face, the skin taut over her cheekbones. No resemblance to the busy bubbly Martha who chatted with him as she dusted and cleaned. This was death in its starkest, uninviting form. Not a believer, he couldn't pray. Instead he said his own goodbye to Martha, briefly touched her cold hands, and moved into the next room where Eileen and her friends were running around with tea and sandwiches for everyone. He accepted a cup of tea and stood sipping alone. He knew no-one and couldn't contribute to their shared memories of Martha.

His reveries were broken by the local priest who had gathered people around Martha's coffin to lead them in the prayers of the rosary.

Putting his cup down, Ed quietly left.

32

Ed Burke needed to get away. Away from the fight with Tucker, the suicide of Fox, away from Dublin.

Once out of the centre of Dublin, he drove west on the N4 to Galway, marvelling at the fact that he could be on a highway leading out of any major Western city. Ireland's spend on its infrastructure was making it look like anywhere else. Good and bad, he thought. He sometimes longed for the single lane, meandering roads between hedgerows festooned with coconut smelling yellow flowered gorse and the blood drops of the fuchsia.

Three hours later he parked in the Corrib Centre in the heart of Galway and walked down Middle Street to Charlie Byrne's bookshop where the shelves bulged with surprises.

Charlie finished serving a customer and greeted him, "Ed, back again! Twice this month and I haven't seen you in years!"

"Charlie, I hope to rectify that. You'll be seeing a lot more of me from now on."

"Great! Listen, I've got a new consignment in. Let me show you." He walked Ed to the shelves at the rear of the bookstore and left him there to browse at his leisure.

Half an hour later, fortified with James Lee Burke's *In The Moon of Red Ponies,* and two of the latest from Galway itself, Ken Bruen's *Priest* and Mike McCormack's *Notes From a Coma,* he felt the pangs of hunger and walked down to McDonagh's where he had a plate of the world's best fish and chips.

Feeling more human already, he drove west out of Galway and began to relax as he drove past Moycullen and through Oughterard into Connemara. An hour later he had negotiated his way through a market day traffic jam in Clifden and was on his final few miles to his cottage in Claddaghduff.

He was blessed with idyllic weather. Blue skies in the daytime and star-filled heavens at night banished the terrible events of recent days. And it would stay that way for the four days he spent here. He had not decided how long he'd stay but that would be decided for him.

A dinner of salmon steaks, floury potatoes, and a bottle of the best Chablis filled him with a feeling of absolute contentment as he sank into the chair in front of a blazing peat fire and opened Ken Bruen's *Priest* with great anticipation.

Sun streaming through the curtains and the silence, always the silence, woke him in the morning. He reached his watch on the bedside table and couldn't believe that it was almost ten thirty. He'd slept like a baby and felt completely refreshed.

By noon he was out in the greenhouse doing his best to resuscitate some geraniums that seemed to survive even the worst neglect. He had to admit that he did not have a green thumb. Oblivious to the world around him, he opened the greenhouse door and, carrying a pot of geraniums in each hand, bumped into Old Mikey Doyle.

"Jeez, sorry Mikey, didn't see you there."

Old Mikey stood there with a big grin on his leathery, weather-beaten face, as he leaned towards

Ed, both hands supported by a hefty stick planted firmly in front of him, " 'Tis a fine day for that."

"Mikey, just the best."

"Are ye stayin' a while this time?"

"Don't know. No definite plans."

Mikey fished a well-worn pipe out of the large bulging pocket of his old topcoat and began to fill it, spluttering all the time. Ed knew he'd have to find a way to move Old Mikey along. Otherwise he'd inherit him for the day. And he couldn't handle that.

"I'm going down to the post office and the shop in a while. I'll take you with me. Save you a walk. I'm sure you're headed in that direction anyway, aren't you?", said Ed, knowing that Old Mikey would end up in the pub next door to the shop while the tourists bought him Guinness just to take his photo and listen to his stories.

Ed didn't wait for an answer before going inside, wiping his hands and getting the car keys. Outside he started the car and reversed it back beside Old Mikey. He got out, opened the passenger door, and gently guided Old Mikey into the seat. But, try as he might, he couldn't get Mikey's seat belt on. Old Mikey sat there, pipe ash dropping all over him, grinning exactly like the mute village idiot played by John Mills in *Ryan's Daughter.*   Ed knew when he was defeated so he left Mikey unbelted and drove away.

At Claddaghduff, the post office was part of the local shop which sat beside Sweeney's Strand Bar. Two petrol pumps and two Eircom telephone booths stood to the right of the post office. Two young men lingered near the telephone booths.   Ed parked between the post office and the pub and helped Mikey get out of the car. As he suspected, Mikey grinned sheepishly at him, held out his hand in thanks, and walked into Sweeney's Bar. Ed turned around, right

into the two young men, one of whom stuck a microphone in his face while the other filmed him.

"Mr. Burke, my name is Declan Stephens and I am a reporter for *Prime Time*. May I ask you some questions?"

"No, you may not! How did you find me?"

"You are news! And it wasn't difficult to find you. We're doing a follow-up program on the murder of the Tánaiste's wife. We thought it would only be fair to give you a chance to speak for yourself."

"I have nothing to say!"

"Nobody's been arrested for her murder and many people link your name with her death.   We think our programme gives you an opportunity to clear that all up.   What can you tell us about your relationship with Pia?"

"Look, I've already told you, I have no comments on the matter. Didn't you hear me? Not a single comment!   Now, please get that out of my face!"

Burke, now visibly angry, pushed them aside. He knew this would be on national television so he felt compelled to restrain himself.   Otherwise young Mr. Declan Stephens would be lying on his arse on the ground by this time.   He decided the few items he needed from the shop could wait, as did the letter he had to mail, so he jumped into his car and reversed out of there.

33

Ed Burke took his shoes off when he reached the beach at Claddaghduff. He checked his watch: 12 noon. He was late today. For the past three mornings he'd finished his five mile hike in time to get back for coffee at 11 am. Today, time had run away from him. And, as he contemplated that, he realized that that's exactly why he'd come here. To wind down. To restore his mind, replenish his system. To let time run away from him.   And then he laughed and thought, *In America I'd spend a fortune for days like this at some up-market spa. And here it's free and natural. And the best!*

He walked to the water's edge and felt the wet sand squelch between his toes connecting him umbilically to the sea. To the Atlantic Ocean. Looking at the horizon he thought that, if the earth had been flat and he had a magic telescope, he could look into the windows of the houses in Cohasset, south of Boston. *The next parish over,* as they say here in the west of Ireland. With his mind wandering he didn't hear his mobile phone at first but its incessant ring-tone finally penetrated. Fishing in his pocket, he opened the phone and answered:

"Ed Burke"

"Jesus, Ed, that's the third time I called. You said you'd keep your phone open for me."

"Sean, take it easy. My phone is open. But there's black spots here in the hills where's there's no coverage. You're lucky you got through at all. I'm on the beach right now. My toes're in the Atlantic. A world away from mobile phones."

"Yeah, I know. Thought something might have happened to you, that's all."

"Something happen to me!   Here in Connemara? The safest place on earth!"

"OK, OK! But that place doesn't exist and you know it."

"What place? Connemara?"

"No, dammit!   *The safest place on earth.* There is no such place!"

"Sean, Sean, you didn't call me to engage in this banter now, did you?"

"No. It's Cosgrave, the Minister of Justice. He wants to see you. Now, he said, if not sooner."

"Did he tell you why?"

"No. All he said was that it was a very serious matter. One that you'd want to see him on right away. So I think you'd better get back here. Now!"

"Goddam it! I was just beginning to relax!"

The traffic was light on the roads to Dublin and he'd left early enough to beat the rush hour traffic in Galway and elsewhere. Normally congested places such as Loughrea and Kinnegad now had new bypasses. Traffic flew through places that used to take a good half hour to negotiate. As a result, Ed Burke reached Dublin by 5 pm. He had put a call through to Minister Cosgrave when he was midway there, at Athlone, and the Minister told him to meet him at the State Pathologist's office.

34

Minister Brian Cosgrave was already in the State Pathologist's office when Ed Burke arrived and he made the introductions, "Ed, this is Dr. Mona Kennedy. I have briefed her on you and on the background to this case."

Dr. Mona Kennedy, stood up and reached out her hand to Ed Burke, "Glad to meet you, Mr. Burke. Thank you for coming."

A tall lithesome blonde, observed Ed, expecting that the State Pathologist would be a prim schoolmistress type, as he shook hands with her and said, "I'm sure the Minister has filled you in on my involvement in this matter. And on its implications."

"Oh, he most certainly has. And that's why you're both here. So I'll get directly to it. Johnny Fox did not commit suicide. He was murdered.   I understand that you suspected that, Mr. Burke."

"Yes, I was pretty sure. Fox had no reason to kill himself. But others had plenty of reason to kill him. He knew too much."

Saying,"I'd like you both to follow me," Dr. Kennedy left her office and walked down a long corridor, lit by naked fluorescent tubes, until they reached a large double door. She inserted her security access card, entered her password, and ushered them into the main body of the morgue. Dissecting tables, disinfectant smells, and a scrubbed clean look gave

Burke a sense of unease. Cabinets lined the side of the room. Dr. Kennedy strode towards the fourth cabinet and turned to them.

"Hanging is a fairly common method of suicide. In Fox's case, he hung himself by putting a slip knot in his bed-sheets, hanging himself from the bars on his cell window, and kicking the bed away beneath him. His neck wasn't broken. In most suicide hangings, the victim suffocates to death – slowly. This doesn't happen in executions. There, the neck is broken and the spinal cord crushed by dislocated vertebrae. Supposed to be painless. But has anyone come back to confirm that. Fox choked to death. That's definitely not painless!"

She pulled out the cabinet and drew down the cover from Fox's head. "This is the body of Johnny Fox.   In a suicide there would normally be a 'V' shaped bruise on the neck, but take a look. You can see that there's a straight line bruise on the neck as well.   There's also some abrasions and contusions. Here, and again here. What you don't see are the fractures of the thyroid cartilage. They're usually caused by the victim struggling while his neck is being squeezed."

"So, you will be confirming that Fox was murdered?" Burke said, rhetorically.

"I have already done that. My report is with the Justice Minister here and also with the Governor of Mountjoy."

Brian Cosgrave cut in, "Thank you, Dr. Kennedy. I had to see for myself. Ed, I have set up a meeting with James Rice. The Governor's not back from Strasbourg yet. He added on a few days holiday. Can't blame him. Tough getting away from his job."

"But I'll bet he won't enjoy a day of it when he learns about this," said Ed Burke.

They walked back with Dr. Kennedy to her office, thanked her and left. The meeting with James Rice at Mountjoy was set for 9 am in the morning.

At exactly 9 am next morning James Rice sat tight-lipped behind his desk. From lean, sharp and agile he had turned into ramrod straight and clenched fisted. He looked across at Brian Cosgrave and Ed Burke, "The impossible happened! On my watch!"

"James, this would have happened even if the Governor had been here," said Brian Cosgrave.

"But he wasn't here. I was," affirmed Rice.

"So what are you doing about it?" asked Ed Burke.

"I have sealed Fox's cell. No one gets in until it's thoroughly examined by forensics. Brian, I've asked you to take charge of this investigation. The prison will not investigate itself," answered Rice.

"The Garda Commissioner has appointed a special investigation team. The best people. They'll get here soon. And they'll have full charge of this investigation, " said Brian Cosgrave.

"Right. I've asked my officers to cooperate fully. They'll have access to anything they need. The duty officers on the night Fox died will be available for interview immediately. I can't imagine that one of them murdered Fox. They're all long-time career officers with excellent, unblemished records," said Rice.

"Everyone is a suspect. You know that," said Cosgrave.

"I know. I know. That may even include me," answered Rice.

"It does include you. Everyone with access to Fox is considered a suspect. The stakes in this one are a lot bigger than you. Bigger than Ireland itself, maybe!" replied Cosgrave.

A gentle knock on the door announced the arrival of Rice's secretary with a tray of coffee. She served it, unobtrusively, and immediately left the room, closing the door behind her.

Replenished, Ed Burke put down his coffee mug and said, "We need to find out who killed Fox soon. This investigation musn't be permitted to drag on."

Brian Cosgrave said, "This team are our very best. They know they'll be tested on this one. And it won't be easy. They know it's top priority."

"I'm sure you're right. But whoever did this will have been clever enough to leave no evidence behind. And I believe that forensics will find nothing in Fox's cell. Nothing that shouldn't be there, that is. Which means the evidence may be hiding in plain sight and the best investigator in the world won't find it, "said Burke.

"You're talking in riddles," said Cosgrave.

"Look outside the paradigm on this one. Look outside the prison. That's where we'll find the connection to this killing," said Burke.

"Explain," continued Cosgrave.

"Let's say one of your unblemished officers has a dark secret. Something that would compromise him if it became public. Would he kill to prevent that?" asked Burke.

"That's wild speculation, Mr. Burke," said James Rice.

"No, it comes from a place that seldom fails me. My experience in the murky world of New York crime," said Burke.

"Ed, you must stay out of this," chipped in Brian Cosgrave.

"Stay out of it! You wouldn't have had the Fox opportunity that we lost if I had stayed out of it," protested Burke.

"Mr. Burke, it seems to me that your opportunity has brought us plenty of grief. Why don't you leave it to the professionals now," advised Rice.

"Ed, listen to me, if you uncover evidence illegally, without a search warrant, it would compromise everything we're doing. It wouldn't be permitted as evidence. That's the law. And if you were right, and it pointed to the killer, then you'd have given him a free ticket. As a lawyer, you surely understand this," said Cosgrave.

"Brian, please, please! I promise not to compromise the investigation. But I can't promise not to help find Fox's killer," said Burke, getting in the last word.

Just in time as James Rice's secretary buzzed him, "Sir, Chief Inspector Cowan and two detectives are here to see you."

"Thanks, Rosie. Tell them I'll see them in a few minutes," and, arising from behind his desk, he shook hands with Brian Cosgrave and Ed Burke and ushered them from his office.

Outside, Chief Inspector Cowan seemed taken aback at seeing the Minister of Justice emerge from the Deputy Governor's office. He scrambled to his feet, as did the two detectives, and greeted Brian Cosgrave with a body language that clearly showed an acknowledgement of the chain of command.

"Good morning, Chief Inspector," said Cosgrave, giving a nod to the two detectives.

"Good morning, Minister," said Cowan.

"Good luck with your investigation. I'm sure the Commissioner has emphasised the importance of this. There's a lot at stake here. If you need my support in any way, call me. My office has been instructed to let you through to me whenever you call," said Cosgrave.

"Thank you, Minister. We will keep you informed," said Cowan.

"Good luck," said Cosgrave as the two detectives stood, almost to attention, in the background.

Ed Burke checked his watch as they left. It read 10.30 am. But he had the sense that they'd been there much longer.

35

Burke and Coyne set out to find Fox's killer. They knew he had to be one of the prison officers.

Sitting over coffee in Burke's kitchen, Coyne asked Burke, "Where do we begin?"

"The process of elimination. That's the only way."

"You mean, the prison officers?"

"Right. We need to find out how many are on the night shift at Mountjoy. And then how many would have had access to Fox."

"That's a tall order."

"You're the best investigative reporter in Dublin. If anyone can do this, you can. You don't have to hide. You have a right to ask questions. You'll be covering Fox's murder for the *News*."

"OK. I do have sources I've used before. I'll tap them again. Maybe I'll get lucky. What about you?"

"They've told me to stay out of this so I can't be seen to be pursuing it. There're other ways. We have Tucker and we need to know who gives him his orders. Maybe it's the same person who ordered Fox's murder. That makes sense, doesn't it?"

"So if you get Tucker to talk, maybe we don't need to find Fox's killer."

"No, no! We can't take that chance. We need to move on both fronts."

36

Burke's hard sell on Justice Minister Brian Cosgrave paid off.   He got permission to see the Garda Commissioner on the Fox murder case. Commissioner Clooney welcomed him into his office, " Mr. Burke, let me say this up front. I never believed that you killed the Tánaiste's wife."

"Thanks, Commissioner!   Now you know that I didn't.   The DNA you found belongs to Brendan Tucker."

"That's brand new evidence.   And it hasn't been released to anyone. I'd sure as hell like to know how you got your hands on that."

"Look Commissioner, I have lots of good old friends. None of them believed I did it either. And some of them thought it was a set-up.   That I was being railroaded. That's all I can say."

"Mr. Burke, I won't pursue the matter."

"Commissioner, please call me Ed."

"OK, Ed.   Justice Minister Cosgrave believes in you. He's in your corner. You must know that. Otherwise you would not be sitting here."

"I know, Commissioner. The Justice Minister believes what I believe. I think."

"And what exactly is that?"

"That David Manning is corrupt. That he had his wife killed. Revenge! Against her and against me. Had to get me off the Mortimer case because I was getting too close. Mortimer's in it up to his eyeballs. And I'm sure he's behind the murder of Marty Rainey. Maybe it can't be directly connected to him. But the dots link up somewhere. Once we find all the dots we'll be able to make that link. But we don't have much time. I think Manning will be the next Taoiseach. God help us all if that happens!"

"That's a huge array of charges you're levelling! I'll be honest. I do not like the Tánaiste. And I think he's out for himself and no·one else. But it's hard for me to buy your grand conspiracy."

"You don't have to. Not yet. All I'm asking is that we find all the dots. When we do, I think you'll reach the same conclusion as me. And the killing of Fox is one of those dots. We need to find his killer. I know you have an investigation team on it. I met them. I'm sure they're a fine team but maybe I can approach it from another angle. Tucker!"

"What's your thinking on Tucker?"

"We've got the DNA linking him to Pia's murder. We're damn sure he and Fox killed Marty Rainey. And he killed my cleaning lady. Who knows, maybe he was there to kill me. I think I'm becoming too hot for them. And he must know who ordered Fox's murder. I'm sure he doesn't know who killed Fox. But I'm damn sure he knows who gave the order. And I'll bet it's the same person he takes his own orders from!"

"We're preparing a file for the DPP charging Tucker with the murder of Pia. We've interviewed him but he clams up. Says nothing. I don't think you'll get anything out of him. But you're welcome to try. I'll set it up."

"I've got to try, Commissioner. Maybe I can convince him to confess and name who hired him by telling him that it's life without parole if he refuses. Who knows, maybe a few years of freedom, even at an old age, holds something for Tucker."

"Well, I wish you success. There's nothing I'd like better than to nail the people behind this!"

37

Sean Coyne's source in Mountjoy told him that four prison officers had access to Fox on the night he was killed. Now the hard investigative work began – how to narrow the four suspects down to one. *May be an impossible task*, thought Coyne, and then cautioned himself, *"One step at a time. Can't beat the 'cop on the beat' approach."*

He already had basic information on each of them:

- Jim Gregory, 32 years old, single, an officer in Mountjoy for only two years; native of Donegal.

- Mick O'Brien, 58 years old, Dublin native, been in prison service his entire life, due to retire soon; wife Mary, two grown-up married children, five grandchildren.

- Billy Nee, 47 years old, originally from County Carlow, been in prison service for twenty years; married to Sally, four children, two in University, two in Secondary School.

- John Lynch, 50, single man, 25 years in prison service; brought up in orphanage, no known relatives.

Nothing sticks out there, thought Coyne, *just four ordinary people.*   Well, he had to start somewhere, so why not with the two single men, Gregory and Lynch. *Let's go alphabetically, Gregory first it is ...*

In the meantime, he'd put the four names out to his usual sources on the street, the sources that fed him regular info on the criminal elements in Dublin. Just to see if 'the dogs on the street' had even the slightest hint of anything.   Looking for 'dots', expecting to find them in the most unusual places.

Starting with Gregory, he found out that he lived alone in one of those new apartments that were springing up everywhere alongside the Liffey. Chatting up the neighbours wouldn't reveal much. Most of Gregory's neighbours were young single professionals, whose apartments were only their bedrooms. Their lives centred around their jobs and their own social circle. Most of them did not know their neighbours. But Coyne's persistence paid off. He learned that Gregory regularly dropped in to his local pub for a few pints.

"He's the salt of the earth," said Paddy, the bartender, "sure all Donegal people are like that anyway."

"When does he drop in?"

"Usually on Friday nights, once in a while on Wednesdays. Said you haven't seen him in a while, did you?"

"Right. Don't know if he'll remember me or not. Maybe I'll drop in on Friday and buy him a pint."

"Sure, why not. You're welcome. Can I get you another?"

"No, Paddy, got to go."

"Ah well, if you must. Sure we might see you on Friday then, mightn't we?"

Next day being Thursday, Sean Coyne decided to spend the day on John Lynch. Despite his loyal career in the prison service, or because of it perhaps, Lynch was a loner. No relatives and no friends either, it seemed. After the orphanage he had worked at a variety of jobs before joining the prison service. He lived alone in a small red brick row house in a gentrified section of the Liberties, Dublin's lower working class neighbourhood. People were easy to talk with in the Liberties and Coyne got all his information in less than an hour from the proprietor of a small corner newsagents.

"An odd fella, he is. When he's not workin' you'll find him up the street in the chapel. Goes to mass every single day."

"So he's very religious then?"

"Agh, you wouldn't know, would you, maybe it's somewhere to go for him, that's all."

"And he has no friends?"

"Well, nobody he hangs out with, if that's what you mean. He's friendly enough. Says hello to everyone. But he keeps to himself."

"And what about girlfriends?"

The man doubled over with laughter, "Girlfriends? Are you kiddin'? He's never had a date in his life. I tell you, the man's a virgin. That's what he is. Now, don't get me wrong, he's not gay or anything. I think he'd run a mile if a woman made a pass at him. And it's too late now. He'll never change now."

Every word about John Lynch rang sound as a bell in Sean Coyne's ears. There was no way that Lynch could be the killer. So that eliminated the two single prison officers. Only two left, Mick O'Brien and Billy Nee. Coyne wasn't feeling optimistic.

But his luck changed with one call from his 'snitch', "We think we have somethin'"

"What did you find out?"

"Not on the phone.   Meet me at Ryan's. Eleven. OK?"

"OK.   I'll be there."

38

Coyne's 'street source' had lived by his wits all his life. He stayed alive because he had 'the goods' on many people. That was his insurance policy. Known simply as Butch, he sat at a corner table in Ryan's pub as Coyne entered and joined him.

"This'll cost top dollar, Sean."

"I'll have to see it first, Butch."

"And you'll have to pay double.   To an eyewitness. Someone who was there."

"Feck it, Butch! You're talking in riddles!"

At that very moment another man entered the pub and approached them. Sixtyish and stooped, he seemed to creep furtively towards their table. Butch pulled out a chair for him and he sat down.

"This is the eyewitness I told you about."

Sean Coyne stretched out his hand and gripped a limp sweaty palm. The man spoke, "I'm only in this for the money. I'm sure Butch has told you that. When I leave here, you've never seen me, you never talked to me, you don't know me. That's why I have no name. Do you agree?"

"Listen, if Butch believes you've got something I need to know, I'll pay you well for it. Butch can guarantee that. And I don't need to know who you are."

The man shuffled his feet under the table before he spoke again, "I was there. When they made the video. Right on screen with that young lad goin'

135

down on him. Couldn't a been more that fifteen years old."

Coyne waited without moving even an eyelid until the man continued, "He's been in the *Beetle's* pocket ever since."

Finally, Coyne asked the one question he'd been holding back, "What's his name?"

"I thought you knew. Butch, didn't you tell him?"

"He never gave me a chance. And then you walked in. It's OK. Tell him who it was."

"Billy Nee! That's who! Like I said, he's been in the *Beetle's* pocket ever since. You wouldn't want your wife and kids to see a video like that, now would you?"

He shuffled to his feet, never looking at Coyne, and said, "You'll get me my money, Butch," and crept out the door in the same manner as he'd entered.

39

Ed Burke walked into the hospital and the guard outside Tucker's room was expecting him. Tucker barely acknowledged his presence. He sat, propped up, in the bed. An IV dripped into his left arm. Burke didn't sit down. He stood and stared at Tucker, then walked around him and came back to face him. Finally Burke pulled over a chair and sat down , facing Tucker.

"You weren't looking for documents in my apartment, were you Brendan? And you didn't come to kill my cleaning lady! You came to kill me, didn't you?"

Not expecting a response from Tucker, Burke continued, "We know you killed Marty Rainey. And now we have solid evidence that you killed the Tánaiste's wife! Johnny Fox was going to testify. Tell us all about it. That's why he's dead. Isn't it Brendan? To shut him up!"

Burke pulled his chair closer to the bed so that he could look Tucker directly in the eyes, "I want to know who you're working for. Who gives you your orders? You're going down for life for these murders. No parole. You'll never see the light of day again. But, let me tell you this. You tell us who gave the orders and that life sentence might have a parole down the road somewhere. You'd stand a chance of getting out then. How old would you be? Fifty, sixty? Still a lot of years left to you. Personally, I think you should spend your last days behind bars. I'm sorry we don't have the death penalty. But I'm after people even more dangerous than you. You think about this, Brendan."

Ed Burke got up, pushed the chair in, and turned to leave. Tucker cleared his throat and aimed a large frothy spittle at him. It hit the floor inches from his right leg.

"I guess that's my answer, isn't it Brendan? Well, I hope you rot in hell!"

Burke left the hospital, angry. In his subconscious, he had his hands around Tucker's throat, squeezing the life out of him. So he didn't hear his mobile phone until he reached his car in the parking lot. He fumbled to open it and take the call.

"Ed, Sean. Good news! Think I know who killed Fox!"

"Brilliant! I need some good news. Spent the last half-hour with Tucker."

"Did you get anywhere?"

"No, you were right. He's a real bastard! He won't talk."

"Well, we don't need him. I'll meet you at your apartment. In an hour. OK?"

"Absolutely!"

40

At Burke's apartment, Sean Coyne updated him on his search for Fox's killer, ending with Billy Nee, the video, and the *Beetle*.

"I think you should see Billy Nee. Not me."

"We can both go. You uncovered it."

"No! I'm an investigative reporter. He'll clam up. But you're a solicitor. And he won't think you're trying to make Page One at your newspaper. Besides, if this man has killed to protect his secret, what kind of state will he be in?"

"Yeah, guess you're right. But I'll want you at the end of my phone all the time. Understand?"

"If you need me, I'll be there. Now, here's where Billy Nee lives and here's his work schedule for the week."

Burke examined the schedule and said, "It's best that we move on this right away. Looks like he's off during the day on Friday."

At ten a.m. on Friday morning, Ed Burke rang the front door to Billy Nee's house in Sandymount.

Almost immediately, a perky attractive woman opened the door, greeting him with a big smile.

"Mrs. Nee?"

"Yes, hello!"

"My name is Ed Burke. I'm a solicitor and I'd like to speak with your husband on a professional prison officers' matter. Is he at home?"

"Yes, would you like to come in ?"

"No, no. Thank you. It's such a lovely day. I'll stay out here for a while."

"Alright, then. I'll go get him. Shouldn't be long."

"Thank you very much, Mrs. Nee."

The door closed and Ed Burke walked the short distance to the little wrought-iron gate at the front, observing the neatly trimmed grass and the imaginatively arranged flowerbeds. An ordered life, about to end. The opening door interrupted his thoughts and he turned around to see a stocky round-faced man, about five ten in height with a close trimmed haircut, striding towards him.

"Mr. Burke?"

"That's right, Mr. Nee."

"What do you need?"

"I need to talk with you privately about a very sensitive matter. It's best if we do it away from your home."

"Listen, Mr. Burke, if that's your name. Anything you want to say, you can say in my home."

"No! Not this! You would not want us to discuss this in your home. Here's my business card. I am a solicitor and the matter I need to talk about is confidential. My car's right here. We can talk in it, so no need to leave the area."

"Fifteen minutes only. That's all you get. So you better make it good."

140

Ed Burke waited until Billy Nee had settled comfortably into the passenger seat before he began, "Billy, I'm going to call you Billy, you're in a lot of trouble."

"What's this all about, Burke?"

"Come on, Billy.   You're living a lie! I know you've been working for the *Beetle!*"

An angry Billy Nee screamed, "Fuck you!" at Ed Burke and reached for the door.

"I know about the video. The one with you and that young boy. You've been paying to keep that quiet for years, haven't you?"

Billy Nee looked shocked. Taking his hand off the door handle, he sank deep into the seat and placed his head in his hands.

"You must've known this would happen someday.   You were only buying time. You should have told the *Beetle* to go fuck himself! And asked your wife for her understanding years ago.   She seems like a great person. But you're a coward, aren't you?   It was easier to do the *Beetle's* dirty work. Now it's too late."

Billy Nee was crying now, his sobs shaking his body, and his body shaking the car. Ed Burke was almost embarrassed for him.

"You killed Johnny Fox, didn't you?"

But   Billy   Nee   continued   shaking uncontrollably.

"I could turn this over now to the Garda Investigation Team looking into Fox's murder. You'd be arrested right away. But I don't want to do that. I want to give you time to make your peace with your family. Get your affairs in order. More importantly, I want your testimony on the *Beetle*. Everything you know. You'll have to pay for what you did. But you can buy yourself some time. You might think the *Beetle's* the big crime boss in this dirty world. But, believe me, he's only a foot soldier in the game. If we get him, maybe he'll lead us up the chain of command. I know I'm speaking in riddles Billy, but I need you to tell me everything. You have no choice now."

Billy Nee's sobbing had finally stopped. Ed Burke could see his shoulders stiffen, see him finally getting a grip on himself. He lifted his head and looked through red teary puffy eyes, "I know it's over. And, you're right, I've been a coward. But, once I took this road, there was no turning back. So, if I'm going down, I want to take the *Beetle* with me. I'll give you anything you want."

"Good! The Garda Investigation Team might be hot on your heels. So we'd better do this now. Come with me to my apartment. We can record your statement and you can sign and date everything in my presence. Believe me, it'll go a long way with the DPP. When you're finished, I'll bring you back here and you can settle things with your family."

Nee stayed slumped in his seat, a deflated version of the sturdy pumped-up man whom he'd met a mere fifteen minutes ago.

"Do you want me to tell your wife you're leaving with me?"

"Naw, just go!"

At three p.m. Billy Nee stopped talking and Ed Burke stopped recording. Burke had already prepared an affidavit which Nee signed and dated. Burke witnessed the signature. That was it. Enough material to indict the *Beetle* on corruption, murder, subverting the course of justice, blackmail, theft, drug trafficking, prostitution... *maybe enough to get him to spill his guts and cut a deal to save his ass,* thought Burke, *more dots connected, one at a time ...*

As promised, Ed Burke drove Billy Nee back to his house in Sandymount and watched as he walked dejectedly to his front door.   Then he drove away.

41

Ed Burke took the safety deposit box from the bank's assistant manager and walked over to the private cubicle provided. He opened the box, removed Marty Rainey's envelope and put it in his briefcase.

An hour later his taxi dropped him at the front door of the Barton Tribunal, where he was greeted by the sign over the door in Irish and English:

Binse fiosruchain um chursai
pleanala agus iocaiochtai airithe

Tribunal of Inquiry into certain
planning matters and payments

Ushered into Judge Barton's office, he found the judge waiting for him.

"Mr. Burke, I was in two minds about this meeting. It's highly irregular. Last time we met you were appearing before my tribunal defending Mr. Mortimer. I take it you are not acting on behalf of him today. Nevertheless, I don't want to miss any opportunity to get at the facts. Are you an opportunity?"

"Judge, I'm fully aware of your concerns. And the fact that the papers have called me a suspect in the murder of the Tánaiste's wife. I'm sure you've checked me out thoroughly. And you know I didn't kill her. Otherwise I wouldn't be sitting here today."

"That's right. If I thought you were responsible for her death, you would not be sitting here today."

Ed Burke opened his briefcase, removed the folder containing Marty Rainey's documents and handed it to the Judge, "I believe that's your opportunity."

They sat together, in silence, for the next few minutes while the Judge leafed through the folder. Finally he spoke, "Thank you. This might lead us to the evidence we need. It may help us pry open the mouths that have refused to talk. Maybe give our investigators the crucial leads they need to ask for subpoenas. And we'll go back again and ask for information from the financial institutions involved in this money laundering and tax evasion. This does indeed present us with an opportunity."

"Judge, I am sure you've seen some of the names involved. Gerry Donley may have been a shrewd investor but he knew all of this was totally illegal so he kept these records to protect himself. Now you know why Marty Rainey was murdered."

"Yes. I assume that Marty Rainey was the missing witness who failed to show up at my tribunal."

"Yes, he was."

"And you are suggesting that Mortimer had something to do with his death."

"I'm not suggesting it. I'm saying it loud and clear. Mortimer had him killed. He's the murderer!"

"That's a pretty serious allegation. You're a lawyer and you better be able to back that up. Otherwise you can be stripped of your licence to practise."

"Oh, I'll be able to prove it. We have the man who killed Marty Rainey in custody. He tried to kill me a week ago. He's in bad shape but he'll live. He was searching for these documents. That's why I decided to turn them over to you."

"There's something bothering me. Are you the source of the leaked documents that the *News's* been publishing?"

"Judge, I could deny that. But what's the point? Yes, I am."

"Do you realize that you are undermining the work of this tribunal?"

"What do you mean?"

"Oh, come on!. You've warned them. They'll have destroyed all their files and documents. Our warrants and subpoenas will get us nothing. Absolutely nothing!"

"No, Judge. I don't believe that. Mortimer is a hoarder. He keeps every document, every receipt. He won't destroy anything. He thinks he's impervious, untouchable."

"But the documents you released to the press implicated Tánaiste David Manning, not Mortimer. Something I had assumed to be false. Until I read the Rainey documents you gave me."

"I believe this matter is far more serious, far more dangerous than tax evasion. Mortimer may be a fat cat but he's just small fry. A patsy in all of this. I don't think it ends with David Manning either."

"Oh, no! Not another conspiracy theory!"

"The Tánaiste won't have any documents to subpoena. So don't worry about me undermining your tribunal."

"But there's not enough in Marty Rainey's documents to support bringing Manning in front of the tribunal. And I can not be seen to be conducting a witch hunt against the second most powerful man in the country."

"I know that. But I want to smear him in the papers. Prepare the way for his downfall. Get him riled. Get him to make mistakes. Here's another allegation: I believe he had his wife killed. I can't prove that yet. But I'm certain of it. Thought he could get rid of both of us at the same time. It's no secret that I loved Pia. I'll get him if it's the last thing that I do."

"Mr. Burke, Mr. Burke!   Please, please. These allegations surely have no foundation. You're angry and you want revenge.   But you're a professional. You can't proceed with wild threats like this against the Tánaiste."

"Judge, I promise you this. These allegations are true. And I'll smoke him out. He's a danger to the nation. I believe that, as powerful as he is, his strings are being pulled by a much greater force."

"Now you mystify me."

"David Manning is certain to become Taoiseach. He brought his party into this coalition and the latest surveys show that his party will have the majority vote in the next election. He's skilled in European affairs, speaks three or four languages, always gets what he wants when he goes there. What if this 'greater force' wanted to ensure that they had a man in Strasbourg well capable of influencing the future policy making in the EU, ensuring that their plans would not be thwarted by national referendums. Is that worth a murder or two along the way? You bet it is!"

"My God, do you realize what you're saying? "

"Yes. And I am scared. You should be as well."

Judge Barton sat staring at Ed Burke. No, staring through Ed Burke. He looked into the far distance, deep in thought, left hand pulling on his lower lip. Slowly he came out of it, twisting his head from side to side, "If you're right we have very little time to avert disaster. The general election will be held before year-end and, six months after that, Ireland assumes the Presidency of the European Union. The Tánaiste will become Taoiseach. He has no opposition and he's played the voters well – from the unions to the rich and powerful. Within a year he will be President of the European Union!"

"So we have no time to waste, Judge."

"Yes, I will move on Mortimer immediately. I'll subpoena his records and order him to appear before our tribunal. If the wheels move efficiently I'll have him before my legal team one week from now, two at the very latest."

"Thank you. I'll take the Tánaiste."

"Mr. Burke, I must insist that you stay within the law."

"Judge, if I can get the evidence I need, the law will deal swiftly with the Tánaiste."

"And if you can't?"

But Ed Burke only smiled at the Judge as he thanked him warmly and left.

Judge Andrew Barton trusted very few people, not even his own tribunal staff.   But he trusted one member of his staff implicitly: his son, Andrew Jnr. A recent law graduate, top of his class, Judge Barton hired him as staff to the tribunal. Conflict of interest did not apply and, as far as nepotism goes, the job was long, tedious, and monotonous.   But the judge believed that long hours and hard work at the bottom created a firm grounding for a legal career.

An hour after Ed Burke had left his office, he called in his son.

"Andy, I have a very special job for you. Take that large envelope. Yes, on the desk. Right there."

Andy picked up the bulky envelope and waited, knowing that this was certain to be another dirty job that his father didn't want to assign to anyone else.

"I acquired those documents today. They could contain information that will allow this tribunal to expedite the work we've been charged with. I also expect that they could involve people in the highest reaches of this state. People who have supporters looking out for their welfare everywhere. Even in this tribunal. That's why I'm asking you to handle it personally."

"What do you want me to do?"

"Firstly, I want you to examine each and every document in that envelope. If any contain names in our government, hold them aside and bring them directly to me. Separate out any that relate to planning permission, especially any that have Mortimer's name on them.   I do know that some relate to the Ansbacher/Cayman accounts.   Keep them separate as well.   Can you go to work on that right away?"

A day later, Andy was back in the Judge's office, looking tired but also excited, "You were right. This is hot!"

"What did you find?"

"OK, two-thirds of it deal with planning. Good stuff that may give our investigators solid leads. I've set that aside and I think you can assign that directly to staff."

"Good...go on."

"Next the Ansbacher items. Many names on here. Here's a couple that show that Mortimer and his solicitor, Murphy, both placed funds offshore in Ansbacher on at least three occasions. I'd be pretty sure that they paid no tax on any of that. A number of large, very large investments were made in the name of Gerry Donley so we'll probably never know who really invested those funds."

"Murphy, hah! Making millions off us! So that's where he's been stashing it. I want him. Badly! Thanks, Andy!"

"There are four more documents that I've grouped together. Look at them. Some major business names appear repeatedly in them. TP McGrady, George O'Hara, and look here, Shane Braddock. They show a pattern of silent investment, mainly in lands zoned agriculture that were rezoned residential soon after they invested. And this one, here they've invested heavily in land contiguous to Dublin Airport. The same land that the Tánaiste is backing for the new terminal. Interesting?"

"I'll say! Excellent! And that's it?"

"No, I saved the best for last. This one here. See the name: D. Manning. Must have at least a million in Ansbacher.   Only one D. Manning I can think of! The Tánaiste!"

"Hah! It's him alright. But proving it will be something else. There's hundreds of Mannings in the phone directory. It's a common name. No wonder he claimed that the papers were trying to smear him. In effect he's telling us to prove it's him."

"So what can we do?"

"Dig deeper, that's what. Take this document and seek out every source you can. See if you can get some inside info. Go to the Caymans if you need to. I know, I know, they refused our request for detailed information on these accounts.   But maybe there's

150

another way. You're a good looking young fellow and a good communicator. Stay a week or two in the sun. You could use a holiday. Get to know the people who work in that bank. Maybe you can loosen some lips. OK?"

"Well, I'm up for that. Best job you've given me yet."

Andy left the judge's office, a big smile on his face. Visions of tropical beaches, exotic ladies, and summer cocktails by the pool invaded his senses.

Andrew Barton, Jr., never made it to the Cayman Islands. Crossing the street to wait for the taxi that he'd ordered to take him to the airport, he was hit by a car and ended up in hospital with a broken collar bone, two broken ribs, multiple abrasions and a mild concussion. A hit and run, the Gardaí said.

42

At first the ringing seemed to be part of Ed Burke's dream.   When it persisted he struggled awake and turned over to see the time.

5 am! Damn! Who the hell is calling me at this time of the morning? He picked up the phone but didn't answer.

"Ed, Ed, are you there?" Sean Coyne's voice.

"Do you know what time it is, Sean? You'd better have a damn good reason for interrupting my beauty sleep!"

"Bad news I'm afraid. Knew you'd want to know right away."

"What is it?"

"Billy Nee. He's dead. Suicide."

"Aw, no!   I should have moved on him right away. But, dammit, I only left him yesterday and I wanted to do the decent thing. Give him time to talk with his wife, his family. Let him take care of matters at home before he turned himself over to the Gardaí."

"It's worse than that."

"What do you mean? How could it be worse than that?"

"His wife is dead too. He shot her first, then he killed himself!"

"Oh, my God!"

"You couldn't have known he'd do this."

"That doesn't help. This is what he considered the *decent thing* to do. If I'd only known."

"You can't blame yourself."

"What about the kids?"

"The two school kids were picked up by the wife's parents. And the church has sent priests to Trinity and UCD in Dublin where the two eldest kids are studying."

"What a tragedy!"

Burke was now wide awake even though it'd been a late night for him. Hadn't got to sleep until one in the morning. With the phone to his ear, he reached for a towel and headed for the shower.

"I'm going to Commissioner Clooney as soon as I can. I want to turn over Nee's statement and affidavit now. Time to move on the *Beetle*."

And as an afterthought, "Find out where Tom Flanagan is today. I'd like to suggest a trust fund for the Nee kids."

43

The K Club stands in the middle of 550 acres in County Kildare. A luxury hotel and golf club, it was built around Straffan House, the home of the Barton family who gave their name to France's B&G wines. One of its courses has been designed by Arnold Palmer, and it's been host to the 2006 Ryder Cup.

A fitting place for the four men who met there over lunch. Perfectly fitting – or as they say in Irish : *Aithnionn ciarog ciarog eile · one cockroach knows another* – more often expressed as 'birds of a feather fly together'.

These men accounted for a major percentage of Ireland's GDP and significantly influenced the rest.   From   industrial   conglomerates   in   five continents to prize racehorses, five-star hotels and prestigious country clubs, billions sat at this lunch table today.

Long-time partners TP McGrady and Jack Simpson sat facing Shane Braddock and George O'Hara. The morning's golf conversation out of the way, TP McGrady looked at his colleagues and said:

"We all know why we're here, don't we? As much as we like golf and the K Club, we wouldn't have been here today."

"TP, damn right," said O'Hara, "I should be in New York at the quarterly meeting with my North American business."

And Jack Simpson added, "Yeah, we should all be elsewhere. This is bad."

Shane Braddock knew that they were all looking at him, " I know, I know. You invested in this one because of me. But we all agreed that this investment was absolutely essential if we wanted to control the direction of this country, if we wanted to ensure our survival and our growth. Isn't that right?"

McGrady rubbed an imaginary itch under his collar while the others shuffled their feet. Yet they all grudgingly agreed and nodded their assent. Each of them knew that there had been complete agreement on this investment.

McGrady again, "You're right Shane. But David Manning is still yours. I believe you need to advise him about the downside if he continues to put our investment at such risk. Don't you agree?"

Everyone knew what 'downside' meant. These men had built their empire on an equal measure of shrewdness and ruthlessness.

Twenty-five years earlier, TP McGrady had been an IRA prisoner, on hunger strike, in the notorious Long Kesh prison. Rumour had it that it was IRA money, the ill-gotten gains of criminal activity, that McGrady used to fund his first business venture. But no-one doubted that it had been McGrady's innate acumen and brilliance that was behind the phenomenal growth of his empire. An empire that stretched, nationally and internationally, from agriculture to food, from pubs to hotels, and from real estate to banking. Wealth and good living hadn't softened him. He remained as ruthless as he'd been in his early days with the IRA.

Jack Simpson was the odd man out. Born in the extreme loyalist Shankill in Belfast, he should not be here. Instead he should still be living in the north, a stalwart Unionist and an ardent member of his local LOL, Loyal Orange Lodge; a Brit to the core, to whom it would be anathema to sit at the table with these Catholic Irish. But Simpson, at only twelve years of age, had already rejected the entire Protestant vs. Catholic sectarian climate that he was growing up in. He couldn't believe in a God that Christians fought over so he rejected it and became an atheist. At fifteen he discovered that his only God was money. And when he looked south across the border he saw the new energy and the new money. So he crossed the border to a new birth, a new future. With his Scots-Irish genes and his Presbyterian work ethic, it didn't take him long to make his first million.

At about the time that Jack Simpson made his first million, George O'Hara returned home from England and made money collecting people's garbage. Waste disposal he called it. With the money he made he started *Hara Homes*, a new construction company. Soon he had put the *Hara Homes* stamp on many of the new residential housing developments. He then branched into hotels and banking and insurance. A prominent backer of Irish charities, a weekly mass goer, and a major contributor to the Roman Catholic Archdiocese of Dublin, George O'Hara had become a pillar of the community. No-one would ever believe that the real George O'Hara sat at this table today.

Shane Braddock, the youngest member of the group at forty-three, was perhaps the most ambitious. A geologist, he had leveraged his knowledge of the oil industry, and of greedy dictators in oil-rich third world nations, into lucrative drilling rights around the world.   He had amassed an immense personal fortune along the way. He knew that control of governments and politicians was the key to power.   Now he wanted to play a guiding hand in the direction of the European Union.   He had judged Tánaiste David Manning to be the key into this club.   Once in, he reckoned that greed and avarice would smooth the way.

44

Tom Flanagan took the phone call from Ed Burke and agreed to meet him immediately. Burke was in Connemara when he called. That was propitious because Flanagan was on his way to an industry meeting in Galway, with Michael O'Leary of *Ryanair* and Padraig O'Ceidigh of *Aer Arann*. None of them were satisfied with the expansion plans for Dublin Airport and each thought that the Tánaiste was playing a game with them. They knew that a *quid pro quo* was required to gain the Tánaiste's support and they were highly concerned about that. Seems that the Tánaiste had been meeting with each of them, individually, and he had had a slightly different story for each. It looked like he was playing them off against each other. So, even though each of them was a ferociously independent competitor, they felt that they needed to join forces on this one.

Flanagan was staying overnight at the Radisson but they wanted to avoid all the 'right people' so they decided to meet elsewhere. Burke chose the King's Head, a good pub right in the heart of the city and a place unlikely to be frequented by any of Tánaiste David Manning's social circle.

Burke was already there when Flanagan arrived at five p.m. He'd staked a claim to a corner table, not too far from the front door.

Flanagan greeted him, "Do we need to make a quick exit, Ed?"

"That's funny, Tom! I've been making a lot of quick exits lately. Thanks for coming."

"Well, as I told you, you simply beat me to it. I had intended to call you. Ever since Pia's wake."

"You and Pia were close. Neither of us had a chance to thank you. For the apartment, your discretion, and everything. Now it's too late."

The waitress arrived with another Carlsberg for Ed and a Guinness for Tom.

"Ed, I didn't know you but I was close to Pia. And if she loved you, that was good enough for me. She'd made an unfortunate choice in her partner. She deserved better."

"So you're not a big fan of the Tánaiste. I was hoping you'd say that."

"Big fan! I hate the man! He's a power-mad, self-centred prick! Why do you think I'm in Galway today? He's been playing us all for fools over the expansion plans for Dublin Airport. Holding out for the best deal. For himself, of course. Doesn't give a shite about the airline industry! Figures we'll be pressured into letting him have his own way. He has a major stake in land close to the airport where he wants to build the new terminal."

"He has a stake! But he can't ... that's conflict of interest!"

"Oh, he's clever. The stake's being held for him by a consortium of our major business players. If you challenge him, he'll simply deny it because it's not held in his name. But I have a source and I know. Wonder what he did for them to justify such a stake. Or what he's going to do for them."

"This consortium ... you know who they are?"

"As I said, I have a source close to the financial centre of one of the members of the consortium.   And, sure, I know who they are. Household names, they are!"

"Who are they?"

"Are you ready?   Jack Simpson,TP McGrady ,Shane Braddock, George O'Hara."

"Jesus Christ!"

"No, he's not a member", laughed Tom, "they don't need him. This gang controls politics in this country.   Where do you think the party gets most of its funding from?"

"Tom, this is exactly why I wanted to see you. Now I think you've put names on my nightmare."

"Nightmare?"

"Guess I sound melodramatic to you.   So, let me tell you about my nightmare."

Ed Burke went back to Pia's murder and brought Tom Flanagan current on all the events since then: the Rainey documents, Marty's murder, Johnny Fox, Brendan Tucker, his belief that Mortimer had ordered the murder of Marty Rainey, his belief that Mortimer and Manning were linked in everything, his meeting with Judge Barton and the turning over of the Rainey documents to the tribunal, and worst of all his fears about Tánaiste David Manning.

"I believe the Tánaiste had his wife killed. I can't prove that yet. But I'm certain of it. Thought he could get rid of both of us at the same time.   And, as I told Judge Barton, I believe that his strings are being pulled by a much greater force. A force that wants to ensure that they have a man in Strasbourg who can influence the future policy making in the EU.   The Tánaiste is certain to become Taoiseach. You can bet he'll get what he wants when he goes there."

Tom Flanagan had not interrupted even once. He sat absorbing everything that Ed Burke had to

say. His only movement was the steady sipping of
his Guinness. Now he leant back and took a deep
breath.

"If your theories are right, then this is a
nightmare."

"And what if my 'greater force' is your
consortium? That's one that we need to counter.
Right now, Tom!"

"You're right. I agree!"

"Now you know why I wanted to meet you."

For the next hour, they plotted and planned. Tom
Flanagan agreed to set up a counter-offensive by
bonding together many of his powerful friends. Bond
them together to counter the consortium. He'd get
his friends to start lobbying the government
intensively with plans and proposals that ran counter
to the Tánaiste and his consortium. And he'd start
immediately with a subject close to his heart: the
new terminal at Dublin Airport.

"I'd love to be a 'fly on the wall' when that
consortium meets," said Ed Burke.

"It's their emails and internet and blackberrys
that you need to listen to."

"You're a genius!   And I know just the man
who can do that. I'll take that on. Anything of value
I'll feed back to you and your counter-offensive
partners."

"Remember, if you do this it must not be
traceable to us, or to anyone."

"Tom, Tom, trust me, I won't do it otherwise."

"Can you get someone to run an investigation,
discreetly of course, on all the members of this
consortium?"

"Yes, Sean Coyne would be happy to do that.
He has a stake in all of this. And he's a good
investigative journalist. What's your thinking?"

"You never know what skeletons might be hiding in their closets. Stuff that can soil their squeaky clean image. If Sean found anything, he could put it on Page One. Nothing as good as bad press!"

At the end they had an action plan, something that the President of *FlanAir* could relate to and Burke no longer felt like Don Quixote.

45

Ed Burke and Sean Coyne caught the 9:30 am *RyanAir* flight from Dublin to Dyce Airport in Aberdeen. An hour later they left the airport in their rented car and headed north on the A96 to Inverness. But they weren't going very far. Within fifteen minutes they took the Inverurie exit and drove down through the centre of town, past the town hall, and took a right over the bridge to Old Meldrum. About a quarter of a mile on they passed the ancestral estate of the Keith clan and, a few hundred yards later, turned right between two imposing stone pillars that guarded the entrance to a long winding driveway. Turning a corner, manicured lawns fronted a large baronial mansion.

They had come to Scotland to see Sammy Begley. Ed Burke knew him well from their days at Trinity together. Like many Scots, such as Sean Connery and Billy Connolly, Begley's ancestors had left Ireland for Scotland in the nineteenth century, often to find work in the fields picking potatoes or carrying bricks on a building site. Sammy had left Scotland for Ireland and Trinity College in Dublin. Trinity College grads were forming software start-ups and an exciting frontier beckoned. Sammy was an original, a creative genius in programming and software design. But he was also a trickster, born with a penchant for practical jokes. One practical joke backfired when he was unmasked as the hacker who had been entering protected government data bases in Britain and Ireland. Not to steal or spy. No, Sammy left jokes and messages instead. But it had backfired. He was caught and his crime was not deemed funny. Sammy spent two years in jail. Time that he used to think and plan. In some ways, time well spent. After his release, he and two Trinity colleagues started a software company and success followed success. During the dot.com bubble, he sold his share of the company for four hundred million. And five years ago, after a bitter divorce and a custody battle for his two kids, Sammy returned to Scotland and the lifestyle of the Laird of the Manor.

Ed Burke had called days earlier and Sammy had been only too happy to see him after all these years. Ed told him he was bringing a friend to discuss something of great importance. And Sammy's eternal sense of curiosity made him look forward to the meeting.

He met them at the front door, gave Ed a huge bear-hug, and crunched Sean's hand in his grip. His burly, strong, outgoing nature belied the scientific mind that could quietly pursue technical puzzles for hours on end.

Late breakfast, Scottish style porridge and kippers, awaited them in the dining room. While they ate, Ed briefed Sammy on the murders of Pia and Rainey and the events of recent days. But it was the conspiracy centred around David Manning that he dealt with at length. A conspiracy that he couldn't prove but one that he'd stake his life on. And that's what he was doing. Staking his life. And he explained how Sean Coyne had become a believer too and had joined the fight.

"So we've come here looking for your help, Sammy. Your technical help."

"What do you want?"

"We want to be able to get into a computer system. One that's protected by the toughest security that money can buy. It's TP McGrady's and we think he sits at the head of the biggest conspiracy in the country, in the EU for that matter. He's the power behind Manning. We need to get in, see what he's doing, who he's contacting, read his emails, his correspondence. I know it's encrypted but we need to see it before it leaves his system, before it becomes unintelligible."

"You're asking me to hack into McGrady's system? Are you crazy?"

"No, Sammy, we're not asking you to do it. We are asking you to get us the tools so that we can do it ourselves."

"But that's the same thing. Every piece of hacking software like that is traceable."

"Sammy, there must be a way. Can you do it?"

"You're asking me to commit a crime. You know that, don't you?"

"No! All we're asking you to do is give us the tool to 'break and enter'. Nobody'll know I got it from you."

"Are you kidding? Symantec, McAfee, MI5, the Special Branch ... they've all got computer scientists who police the internet. And they know the style and signature of almost every hacker on the planet. I don't want to spend another two years in jail."

"Can't you create one that doesn't have any fingerprints on it? We need to find out what these people are planning. And we need to know now!"

"I find it hard to believe that the Tánaiste, your Deputy Prime Minister, is planning to control the state, even the EU, for his own power, his own greed."

"But you believe me, don't you?" said Ed.

"I believe that you believe it. And I suppose that's good enough for me."

"So you'll do it?"

"I'll have to think about it. It's not easy to create what you want. It'll have to be brand new. All the old virus tricks are known. Most of them are caught by very sophisticated virus protection software."

"Will you consider it?"

"OK, here's what I'll do. Only as a mental exercise at this point. I'll see if I can design something new. And, if I do, I'm not saying that I'm going to give it to you. That's all I can promise."

Ed Burke and Sean Coyne left Scotland with a sense that they had succeeded. They had challenged the genius of Sammy Begley. And they knew that Sammy would not be able to avoid the temptation. That was the only incentive. Temptation and a challenge. Sammy couldn't be tempted by money. He was already a multi-millionaire.

46

Shane Braddock looked angrily at David Manning:

"You stupid fuck!"

"You can't talk to me like that!"

"I can and I will.   Do you think I'm an imbecile? I know your hand is dipped in your wife's blood. Don't fucking deny it.   Don't even try!"

"You're crazy! Why would I do that?"

"Why?   Why?   Because power has gone to your head and you think you can get away with anything. That's why!"

"Pia hated your guts.   What do you care anyway?"

"Oh, I care!   I care a lot.   You're a major investment. And we're expecting a very high return on our investment."

"You've done well on your investment so far. You wouldn't have your billions today if I hadn't bent the rules for you, rezoned land, removed regulations, created tax incentives, got you inside deals. You owe me!"

"Don't press your luck. I control the voters. The unions vote the way I want them to. And the public vote for anybody I recommend. "

"Don't be so damn sure. Those voters are committed to me. They'll stay with me. You're just another blackmailer!"

"No, Tánaiste, you're wrong. I'm a businessman. I take opportunities when I get them. And you were an opportunity that I turned into an investment. And I like my investments to perform well."

"Businessman, hah! You're a robber baron, that's what you are. And you need to control the government so you can hold on to your empire."

"Robber baron! In America, that's what they called men like Rockefeller and JP Morgan. But those men built a nation. You don't think it was Jefferson and Adams and their starry-eyed idealist founders. Hell no, it was your robber barons who conquered the west, built a nation, and today control Wall Street and the world economy. I am a nation builder. The new Europe needs nation builders like me. If we don't do it, your European Union will sink into mediocrity, mismanaged by warring bureaucrats and incompetent leaders. That's why you're an investment that I must protect at all costs. You will be *Taoiseach* and you will hold the Presidency of the EU. And you will steer Ireland and Europe in the direction that we want."

"Oh, I'll be *Taoiseach* alright! But you can't take the credit. I'm not your patsy. We're partners in this and I've got as much at stake as you. So you don't need to lecture me about protecting our investment!"

With that the Tánaiste reached for the door handle, swung the door open, stepped onto the pavement, and walked away from Braddock's Mercedes saloon.

Braddock sat for a minute, contemplating the state of things.   Power had gone to Manning's head, power that had blinded him and made him feel omnipotent. Their investment was now high risk.   If they couldn't turn it around, they might have to write it off

47

Sammy Begley's 11 am *Ryanair* flight from Dyce Airport in Aberdeen landed at Dublin Airport at 12 noon. Ed Burke greeted him warmly as he emerged into the Arrivals lounge.

Thirty minutes later, their taxi dropped them in Ballsbridge Gardens. Once inside his apartment, Ed said, "First things first," and poured four large measures of coffee into the cafetiere, "will you settle for fresh bagels, Sammy?"

"Ed, that's perfect."

Sammy opened his dark blue carry-on bag, removed a DVD and handed it to Ed. Ed turned it over and read the insert: *The 'K Club' – Highlights of the 2006 Ryder Cup.*

"Sammy, that's lovely. But I'm not really into golf."

"It's not for you. It's a present for one of golf's biggest Irish fans, TP McGrady."

Ed Burke stopped pouring coffee into the two mugs and held the cafetiere in suspended animation. It had finally struck him.

"You did it, didn't you? This is it, isn't it?"

"Yes, that's it."

"Brilliant! We should be drinking something stronger than coffee. We'll leave the adult beverages till this evening."

"I won't be staying. So let me tell you what this will do and how to use it."

Euphoria gone and the coffee too, Sammy Begley lifted a laptop carrier bag from the floor beside him, unzipped it, removed the laptop and placed it on the kitchen table. He opened it and turned it on. Nothing unusual. Windows XP loaded and the start-up sequence commenced. Only one user appeared on the screen. Sammy placed the cursor over it and clicked. The usual desktop display icons appeared, with one exception: a folder named *TROY.*

"*TROY* is housed on a site in Islamabad, Pakistan. Everything will go first to that server in Pakistan and then it'll be forwarded to this laptop. If anyone tries to locate it, they'll discover that it's also in Islamabad. And if they try to find the server in Islamabad they'll only reach a dead-end. So you see, nothing can be traced to you or me."

Ed Burke had never doubted Sammy Begley's ability. Ed's usual loquacity now failed him and he simply nodded, knowing he was in the presence of a genius.

Sammy continued, "Let me explain how it works. You have broadband, right?"

"Yes, I do."

"OK, the Ryder Cup DVD is the key. Find a way to have McGrady run it on his computer. Shouldn't be too difficult seeing that he's such a big fan of the game. When he runs the DVD, it will download special software onto his hard drive. When he goes on-line, that software will send all the files on his system to this laptop. It will also send you a copy of every email he sends and everyone he receives. He will not know that this is happening. Most

171

importantly, you must boot the laptop, open TROY, connect to broadband and leave it on all day. It must be on *live standby* at all times so that it can receive from McGrady's computer. Do you understand, Ed?"

"Absolutely!"

"Can you get McGrady to run the DVD?"

"We have someone in his organization."

"Good."

"How can we ever repay you?"

"No need. This got my juices flowing again. You knew it would, didn't you? So, get the bastard for me too! That will be ample payment!"

48

True to his word, Tom Flanagan moved fast on his counter-offensive, fighting *'fire with fire'* or, in this case, *'money and power'* with *'money and power'.* Opposition party TDs launched an onslaught of questions in the *Dail* about the deals being done to acquire land for the new terminal at Dublin Airport. Editorials in the major newspapers explored the whiff of corruption in the body politic. *PRIME TIME,* the television showcase of investigative journalism, scheduled an entire programme on the subject. McDevitt, the *News's* managing editor, had withstood a grilling over their recent *Page One* headlines on corruption and off-shore accounts. Without naming names, and while continuing to assert that he didn't know the source of the leaked documents, he accomplished his objective. When the programme ended, that whiff of corruption in the body politic floated dangerously close to the Tanaiste.

Ed Burke and Sean Coyne arrived at *FlanAir's* headquarters in Custom House Docks, adjacent to the IFSC, the International Financial Services Centre, the hub of international banking and finance in Ireland. They took the lift to *FlanAir's* tenth floor executive offices.

Tom Flanagan met them at the door, "Ed, Sean, come in, come in."

"I'm impressed," said Ed.

"That's the intent. As my mother used to say *'if you have a cow you'll get a cow'*. Our offices here are an investment in *FlanAir's* image."

He then guided them through the large double doors into the reception area, smiled at the smart looking young receptionist, and led them back to his office. On the tenth floor corner, it commanded a view of the River Liffey and the bustling city below.

"Marvellous view! How do you get any work done here?"

"It inspires me. *FlanAir's* feet are in the air, not on the ground. But we didn't come here to talk about that. Let's sit."

They gathered around Tom Flanagan's desk, which wasn't a desk at all. A round mahogany table, it could seat six comfortably, and acted as a conference table as well as a desk.

"I reckoned we'd be here over lunch so I took the liberty of ordering lunch. Hope you don't mind."

He pointed to a credenza that ran the length of the wall behind him. It supported an appetizing display of ham, wild smoked salmon, brown soda bread, strawberries and other fruit.

While Ed and Sean salivated over the offering, Tom said, "We're waiting for one more person. My inside source in the consortium."

As he said that, his phone buzzed, "Yes, Cathy? OK, please send her in."

Moments later, they turned around to see the new arrival. Ed Burke had expected another man. Now he pushed his chair back and stood in surprise.

"Maria, thank you for coming," said Tom Flanagan, rising to greet her, "I'd like you to meet Ed

Burke and Sean Coyne." And turning to them said, "Ed and Sean, Maria Lane."

Sean shook hands with her and then she turned to Ed, "Mr. Burke, you've become a household name lately. Pleased to meet you."

As they shook hands, Ed felt drawn into the deepest blue eyes he'd ever seen and realized that Maria Lane stood tall, easily matching his own six feet. Blonde, Parisian cut hair, framed her beautiful face, a face strengthened by a firm jaw line. A tailored dark business suit completed her no-nonsense image.

"Believe me, that kind of publicity I don't need. And please call me Ed."

"OK, everyone, let's have some lunch before we get serious," said Tom Flanagan.

Twenty minutes later, appetites sated, they once again convened around Tom Flanagan's round desk.

"Maria is fully briefed on why we are here. She has my full confidence but I'll let her speak for herself," said Tom Flanagan.

"Thank you, Tom. I am the Administrative Assistant to TP McGrady. Even though I don't have full membership of their little club, I do know the threat they pose to this country. And, before you ask me, I don't work for any organization, Secret Service, MI5, MI6, CIA ... might as well name drop them! I do have a personal reason for doing what I'm doing. But I'm not going to talk about that. Except to say that I want to stop McGrady and his friends. Tom has told me all about your fears, Ed. And I am not surprised. Or shocked. I think you're right. And that's why I am here. I want to help you stop them."

Ed Burke had brought the laptop and the *Ryder Cup Highlights* DVD with him. He placed the laptop in the centre of the desk and briefed them fully on the technical details. No-one interrupted.

"Perfect!" said Maria, "I can get McGrady to run that DVD on his system. He's often on the net. Big fan of the technology. And he loves golf. He was a *Ryder Cup* special guest at *The K Club.* So he'll love this. It'll sell itself."

"This software cannot be traced back, to this DVD or to anyone else. As soon as it downloads to his hard drive, it immediately erases itself from the DVD. It burns its bridges. So, it cannot be traced to you. You won't be compromised. OK?"

"You seem to have great faith in it. But I'm willing to take the risk. Getting McGrady is well worth it."

Ed closed the laptop and turned to Sean Coyne, "Sean, you have a contribution to make, don't you?"

"Thanks, Ed. I've been looking into the closet of every one of these upstanding people. And I think I've found something. In O'Hara's past. Looks like he has left this country with a collection of illegal dumps, some of which may be toxic. At least one big dump across the border in Northern Ireland. That'll make the UK government real happy! They date back about fifteen years. When he was on the bottom rung of the ladder and owned two waste disposal companies. He sold them later at a huge profit, funding for his next investment. He was aggressive and unscrupulous. Hardly the image that he projects today as the darling of the Catholic Archdiocese and the *holier that thou* champion of the morals of the nation!"

"That's exactly what we need, " said Tom Flanagan, "will your editor publish this?"

"McDevitt's on board. He's a believer. But we have to get hard evidence first and I'm sure we can."

Ed reached across and handed the DVD to Maria, "I'll give you my mobile number. Call me if you have any problems" and, as Maria took the DVD, he added, with a smile," Call me even if you don't."

Then, looking at Tom Flanagan, he said, "Let me bring you up-to-date on where we are before I go. I turned Marty Rainey's documents over to Judge Barton. That enabled him to subpoena Mortimer. He's asked for full disclosure of all of Mortimer's files. We can only hope he finds a *smoking gun* linking him to David Manning. Mortimer is trying to stall the tribunal. But the judge will jail him if he tries that. At any rate I hope it's giving the Minister some sleepless nights and shaking up our cosy little consortium. "

Tom said, "And maybe if we shake them up, they'll get careless. And, Maria, if they do, you might get the evidence on Manning that we need."

Ed said, "I don't think the tribunal will find anything linking Mortimer to Marty Rainey's murder. But I believe that I can tie him to Johnny Fox's murder in Mountjoy. The guard who did it recorded and signed a statement before he killed himself. I've turned that statement over to Commissioner Clooney and he's delivered it to the DPP. It clearly indicts a man called Joe McGinnis. You probably know him, from the tabloids, as *The Beetle*. I'm sure *The Beetle* was taking orders from Mortimer, maybe even Manning himself. We'll have to see if he'd prefer to cut a deal or rot his arse in Mountjoy for the rest of his days."

The meeting over, they agreed to meet again in ten days, sooner if necessary. As they left, Maria said, "Ed, I'll call you."

49

Denis Rainey was an only child. His father Thomas had died from a cerebral haemorrhage, only seven years ago. But not before he had moved his family into a new house, one with a separate apartment for Denis. He and Denis's mother, Ellen, had long ago realized that Denis would never be able to function alone in that wide, wide world. He lacked all cognitive reasoning and was unable to function in groups. He didn't even have one friend. Computers were his only friend. He was not a savant but he had the Asperger gift of acquiring knowledge in a very specific area, often something in science or maths. With Denis it was computers. At thirty-six years of age with the mentality of a teenager, he still managed to hold a key software development job with SUN Microsystems at their offices in Eastpoint Business Park, thirty minutes by bus from his own home.

Denis needed to function in an exact routine every day. His work accommodated that and he was always home at five thirty every day. Usually he went home to his own apartment, seldom stopping in to see his mother. They shared the same roof but led separate lives.

Arriving home at five thirty-five, he put an Indian meal, chicken korma, in the microwave, heated a nan bread, and filled a tall glass with water.

He didn't cook and he never drank anything stronger than water. Loading everything on a large tray he sat at the kitchen table beside a huge pile of newspapers that had taken over at least one half of the table. He took another one out of his briefcase and added it to the pile. As he ate, he sifted through them again, all first page stories by a reporter called Sean Coyne covering everything from the murder of his uncle Marty to the killing of Johnny Fox, the suicide of Billy Nee, and the on-going testimony of Mortimer before the Barton Tribunal. Mortimer, the man his Uncle Marty had been so afraid of, the man he refused to testify against. His uncle Marty had told him that. He liked to confide in me, Denis confirmed to himself. This had been Denis's daily ritual since his uncle's death. Reading the headlines, following the story, seething inside.

Finishing his meal, he took the tray to the sink and then crossed the room to the table in the corner that he had turned into a shrine to his Uncle Marty. In the centre stood a large framed photo of Marty and himself, both of them smiling ear to ear. Marty had his arm tightly around him. A brass candlestick holder stood on each side of the picture, the candles worn down half-way. Denis scratched a match and lit them. He stood there for almost five minutes and then, as though he had made a decision, he turned smartly away.

Out in the hallway, he rooted through a pile of stuff in the bottom of the closet and found what he was looking for, a large old tea caddy, an antique. He brought it back to the living room, sat down and looked at it. It had come out of their old house. Used to be hidden under the floorboards. His mother had decided to get rid of it but he had taken it. She had always thought that one of the workmen on the site had stolen it.

He opened it and took out a bundle of oily rags. Unwrapping them he looked at the small pearl handled revolver, the one his grandfather had used during the troubles in the twenties, the one he'd hidden for ever. It seemed almost new. A package of bullets rested at the bottom of the tea caddy. He took one and inserted it in the revolver and spun the chamber, marvelling at its workmanship.

Then he took the gun and the rest of the bullets and placed them in an inside pocket of his briefcase.

50

Rain lashed the windscreen in sheets as Burke pulled his car into the parking lot of the Schoolhouse Hotel in Clontarf.

Coyne cursed, "Fucking country!   It never stops raining. Makes me want to go live in Florida. Or Spain. Or anywhere the sun shines!"

Burke said, "You don't have to dig out of six inches of snow in the morning like I had to in New York. Believe me, I'll take this any day. Sure it's a fine soft day. Anyway, this is as close as we'll get."

"Yeah, guess the Gardaí have the place sealed off. But I've got my press badge. That'll get us as close as we can."

Burke zipped and buttoned up his raincoat and pulled the hood over his head. Coyne only had a *mac-in-a-sac* but it'd have to do. They closed the car door and made a run for it. Out onto Clontarf Road and back towards a complex of up-market apartments tucked away, hidden behind the big old mansions that fronted the road.

Police tape sealed off the avenue leading to the apartment building where Mortimer had been shot. Journalists and TV news-people huddled under umbrellas or spoke into microphones while cameras captured every word for Sky, CNN, the BBC, and

RTE. They were all here. And Sean knew most of them.

Two young guards, looking miserable in the downpour, stood behind the tape to prevent anyone from entering. They could see three police cars about a hundred yards ahead, barely blocking their view of a tent erected at the entrance to the apartments. Probably concealing the State Pathologist as she examined the body.

Charlie Crowe from RTE approached.

"Charlie, hell of a day."

"Hello Sean, miserable indeed," said Charlie, looking intently at Ed Burke.

"What happened?"

"We don't know very much.   Apparently Mortimer was leaving the building when he was shot. High price to pay for a *quickie*!"

"A *quickie*? What do you mean?"

"Oh, come on!   Many people knew that Mortimer's mistress lived here. He often popped in at lunchtime."

Finally recognition dawned on Charlie Crowe as he recognized Ed Burke and said, "Aren't you Ed Burke?"

"Yes, I am."

"Weren't you defending Mortimer at the Barton Tribunal?"

"I was. But I resigned. You know that, don't you?"

"You're right. But I don't know the full story. You disappeared after the Tánaiste's wife was murdered. Shouldn't you clear this all up?"

"What are you suggesting, Charlie?"

"An interview with me. Prime Time exclusive. Clear your name. Give you an opportunity to tell your side of the story."

"That would be good for you. But not for me."

"I have a sense that you know a lot about what's going on here. The Tánaiste's wife's murder. The Rainey murder. The Fox suicide. Now the Mortimer killing. They're all connected, aren't they?

"Charlie, you're the best investigative reporter in this country. And I can only say that your senses do not fail you. But I cannot be quoted for even saying that."

"So what can you tell me?"

"At this time, nothing. But I'll promise you this. When this is all over, I'll give you your Prime Time exclusive."

Sean Coyne chipped in, "Charlie, you got what you wanted. Ed's promised you an exclusive. So you owe us one. What more do you know about what happened here today?"

"I know very little. Mortimer was shot as he left the building. He fell down the front steps. Then the gunman walked up and finished him off. Shot him in the head. We managed to get that from an eyewitness who called us from one of the apartments. Wants to stay anonymous, of course."

"So who shot him? Do you know?"

"Don't you know? The Gardaí caught him down at the Eastpoint Business Park. He worked for SUN Microsystems. Did this on his lunch-hour."

"His lunch-hour?"

"Yeah, he must've been stalking Mortimer for some time. Knew where to find him, and when. Today he got lucky."

"So who is he?"

"Oh, his name explains it all! This was an act of revenge. He's Denis Rainey, Marty Rainey's nephew."

51

Archbishop John McCready sat at his desk fingering the rosary beads in his right hand. These days he did not say the rosary every day with the rigour and discipline he had experienced at his mother's knee. Rosary every night, everyone in the family on their knees, his father acquiescent but unwilling. And the trimmings at the end: the prayers for all the dead, all the neighbours, every sick person in the neighbourhood, and the world; endless, with his father dozing off in the middle of it. But now he used the beads as worry stones, as aids to contemplation, as doors to his deepest thoughts. Dressed in a simple cassock with the sleeves rolled up, his bald head and ordinary looks gave no hint of his imperious rule as Archbishop.

A knock on his door announced the entry of a young priest.

"Yes, Father Thomas?"

"It's Mr O'Hara. He's here."

"Alright, send him in. And make sure I'm not disturbed."

George O'Hara entered the room with his usual familiarity. Robust, red cheeked and cheery of manner, George O'Hara could easily have passed for a jolly member of the church hierarchy.

"George, good of you to come on such short notice."

George O'Hara had many more important matters to take care of, yet he said, "Nothing more important than yourself, Archbishop." He took a seat in front of the Archbishop's desk and waited.

"I'm very worried. These newspaper headlines. Illegal dumps and implications of corruption."

"Yellow journalism. Tabloid smears. That's what it's all about. Sells newspapers."

"I wasn't born yesterday, you know. These newspapers are not stupid. If they're lying, they'd risk a lawsuit from you, wouldn't they?"

"They know I won't do that because it would keep it in the headlines. Help them sell more papers. They know I'm hoping that it'll disappear soon, replaced by some other hot topic."

"But damage has already been done."

"What do you mean?"

"You must know that your reputation makes you our best advocate with this government. You sit on the group led by the Tánaiste that's deciding how much we pay in compensation for the victims of abuse by some of our clergy. You're close to arranging a most favourable settlement. We are having some difficulty there."

"I don't understand."

"I've had some calls from other members of the group. They don't feel comfortable having you there. They plan to ask the Tánaiste to remove you."

"Nobody's said a thing to me. Are you sure this isn't a ploy to get me off the group? There are a couple of people who think our proposed settlement is millions short of what the church should be paying in compensation. With me removed they stand a better chance of convincing the others to see it their way."

"George, believe me, this is no ploy. I've already spoken to the Tánaiste but his hands are tied. If these allegations in the papers turn out to be true, we will lose you. And that will be a body blow to this church. Do you understand that?"

"I   think   you're   overestimating   my importance."

"No! The church needs allies today. We need people like yourself at the helm of power. We need governments that can be persuaded to see the world from our point of view. We are not protected by the constitution any more."

"Oh, yes, Article 2's gone. Well, we had to trade that off for a peace settlement in the north."

"I was opposed to that, as you know. But I'm afraid that our influence has diminished. Your Ireland now preaches cultural diversity. Cultural diversity! Hah! Those are code words for the erosion of Catholic teaching, for the destruction of our ethos, our beliefs, and our culture. With this diversity we've got divorce and next it'll be abortion and heaven knows what else. We're losing control of the schools and there's even talk of taking cultural diversity into the teaching of religion, talk of teaching evolution instead of our biblical belief in creation."

"But, Archbishop, I am insignificant when it comes to that great struggle."

"No you are not. When Europe was in the dark ages, our monks took the light of Christ to the darkest corners of Europe. Often, just one monk at a time. And they convinced Kings and Queens and governments. But mostly they convinced the people.
"

Archbishop McCready had been playing with his rosary beads all this time. Now he self-consciously placed them on the desk, got up and came around and took a seat next to George O'Hara.

"George, we are in a new dark age. And we need to go back to the continent again, back to the halls of power, back to the EU. We need to do what those Irish monks did. Convince them! Let us re-establish great seats of learning again. Bring God back! George, we can only do that if we have the right people in the right places. You are in the right place for us now. And the Tánaiste will lead this country soon. He will roll back these abominable changes in our laws."

George O'Hara had never seen such a messianic look in the Archbishop's eyes, thought he should offer some words of comfort, "Archbishop, I'll talk with the Tánaiste. I'm sure we can reach a settlement favourable to the church. And my reputation will survive these smears. I promise you that. We'll be on firm ground once the Tánaiste becomes Taoiseach."

Archbishop McCready stood up, laid his hand on George O'Hara's head in a symbolic act of absolution, and returned to his desk. O'Hara left.

52

The Beetle's eyes narrowed and the veins bulged in his reddening neck. The day's sweat had overridden his daily splash of cologne, giving off a repellent odour. But no one was there to notice.

He slammed the phone down and, just as fiercely, lifted it and dialled again, "Listen, get the lads together. Seven tonight. You know where."

Finished, he again slammed the phone back on the receiver, shouting out loud, "Brendan, the stupid fuck! Screwed up big time! If he talks, I'm fucked!"

At exactly seven pm, the Beetle and four of his team met. At nine pm the meeting ended. They left with a mission: *Free Brendan Tucker!*

At five the following morning, the hospital was quiet. Two or three people slumped over chairs in the Accident & Emergency waiting room. Twenty more lay on trolleys in the hallway, waiting for beds. Some of them had lain there for over twelve hours. They were all ignored by the two Gardaí who wheeled Brendan Tucker through A&E to the unmarked Securicor prison transport van outside.

"I'm not a fucking invalid, ye know," protested Tucker.

The Gardaí didn't answer.

"Did ye hear me? I said I'm not a fucking invalid!"

The younger guard, not accustomed to such abuse, couldn't contain himself, " You get the same treatment as any other patient. We take you in a wheelchair from the ward to your car or ambulance. In your case it's straight to Mountjoy! And I hope they throw the key away!"

The older guard glowered, shook his head, and held open the outer doors while his partner pushed Tucker through the exit and right up to the already open rear door of the white prison van. One Securicor guard handcuffed Tucker and joined him in the rear of the van. The second signed the papers, closed the rear door, and climbed into the driver's seat. In a minute he had traversed the hospital parking area and exited the grounds. Transfer accomplished in less than five minutes.

They moved slowly through the streets. Lights began appearing in windows, signs that life was stirring. Dry morning, good forecast, no traffic – all of that and the soothing sounds of classical music from FM 100 relaxed the driver. *No rush,* he told himself, *piece of cake.* They'd deliver their passenger to Mountjoy in twenty minutes.

The intermittent traffic lights stayed green, *almost as though they are in collusion with me,* thought the driver. With no merging traffic to avoid at the roundabouts, he glided through each with only a glance at the cross streets. A milkman up ahead closed the doors on the rear of his delivery van. A rare and disappearing sight these days. Most people picked up their milk at their local supermarket. But

some senior citizens and shut-ins still depended on
their daily milk delivery.

As they reached the next roundabout the
milkman pulled his van out in front and stalled. The
Securicor driver almost rear-ended him. With his
emergency lights flashing, the milkman walked
around his vehicle seeming puzzled. Looking up at
the driver, he shrugged his shoulders and shook his
head in frustration. The driver couldn't get out to
help the milkman. So he sat there for a minute and
then decided to reverse. As he did so a large black
SUV pulled out of a side street and moved behind,
effectively blocking him.

Two men, wearing balaclavas, jumped out of
the SUV and ran to the prison van. One of them fired
a shotgun through the door of the van, forced the door
open, and dragged the driver on to the road. The
blast had severed an artery in his leg. If he didn't get
help he'd soon bleed to death. They put a gun to his
head and threatened to kill him right then if the
other guard refused to open the door. The second
guard had no time to think. Saving his friend seemed
more important than taking Brendan Tucker to jail.

So he opened the door. One of the men pulled
him on to the street, saying "Gimme the keys to the
cuffs!"

He did and they uncuffed Brendan Tucker and
put him in the SUV. Within a minute they had
reversed and left the area.

"Holy shite!" gasped Tucker, breathless from surprise
as much as shock.

"You look surprised, Brendan", said Tommy
Keegan.

"I feckin' am, Tommy. Never expected this."

"Come on, surely you didn't think the boss was goin' to let you rot in the 'Joy !"

"I dunno. I fucked up. I dunno."

"Well, the boss owes you, man. He believes you're better off outa the 'Joy."

"I dunno. I fecking don't know!"

"You think he'd go to this trouble if he didn't think it was a good idea. Wait'll you talk to him."

They gave Tucker a flask of hot tea and a roll and he settled in to enjoy it, thinking that freedom 'on the run' was a lot better than an all-expenses paid cell in Mountjoy.

They drove west out of Dublin on the N6. The road going east to Dublin was already beginning to fill up with early morning commuters. At Tyrellspass they left the main road and took a meandering secondary road for at least ten miles. Then they turned left into a single track boreen, bordered by unkempt hedgerows and clumps of blazing red fuschia. Half an hour later, they pulled into a narrow lane that ended at the front door of a small thatched cottage. *Must be the last one left in Ireland*, Tucker speculated. Once inside, he discovered a modern comfortable interior with an open plan kitchen, dining, and living area. A new-looking pine staircase led to an open loft bedroom framed in similar pine.

"Make yourself comfortable, Brendan. The boss'll be here in a couple of hours. Plenty of food and there's beer in the fridge. Help yourself."

"Where are we?"

"Where nobody can find you! Isn't that what you want?"

"Very funny! You know what I mean."

"Yeah, well, we're in the ass-end-of-nowhere, that's where we are. This house isn't on any of the Guards maps. You're safe here for now. I'm sure the boss will fill you in on his plans. So relax, have a beer man, chill out! We'll keep a look-out."

Tommy left to join his partner who'd remained outside in the SUV. Brendan checked out the fridge and chose a beer over the Guinness. He sank into a large over-stuffed armchair in the living room and reached for the TV remote. Switched on and was amazed to find that he had SKY on satellite. *Fucking great little cottage*, he said out loud to himself. Hezbollah had fired another two hundred rockets into Israel and the Israelis had bombed Lebanon again. *Could be a lot worse*, he thought, *could be in the middle of that shit!*

Lulled into a trance by the sheer boredom of the news, he almost missed the *news flash* on the bottom of the screen:

Brendan Tucker escapes from prison van in bold early morning attack in Dublin ... more on the one o'clock news...

Shite! I'm famous! he shouted, then immediately thought, *Shite, shite, shite! Now every fucker in the country'll be lookin' for me!* Adrenalin running high, he jumps up and takes two more beers from the fridge, to save himself from getting up too soon again.

He made certain to tune in to SKY news at one, biting his fingernails as it seemed the only news in the entire world was the Israel/Hezbollah war. Then, at twenty minutes past the hour, SKY switched to Dublin and the Tucker escape. A reporter stood on the street where he'd escaped from the prison van, giving a description of the event. Brief flashes showed his picture and advised people that he was extremely dangerous and to contact the Gardaí if he was seen. It went on to say he was wanted for the murder of the Tánaiste's wife, giving some background on that, including a snippet showing Ed Burke, refusing to talk to a reporter. The sign over the door in the background read in Irish and English, *Oifig an Phoist Cladach Dubh, Claddaghduff Post Office.*

   Smartass prick, thought Tucker, *shoulda killed him when I had the chance!*

53

"Some people have a great life, lying on their ass, doing nothing all day!"   The Beetle's unmistakeable voice overrode the drone of SKY and penetrated Tucker's beer induced sleep. Tucker struggled awake and The Beetle reached for the remote and shut off the TV.   Looking at Tucker, he asks, "Aren't you going to say anything to me?"

"Thanks for getting me out! I can't believe you'd do that!"

"Why not? What the fuck do you think I am? Man, you took care of me and I owe you. No way I'm going to let you rot in Mountjoy. Now your partner was a different matter. Fox the informer! And you know what we think of informers in Ireland? But we got his ass. He won't be informing on anyone."

"You killed Fox."

"Well, let's just say he saw the error of his ways and took his own life."

"They don't believe that. They know he was murdered. And they're tryin' to find out who did it."

"How do you know that?"

"That fella Burke came to see me. The bastard who put me in the hospital. Tried to cut a deal with me. Tried to get me to rat on you. But I said nothin', not a feckin' word! I screwed up there. Shoulda killed the prick!"

"So they tried to get you to talk?"

"Yeah, but there's no way I'd ever tell them anythin'. You know that, don't you?"

"Brendan, Brendan. Of course I know that! You're not Johnny Fox!"

The beer had filled Tucker's bladder so he headed for the john. The Beetle got himself a bottle of Ballygowan still water from the fridge, telling himself that he'd moved just in time. Tucker came out of the john, looked at the Beetle, seemed to want to say something, cleared his throat and said, "They know I killed the Tánaiste's wife."

"Jaysus! They're playing with your head!"

"Naw, naw! They found that stuff, DNA. Said it was a match for me. You know that stuff's better that fingerprints. They're not bluffin' They got me."

The Beetle walked around the room thinking about this. It was new news to him and he thought that it was as well that he'd sprung Tucker before they made him talk. So he said, "Just as well I sprung you. You'd have been in the Joy for the rest of your days, me boy!"

"I'm all over the feckin' news. Everybody'll be lookin' for me."

"No, they'll be looking for Brendan Tucker. Not for you."

"Whad'ye mean?"

"I'm going to get you a new ID, new papers, maybe even a new look."

Brendan Tucker looked hard at the Beetle, thinking to himself, *Why is he doing this? I'm only small fry.* And then thinking, *I don't believe it. He's foolin' me. But I won't be able to prove that. Until it's too late.* So he said, "Why are you doing this for me?"

"I'm doin' it to protect the Tánaiste. I want you out of their filthy claws. I don't want them

195

anywhere near the case of his wife. I can't explain any more to you. You'll just have to trust me on this."

"So, when can I leave here?"

"Not for a while. It'll take some time to get the proper identity papers for you. And to plan your new life. You're safe here in the meantime. I'll make sure the fridge is well stocked and the lads can get you anything you want."

With that he gave Brendan a huge bear hug and left. Tucker opened another can of beer, sat down, pulled the ring and took a deep slug. He went over everything a dozen times, from the moment Burke came to see him in the hospital to the instant the Beetle closed the cottage door behind him. And he came to only one conclusion: *I'll never leave this cottage. I am a dead man!*

54

Whenever he could find the time, TP McGrady spent the weekend at his house in the Churchfield estate in the grounds of the K Club in County Kildare. Close enough to Dublin, the house overlooked one of the K Club's golf course lakes.

This weekend he had managed to get away on the Thursday for a long weekend and had asked Maria Lane, his Administrative Assistant, to put together a briefcase of important business documents and bring it out to him on Friday. He hoped to find time to study them over the weekend. Maria thought that the place and time couldn't have been better if she'd managed it herself. Just the place to give him his Ryder Cup DVD.

She arrived mid-afternoon on the Friday and was ushered into TP's Churchfield house by a smartly dressed young man, seemingly a valet/waiter/jack-of-all-trades. TP's 'Man Friday' , she thought. He guided her out through the sun room to the garden terrace where TP stood looking out at the golf course.

"Do you play, Maria?"

"No. I've never been interested. But I suppose I've never had the opportunity either."

"Well, if you change your mind, I can arrange some lessons from the pro here."

With that, he turned around and led her back through the sun room to the expansive drawing room, dominated by a Waterford crystal chandelier and a marble fireplace framed by full length marble carved Celtic figures. He stopped and put out his hand for the briefcase she'd brought.

"I have something else for you. Something special that I thought you'd like."

Looking at her with curiosity, he waited as she fished inside the briefcase and retrieved the Ryder Cup DVD and gave it to him.

"What's this?"

"It's some marvellous highlights of the Ryder Cup taken here at the K Club."

"Go on!"

"Yes, yes! I knew you'd like it!"

"Like it. I'll love it! Where in the world did you get this?"

"I have some friends in the media who are preparing a special for one of the Sky Sports channels. These are very special outtakes. They will not be available anywhere. It's how would you say, a 'one-off'."

"Maria, fantastic! I want to see this now. Let's go."

He left the drawing room and crossed the entrance room to his office with Maria in tow. Once there, he sat at his desk , plugged in his laptop, booted it up, and inserted the DVD.

"I'll download this to my server. Then I'll be able to watch it anywhere I happen to be. I don't have time today but I have to see it to believe it!"

Enraptured like a child, he watched the opening five minutes of the Ryder Cup, then shut down the system, thanked Maria profusely, and insisted that she let him buy her lessons from the K Club pro.

55

Next evening Maria Lane and Ed Burke met for dinner and immediately discovered that they both loved good red wine. Maria had left her tailored, no-nonsense image at the office. Dressed in a flattering mauve dress, her beautiful face softened by the candlelight, Ed felt that this is where he should be tonight and this is the woman he should be with. A match of equals, he thought, then dismissed the legal mind that seemed to be overruling his other mind, the one of intuition and emotion.

"How did you get him to run the DVD so easily?"

"Easier than I thought it'd be. He's spending this weekend at his house at the K Club. I had to deliver some business papers to him yesterday. Said he wanted to read them over the weekend. So I took the Ryder Cup DVD with me. Told him I'd got it from a friend in the media. He never questioned me on that. But he insisted on running it before I left. Just to make sure it was OK. I watched him as he looked at the opening few minutes. He uploaded it to his server so that he could watch it from any of his computers."

"I'll drink to your success!" said Ed, raising his glass of red and clinking Maria's.

Maria could see that Ed seemed to be in deeper thoughts. The wisps of grey hair gave his dark good looks a debonair dash. She felt his blue eyes looking deep inside her.

"Penny for your thoughts", she said.

He laughed, "Oh, they're not worth it. Just day-dreaming. I'm sorry."

"You did seem to be somewhere far away."

"Well, I wasn't very far away. I was right here. Do you really want to spend that penny?"

"Yes, I do."

"OK. I was thinking how good it felt to be here with you. That may sound crazy. And presumptuous. You see, now you're embarrassed."

"No, no! Actually I'm flattered."

An awkward moment relieved by the waiter arriving with the menu. They spent the next few minutes discussing the entrees, finally settling for the rack of Connemara lamb. A match for their red wine.

"Why are you doing this, Maria?"

"You mean spying on McGrady?"

"Well, I didn't put it like that."

"It's a long story. And a very personal one."

"I'm not prying. Just wondered why. You don't have to tell me if you don't want to."

"No, it's not that. It's something that I'm not accustomed to talking about."

"If it makes you uncomfortable, I don't need to know."

"No, you do need to know. What you're doing means everything to me."

The waiter arrived with their second bottle of red, refilled their glasses and left. Maria played with the stem of her glass but didn't drink. Then she stopped, straightened her shoulders and looked at Ed.

"TP McGrady killed my brother."

Stunned, Ed could only sit in silence as Maria continued.

"It was a long time ago. But it seems like yesterday to me. I was only ten years old when my brother, Dara, died. He was my hero. I loved him, I looked up to him. And he always looked after me. At school, when I was only six, I remember how he protected me, how he stood up for me."

She paused, tears in her eyes, and wiped them with her napkin before she continued.

"Time's got bad in Derry. Violence on the street. RUC batoning the kids, shooting rubber bullets at them. Dara got caught up in it all. And he found a hero, TP McGrady, who led him into the IRA. But Dara didn't know what he was doing. He was an angry young man. They came for him in the middle of the night. Dragged him out of bed, bundled him into an army tank, and threw him into Long Kesh with McGrady. Dara never came out of there. Two years later in 1981, the same year that Booby Sands died on hunger strike, Dara was dead. Brutalized by the guards and abused by other prisoners, he didn't wake up one morning. They say his heart gave out but I don't believe it. He was murdered and I blame McGrady for his death."

She stopped to wipe the tears again and Ed asked, "Doesn't McGrady know how you feel?"

"Oh, he thinks he's making amends by giving me this job. And I went along with it to get close to him. I only wanted revenge!"

"And now?"

"Now? Now I want justice. What I've seen of McGrady business only confirms my belief. He's ruthless. And he's dangerous. He's only in the game for one person. Himself! And he doesn't care who he tramples on."

201

Ed reached in his pocket, took out a brand new handkerchief and gave it to Maria. She thanked him and dabbed at her eyes. Then she burst out laughing.

Ed was thrown off guard, disturbed by her rapid change of emotion, until she said, "Oh, Ed, please forgive me. I couldn't help it. " She fluffed out his handkerchief to show the yellow embroidered face of Bart Simpson!

Ed started to laugh too, "Oh, God, I must have made a mistake when I put that in my pocket this morning. It was a gift from my ex. One of the only things from her that I held on to. Couldn't throw Bart in the bin! But that's a story for another day."

"Well, if you want to talk about it sometime"

They finished their meal and Ed called a taxi. He dropped Maria home and then directed the driver to his apartment in Ballsbridge. On the way he kept telling himself not to get involved, not to get burned again. He was afraid to lose again.

56

Tucker waited till dusk before making his move. He'd already decided to leave and he suspected that Tommy Keegan and his partner may have been instructed to prevent that. If he's right, they've most likely been given orders to take care of him, probably when he's asleep tonight. So he'd try to make them believe that he suspected nothing. He could see them sitting on two green plastic chairs beside the SUV. He opened the door and walked towards them. He was sure he could see them tense up when they saw him.

"Nice evenin' fellas. You know what I'd like. Saw some chopped mince in the freezer. Maybe we could make up a bunch of burgers. You don't think this old cottage might have some kind of a barbecue do you?"

They both looked at him in amazement, totally disarmed by his request. Then Tommy said, "Jeez, I dunno. A barbecue out here? But you never know these days. You hang out with Joe here and I'll take a look in that old garden shed."

"Thanks, Tommy. I have this feeling that you'll get lucky. And I make a good burger, so dinner's on me."

As Tommy headed off towards the shed, Brendan asked Joe for a smoke. Joe offered him his cigarettes and he fished one out of the pack. Then he lit it from the end of Joe's and, as Joe reached up to get it back, Brendan hit him on the side of the head with a rock he'd picked off the ground. Joe fell back over the plastic chair and Brendan hit him again and again until he lay completely still. Then he reached under Joe's jacket and took the gun from his inside pocket. The keys were in the ignition of the SUV. He started the engine and reversed just as Tommy emerged from the shed. Screaming at the top of his lungs, he held a gun between his hands and started firing at Brendan. Brendan held the accelerator to the floor and reversed at full speed. Tommy tried to get out of the way but he was too late. The SUV crushed him up against the wall of the shed and he slid to the ground, blood seeping from his lips. Brendan shifted into drive and took off down the lane to the boreen until he reached the road where he turned right. He knew he was only a few miles from Tyrellspass and the N6 to the West. But he also knew that he'd be a marked man in the SUV. He'd have to dump it somewhere.

Twenty minutes later he reached the junction of the N6. *Came a bit too far*, he judged, so he turned around, dumped the SUV in a clump of trees off the road, and walked back towards the N6. Turning west he started walking, reckoning that he'd start hitching a ride. Still a common practice in Ireland, a place where a certain innocence still prevailed and where every stranger wasn't thought to be a threat.

I know where I'm going, thought Tucker, *west to Connemara and this time. I'll take care of Burke real good. Shouldn't be hard to find him. And, if he's not there, I'll just hang out and wait for him. He'll show up some time. And Connemara's a good place to hide out.*

57

Ed Burke eased himself into the Jacuzzi and felt the pulsating jets massage his lower back. He picked up the glass of red wine from the floor where he'd left it, settled down into the warmth and sipped. Feeling his body relax, he realized that this was only the third time he'd used this Jacuzzi in his apartment since he'd arrived from New York. Drained by the events of recent days, a safe womb-like feeling overcame him.

He'd left the TV on and the bathroom door open so he could hear the one o'clock news. Now the sound irritated him and he cursed himself for failing to disconnect that world out there.

Too late now, he moaned as he listened: *Good afternoon. This is RTE news at one.   Here is today's top story.   A dangerous criminal made a daring escape from a prison van taking him from hospital to Mountjoy Jail this morning.   Brendan Tucker, in jail for the murder of a young Dublin woman and under investigation for the murder of Tánaiste David Manning's wife, Pia ...*

Burke, in shock, clambered out of the Jacuzzi, breaking his wine glass as it toppled onto the floor, and dashed, naked and dripping, into the living room in time to see an interview with the Garda Press Officer who was saying that the Gardaí were following a number of leads and hoped to soon recapture Tucker. A photo of Tucker followed, accompanied by advice to the public that he was dangerous, to avoid contact and notify Gardaí immediately if seen.

"The usual shite!" Ed said out loud to himself, "They don't have a clue where he is!" and, as he turned back to the bathroom for a towel, his phone started to ring and he answered, "Burke"

"Ed, Commissioner Clooney. I suppose you've heard about Tucker's escape."

"Just this very minute on the news, Commissioner."

"I wanted to warn you personally. Tucker has nothing to lose. And he might want revenge. I can't provide you with protection."

"I don't think you'll find Tucker alive."

"What do you mean?"

"Tucker's a loner. Not a fellow who inspires loyalty. So I don't see his friends risking their lives to spring him."

"So what's your thinking?"

"I think he's been sprung to keep him from talking. They've taken out Johnny Fox. Now they want to wrap it up."

"But you failed to get Tucker to talk, didn't you?"

"That's right. And I don't think that Tucker would have talked. Ever! But I'm sure whoever ordered him to kill Marty Rainey and the Tánaiste's wife can't take a chance on that."

"Well, whoever busted him out of that prison van were professionals. It was a military operation."

"And you have no idea who did it?"

"No, we don't. We can only assume it was one of a number of criminal gangs here in Dublin. We're looking into the movements of every one of them now."

"Commissioner, thanks for calling. I'm going to Connemara for a few days. Nobody'll find me there. By the time I return I'm betting you'll have found Tucker's body dumped somewhere."

"I sure hope you're right. We don't need him running around loose."

58

Tommy Keegan woke to the pain. That's all he could feel. The pain. Then the cold and the wetness.

Dawn broke through the clouds and he saw that he lay in a muddy puddle on the ground. It had rained heavily during the night. He propped himself up on his elbows and tried to scream. But he couldn't. Each breath increased the pain. It only eased when he held his breath.

Everything came back to him. Tucker reversing the SUV. His panic and his fear. And the pain. The sense of dying. And then the oblivion.

So I didn't die after all, he contemplated, *but I'm bad, broken ribs at least, maybe a punctured lung. Got to get out of here, got to get help.*

Bits of tree branches had been ripped off by the wind. A sturdy one lay near him. He reached it and, holding his breath, used it to slowly and painfully rise to his feet and lean against the shed behind him. He reckoned that nobody would come to this old cottage so he'd have to leave. Bracing himself on the tree branch, he took one tentative step. Even that small exertion sent unbearable pain through his body. Gritting his teeth, he told himself that he'd have to learn to handle the pain. He took another step forward and then a third ...

Padraig and Rosie O'Malley drove down the boreen in their fifteen-year old Ford Fiesta, at their usual speed of twenty-five miles per hour.   In their seventies, with their two grown sons in Australia, they lived a simple, frugal life. This was one of their two trips a week. Their Sunday trip to mass was the other one. This one took them to their local shop for eggs and bread and milk. Padraig would usually nip into the pub next door for a pint while Rosie shopped and gossiped.

Turning a corner, Padraig slowed to almost a standstill to avoid the five sheep grazing at the verge. Edging past them he suddenly hit the brakes, jolting Rosie out of her reverie.

"Jesus, Mary, and Joseph!   What's the matter with ye, Padraig? Are ye tryin' to get us killed?"

"Rosie, there's something, somebody, lyin' in the middle o' the road."

"Aaghh!   Don't tell me!   It's probably Auld Jamie. Drunk again!"

"Naw, naw. Doesn't look like him."

"Well, are ye goin' to get out and take a look?"

Padraig said nothing.   The years had tempered his reaction to Rosie's quick temper. He eased himself out of the car and walked the few yards to the body in the middle of the road. A man he didn't recognize. Lying on his back, unconscious, beaten and bloody. A broken tree limb lay diagonally across his body. Padraig went back to get Rosie.

"He's badly injured. Unconscious. But I think he's still livin'."

"What're we goin' to do?"

"We can't leave him there. And we can't get him into the car. I'm afraid to move him."

"But we can't leave him in the middle of the road."

"No."

"I'll get out and help. We'll move him to the side of the road. We'll tell them down at the shop. They'll call the ambulance."

Padraig and Rosie, using every last ounce of their strength, dragged Tommy Keegan into the grassy verge. The sheep, normally skittish, stood and gazed at this strange scene.

Tommy Keegan woke up in a hospital bed, chest bandaged tightly, an IV in his arm. Two men sat at his bedside, waiting to talk with him. They introduced themselves as Detectives Mahoney and Sutton from the *Garda Siochana*. Detective Mahoney did the talking.

"We know who you are, Tommy. Nice mess you got yourself into this time!"

"Whad'ye mean?"

"It's a serious offence breaking a prisoner out of jail. They'll put you away for twenty, or thirty, at least. With no parole. You'll never come out alive again."

"Whady're ye talkin' about?"

"Don't play dumb with us, Tommy. We found the cottage where you kept Tucker. And we found your friend Joe. He's dead. I suppose Tucker killed him and tried to do you too, Tommy. "

Tommy said nothing. He knew they'd got him. What could he say? He still burned with anger over Brendan Tucker.

"You're a patsy. A fall guy. You were used. Didn't you know that?"

Tommy looked at them but remained silent.

"We know you work for *The Beetle*. Did he order this?"

Tommy gasped, "I don't know what the feck ye're talkin' about!"

"Don't play dumb with us. Here's the way we see it. *The Beetle* ordered you to spring Tucker from the prison van and take him to that cottage. *The Beetle* planned to kill Tucker. Shut him up like he did with Johnny Fox. Keep him from talking."

Detective Mahoney could see the look of realization spread over Tommy Keegan's face and he knew he had him.

"So you see, you'd be a damn fool to throw away the next twenty years of your life to protect *The Beetle!*"

59

Burke decided there was something hypnotic about Omey Island, something magnetic that pulled him there every time he stayed in Claddaghduff. Today he'd decided to spend the whole day there and let the island have its way with him.

He crossed the half-mile stretch of beach to the island at eleven am and he knew he'd have to be back before the tide came in at four, otherwise he'd be stuck on the island for another seven hours.

Once on the island, he climbed to high ground until he reached the marvellous hexagonal house that belonged to poet Richard Murphy. He could see that it was unoccupied so he sat down, with the house breaking the wind at his back, and took the tuna sandwich from his backpack.

Perfect place for lunch, he thought, *maybe some of Murphy's muse will rub off on me... that's it, Omey's the place to write ... I could get out of the law, just like Grisham ... write a bestseller ... make the movie ... leave this sordid mess behind...* Then he laughed out loud ... *a fantasy! That's all! Never happen ... but it's lovely to let the mind wander ...*

Finishing his sandwich, he turned around to pick up his backpack just as something flashed in the hill above him. Pulled out of his reverie, his mind kicked into high alert. He looked at the hill but saw nothing. Probably the sun glinting on a bottle or a piece of glass or something. *You'd think I was in the South Bronx! Old fears never go away!*

Moving out, he headed for the west coast of the island to find St. Feichin's Well. Renowned for its cures, especially of skin ailments, the emigrants of the nineteenth century often took a bottle of the well's water with them on their journey west across the Atlantic. *Maybe Willie King took some with him to Salt Lake City. I've got to dip my hand in it and connect with old Willie... Jesus! If anybody heard me now they'd have me locked up!*

Reaching the western coast, he stood and watched the Atlantic Ocean crashing into the rocks below. *A terrible beauty*, he thought, and then apologised to Yeats. Turning around to get a better footing, he saw something flash again a short distance behind him. Spooked, he immediately lay down and took cover behind a small hillock. This time all his senses went on high alert. He dismissed his idea of the sun glinting off a bottle and decided that someone had followed him. *Maybe a tourist, maybe something innocent, but hell, why take chances!* He unzipped his back pack, took out his binoculars and focused on the area he thought the flash had originated. Nothing at first. Then he saw movement. Someone was walking down the hillside, about two hundred yards behind him. He centred his sight on the figure and focused. Something seemed familiar. He zoomed in for a closer look.

Fuck! It's Tucker! Then the flash again and he could see that it was indeed the sun reflecting off a buckle or a button or something metal on Tucker's coat. He looked again, to confirm. *Yip, Tucker! The bastard's out to kill me. And I have no weapon. I'll have to give him a run for it.*

Thinking that he now wished he knew the island better, he realized that Tucker most likely didn't know it either. Which might make things even between them but he knew that Tucker had to be armed. St. Feichin's Well lay on the north shore of the little bay on the west coast and he figured, if he made it there, there might be other people visiting the well. *A slim chance*, he thought, as he started to run. Looking over his shoulder, he could see Tucker running too, and he was sure that Tucker was gaining ground on him. He had no plan. *Just keep running,* he told himself.

Reaching the edge of the land ahead, he could see a beach down below. At the same time he heard the gun shot, magnified by the silence of Omey, and he dropped to the ground. Looking back, Tucker seemed so close. He stood in a firing stance, his hands clasping a weapon. He fired again and the bullet struck a rock, only a foot away from Burke. Burke rose and ran in a crouch, weaving back and forth, to deny Tucker a target. He could clearly see the beach below and two fishermen working on lobster cages. He yelled to them and immediately lost his footing, pitching to the ground and rolling over and over. Struggling to get up, he couldn't stand on his right foot. With his ankle already beginning to swell up, the pain was intense. *Now I'm fucked!* he groaned, *I can't outrun him. I'll have to make a stand.* He crawled towards a rock outcropping ahead, lay down behind it and collected all the stones he could find. A bad defence against bullets, but better than none.

Tucker appeared about twenty yards away and Burke yelled, "Don't move Tucker! Drop the gun!"

Surprised, Tucker stood there, temporarily off-balance, then got a grip on himself, " Burke, you have

214

no fecking gun. You're bluffing. That might be OK in your courtroom, but it's no defence here!"

"Tucker, you're a bad judge, aren't you? And a poor fucking shot! "

"Burke, I have a bullet just for you. Think I'll gut shoot you and let you die a slow death out here. Nobody'll find you.   And you can think happy thoughts of me!   Yeah, that sounds better than putting one between your eyes, doesn't it?"

"You're a sick bastard!"

"What's the matter?   Why are you hiding? Can't you run? Did you hurt yourself? That's it, isn't it? You hurt yourself!   You can't run away from me, can you?"

"Just keep fooling yourself!   I'm waiting for you. I want you up close so I can watch your brains spray all over these rocks!   For Pia, you murdering bastard!   That's why I'm waiting for you.   You're fucking stupid, aren't you?"

Tucker seemed to be absorbing all that. Burke could see him clearly through the opening in the rock outcropping. He saw him hesitate. But he wanted him angry, out of control. His only chance lay in Tucker rushing him, too angry to focus. Maybe then he could stone him to death.

Tucker moved from one foot to the other, obviously seething with anger, as he shouted, "I'm goin' to close your big mouth forever, Burke!"

He charged, firing his gun wildly.   Burke threw a stone at him as he closed within ten feet. The stone caught Tucker on the chest, causing him to stumble.   But he kept coming, jumping over the rocks. Burke threw stones at him with both hands. Tucker's next bullet seared the side of Burke's head, setting his brain on fire. Stunned, he fell over and Tucker stood looking down at him.

Raising the gun, he said, "Goodbye, fucker!" and then dropped to his knees, a look of total surprise on his face. The long-handled knife had sunk deep in his chest and he tried to pull at it as he fell to his knees, blood oozing out of his mouth. Seconds later, he fell backwards, the knife pointing skyward like some kind of grotesque marker.

Burke felt hands reaching for him and helping him to his feet. He looked into the faces of the two fishermen before he lost consciousness.

60

Ed Burke regained consciousness with a feeling that his body was bouncing on a trampoline. Squinting, he could see that he was being carried on a litter across a sandy beach. He heard the whirring sound of a helicopter and he could read *FlanAir* on the fuselage as they got closer.

Gently, the two paramedics lifted Ed into the helicopter, secured the litter in place, and the pilot lifted into the air.

Looking up, Ed asked, "Where am I?"

One of the paramedics smiled and answered, "Mr. Burke, you are on board a FlanAir helicopter. We are taking you to the Galway Clinic. Don't be alarmed. Your vital signs are stable. But you need a thorough medical examination. We'll be there soon. They're expecting you. Please rest."

"Thank you, " Ed replied feebly as he felt himself being lulled into sleep again by the sound of the engine and the whirring of the rotor blades.

He woke up again on an examination table in the Galway Clinic. A man, dressed in hospital whites, said, "Mr. Burke, I am Doctor Michael Casey." And looking at a fresh-faced young nurse standing beside him, said, "This is Nurse Mulkerrins. You're suffering from a mild concussion and extensive bruising. We'll be taking you for some xrays and scans. As a precaution. We'll try to do them as quickly as we can. And Nurse Mulkerrins will ensure that you're as comfortable as possible."

Nurse Mulkerrins smiled infectiously and gave his arm an assuring touch.

Doctor Casey spoke again, "You will be kept for observation for a couple of days. We have a room prepared for you. I will see you later this evening. I should be able to give you the results of our examination then.   And, Mr. Burke, this is a precaution From my own examination, you seem to have survived this attack on your life very well.   A mild concussion, that's all.   I'm sure our tests will confirm that."

At nine o'clock that evening, as the nurses were completing their shift turnover, Dr. Casey walked into Ed Burke's room. He could see that Burke was awake, browsing *The Irish Times.*

"I see you're catching up on the news."

"Looks like I've made the front page again."

"Yes, all the nurses will be coming in to get your autograph, I'm afraid!"

They both laughed at the prospect and Dr. Casey said, "Good news. The x-rays and scans turned nothing up.   Neurologically, you're fine.   Just the mild concussion. Lots of rest and some TLC from our nursing staff and you'll be right as rain again."

"Thank you, Dr. Casey."

"Oh, don't thank me.   Thank Mr. Tom Flanagan of *FlanAir.* This is a private clinic and we don't take emergency trauma cases like yours. Normally, you'd have been taken to the regional, University College Hospital.   But Mr. Flanagan didn't want you to end up in the hallway for hours in their A&E waiting for a bed to become available. Mr. Flanagan is one of the investors in this new clinic. So he has influence. A good friend to have, Mr. Burke."

"Yes, he is. I will thank him later. Right now, I'm in your good hands, Dr, Casey, and it's you I want to thank."

Dr. Casey smiled and nodded appreciatively.

Nurse Mulkerrins arrived, "Mr. Burke, I've ordered you some food. Tea and toast and some scrambled eggs."

61

Commissioner Clooney ordered *The Beetle's* arrest.
He didn't need Tommy Keegan's confession.   He
already had Billy Nee's, videotaped and signed.
Keegan's was simply the icing on the cake.

Four gardai, members of the Special Criminal
Investigations Team, arrived in two cars at The
Beetle's home at eleven o'clock at night.   Tom
Buckley sat in the lead car, beside the team's leader,
Captain Terry Farrelly. They would make the arrest.
Their two partners, in the second car, would provide
backup.
    Surprise was the key to success. They wanted
to avoid any confrontation with members of *The
Beetle's* gang. So they chose to arrest him at this late
hour when he'd be relaxing in the privacy of his own
home.
    It was easy. *The Beetle* offered no resistance.
He even offered Farrelly and Buckley a nightcap.
The attitude of a man who considered himself
untouchable.
    Putting on his coat, he reassured his wife,
"Call Doherty. And, don't worry, I'll be back in an
hour's time."

Despite the protests of his lawyer, James Doherty,
The Beetle was detained overnight on the basis that
the charges involved murder.   Interviews were

scheduled for the very next morning. His lawyer was invited to attend.

At ten am the following morning *The Beetle*, joined by Doherty, was taken to be interviewed by Captain Terry Farrelly and Detective Tom Buckley. The interview would be monitored externally by a Chief Inspector and a Detective Sergeant who was not a member of the Special Criminal Investigations Team.

"Good morning, gentlemen. My name is Captain Terry Farrelly and this is Detective Tom Buckley. I am in charge of the Special Investigation Team assigned to the murder of Tánaiste David Manning's wife, Pia, as well as the murders of Marty Rainey and Johnny Fox. Detective Buckley is a member of my investigating team and has been with these matters from the outset."

The Beetle, now seated opposite, glowered at them. James Doherty opened his briefcase and took out a sheaf of papers.

Captain Farrelly said, "You are Joe McGinnis, also known as *The Beetle.* Do you confirm this?"

The Beetle did not respond, until prompted by Doherty to do so. Then he answered, "Yes."

Then the Captain said, "We are prepared to videotape this interview with you, Mr. McGinnis. I recommend that you approve. It is intended to protect all of us, you from any abuse by us during this interview, and us from any false charges levelled at us later. Mr. Doherty will be provided with a copy."

Again, after consulting with Doherty, *The Beetle* agreed.

Tom Buckley activated the Garda Interviewing Recording System and Captain Farrelly continued, "I am going to ask you a series of questions, Mr. McGinnis. I would advise you to answer truthfully."

"Did you order the murder of Tánaiste David Manning's wife, Pia?"

"No!"

"Did you instruct Brendan Tucker to kill the Tánaiste's wife?"

"No!"

"Did you have Tommy Keegan and other associates of yours break Brendan Tucker out of a prison van?"

"No!"

"Well, we have testimony from Tommy Keegan saying that you did."

"He's a fucking liar!"

"Did you intend to kill Brendan Tucker to keep him from talking?"

"I don't know what you're talking about!"

"Did you order Brendan Tucker and Johnny Fox to kill Marty Rainey?"

"Who's Marty Rainey?"

"Come on, Mr. McGinnis!"

"Captain Farrelly, I take exception to this badgering of my client," said Doherty.

"Mr. Doherty, these are serious charges that your client is facing. And we certainly won't accept frivolous responses from him. Now, I'll ask you again, Mr. McGinnis. Did you order Brendan Tucker and Johnny Fox to kill Marty Rainey?"

"No, I did not!"

"Did you order them to find documents in Mr. Rainey's possession? Documents that he intended to turn over to the Barton Tribunal?"

"No!"

"And did it all go wrong? Did they kill Mr. Rainey when he wouldn't tell them what he'd done with the documents? Isn't that the way it happened, Mr. McGinnis?"

"I know nothing about it!"

"Did you order the murder of Johnny Fox in Mountjoy?"

"He committed suicide!"

"No, Mr. McGinnis, he did not. And you know that. Mr. Fox confessed. He was being transferred to the witness protection program in return for testimony he planned to give us. But he died, very conveniently, before he could give that testimony. And we believe that his testimony would have led to your indictment for the murder of Marty Rainey."

"Captain, I must object to this line of questioning. It's pure speculation. You have no evidence to support this. I must ask you to refrain," interjected Doherty.

"Let me assure you, Mr. Doherty, I do not deal in speculation. Mr. McGinnis, do you know Billy Nee?"

"Never heard of him!"

"You have heard of him. He was front page news recently. Killed his wife and then himself. He was a guard at Mountjoy the night that Johnny Fox died. Does that jog your memory?"

"Yeah, I read the papers. So what?"

"I'll tell you 'what', Mr. McGinnis. Billy Nee confessed to the murder of Johnny Fox. He also stated that you ordered him to do it. No, I don't want a response from you. We have an affidavit from Billy Nee, testifying to his sexual indiscretion, your hold over him because of it, and his murder of Johnny Fox at your request. He videoed his confession. And I'm going to play some of that for you now. And, yes, Mr. Doherty, we will make it available to you."

With a nod from the Captain, Tom Buckley hit 'play' on the Billy Nee video and they all sat transfixed as it played out before them.

The Beetle said, "You can't prove anything with that. It's his word against mine!"

223

"That's not all that we have, Mr. McGinnis. You never knew that Billy Nee wired himself when he met with you. Big mistake on your part. Thought he was a mouse, did you? A harmless mouse that you used. Well, we have your voice on that recording telling him that he must take out Johnny Fox. I am going to play that for you now," said the Captain, with a nod to Tom Buckley.

Stunned, *The Beetle* said, "That's not me! That's a fake! Anybody can forge these things now!"

"Yes, Captain, we will insist on our experts examining these videos and recordings," added Doherty.

"We'll be happy to grant you that. When the trial commences. We are preparing a file for the DPP on all of this. Mr. McGinnis, we believe that you were acting on behalf of someone else. Someone much more important in this country. And someone much more dangerous than you. That's the person we really want, Mr. McGinnis. I'd like you to reflect on that before we meet again. And you'll have plenty of time to reflect. We'll be detaining you until you go before the judge in this matter. Probably in a week's time."

"I want my client released. You can't hold him. You have no evidence here. All of this is trumped up," argued Doherty.

"Mr. Doherty, we have the right to hold him. You can ask the Judge to release Mr. McGinnis on bail, pending a trial. It will be entirely up to the Judge to consider if that would be advisable. As I said before, Mr. McGinnis, you will have plenty of time to reflect."

In jail *The Beetle* had plenty of time to reflect. Denied bail and depressed by the Billy Nee

224

confession, he met with his lawyer, James Doherty, five days after his arrest.

"Joe, you can go to trial and fight this. But I'm telling you now, you can't win. The jury will believe Billy Nee."

"Jaysus, Jamey, I know that. I fuckin' know that!"

"Listen to me. They can threaten you with all that other stuff. Manning's wife, Rainey's murder. But they can't tie you to it. Fox is dead and now Tucker's gone too. They don't have a shred of evidence on any of it. Oh yes, Tommy Keegan swears that you broke Tucker out of jail. But Keegan's a criminal and a sworn liar. No jury will believe him."

"So what are you sayin'?"

"I'm telling you that the Billy Nee video will convict you."

"I'm not getting' out, am I?"

"No, Joe. No bail. I tried. I expect the DPP to charge you very soon. Probably by next week."

"Jamey, I want you to take care of things, see that my wife's OK."

"Joe, I might not be able to help her."

"What the hell do you mean? Haven't I paid you? And paid you well?"

"Joe, Joe, yes you have. That's not the reason. The Criminal Assets Bureau is out to get you. They're planning to confiscate your houses, your cars, freeze your bank accounts, get their nasty little hands on everything you own. Your wife will be left with nothing!"

"They can't do that!"

"Yes they can. They were given statutory powers under the *Criminal Assets Bureau Act 1996*. I know for a fact that they're seeking a High Court order on you right now!"

"The bastards!"

"You may say that but, once they sink their teeth into you, they'll strip you naked."

"So I'm double fucked, that's what ye're tellin' me!"

"Joe, I don't want to get your hopes up but I think I could delay the CAB going to the High Court. Maybe even get them to lay off."

"How the hell can you do that?"

"OK, I'll be up front. I've been approached with a deal for you."

"Whad'ye mean?"

"Remember what Captain Farrelly said five days ago. After they arrested you. He said they were after someone much more important than you. He said that that was the person they really wanted."

"So what?"

"Farrelly asked me to see the Garda Commissioner yesterday. The Commissioner convinced me that you worked for a government minister. They want that person bad. Real bad. You know what I'm talking about, don't you?"

The Beetle didn't answer this time. Instead, his mind examined the unthinkable. *Could he 'rat' on the Tánaiste?*

"Joe, we could stop the CAB. Save your property. Let you wife live in comfort. Why don't you talk?"

The Beetle had already decided. But he wanted to be sure.

"If I talk, how can I trust them?"

"You can't. We'll need firm guarantees. I'll want them from higher up, from the Minister of Justice."

"And what about the DPP?"

"I don't know. They won't be inclined to overlook the Billy Nee confession. So I think you'll still go to trial. And you'll probably be convicted.

226

But, let me tell you this, if you give them the person they want, I am sure that the sentencing judge will be asked to take this into consideration."

"So I'm still fucked!"

"Joe, be realistic. Isn't ten years and keeping your property better than losing everything and life without parole?   I'll be back tomorrow for your answer. If you decide to cooperate with them, I'll set it up. They'll want to move immediately. And you'll want to stop the CAB."

"You don't have to come back tomorrow for my answer. Do it. Set up the meeting."

Two days later *The Beetle* was taken under garda escort to meet Commissioner Clooney.   James Doherty accompanied him.   Ushered into a room at Garda Headquarters, *The Beetle* was surprised to find tea awaiting them.   Two gardai stood guard outside the door.   *The Beetle* decided to partake of their hospitality and started pouring himself a mug of tea.   Doherty declined.   With the hot amber brew pouring into the cup, *The Beetle* almost burned his fingers as he heard,

"I hope we can still act in a civilized manner, Mr. McGinnis"

And turned to see Commissioner Clooney and another, vaguely familiar face, standing in the doorway.

"Mr. McGinnis, our Justice Minister, Brian Cosgrave."

The Beetle, lost for words, stood awkwardly with the tea almost spilling from the mug in his right hand.

"Sit   down   and   let's   talk,"   said   the Commissioner, and turning to James Doherty, "Mr. Doherty,   the Justice Minister decided to join us today to show you that what Mr. McGinnis has to say is vital to this nation."

"Commissioner, that is the guarantee we talked about."

Justice Minister Brian Cosgrave, who'd sat silent, looked at *The Beetle* and said, "Mr. McGinnis, let me be truthful. I have no time for you. You've lived off crime all your life. Your drug business has made addicts of many of our young people. You've stolen with impunity. I'd prefer that we lock you up and throw the key away. But, as you know by now, we want the man you work for. We want him badly enough that we're willing to make a deal with you. And I am here to guarantee that. I only hope we won't regret it."

"Thank you, Minister," said James Doherty.

"Mr. Doherty, quite frankly the only person I want to hear from is Mr. McGinnis. Commissioner ..." and he turned towards Commissioner Clooney intimating that the preliminaries were over.

The Commissioner looked directly at *The Beetle,* "Mr. McGinnis, we are going to video these proceedings at this point," and looked at James Doherty for a nod of agreement. Nodding to the two-way window, he turned again to *The Beetle.*

"Mr. McGinnis, who did you take your orders from?"

The Beetle hesitated, drained the last of his tea, cleared his throat, and answered, "David Manning."

Doherty looked stunned. *The Beetle* had just named The Tánaiste, the Deputy Prime Minister, the second most powerful man in the country. He was even more perplexed when he saw the calm looks on the faces of the Garda Commissioner and the Minister of Justice.

"Now, Mr. McGinnis, I am going to ask you a number of questions and I want you to give me as exact an answer as you can to each question.   It would also be helpful if you can offer corroboration of the information you give us."

Opening a leather folder he'd brought with him, the Commissioner leafed a page or two and then began.

"Did David Manning hire you to kill Marty Rainey?"

"No, he didn't."

"He didn't!   Then who did?"

"Mortimer."

"Of course.   To stop Rainey from testifying at the tribunal."

"But Manning knew."

"How do you know that?"

"Mortimer told me.   Said that the Tánaiste wanted documents that Rainey had.   Besides, I'd done work for both of them before."

"Such as?"

"Helping people to make up their minds to sell."

"Sell?"

"Yeah.   Sell their houses.   When they stood in the way of development."

"Can you prove in any way that Manning knew?"

"No.   You just have my word for it."

"And Mortimer's dead.   So we can't ask him."

The Beetle had the inkling of a smile on his lips as Justice Minister Cosgrove got up to leave, saying,   "Mr. McGinnis,   if you want a deal you'll have to do better than this."

The Beetle's smile became more noticeable.

The Commissioner continued, "Mr. McGinnis, when and where did you last see David Manning?"

229

"That's easy. A few weeks ago. We met in Lucan. At the Finnstown House Hotel."

"Was there anyone else at the meeting?"

"No."

"Did anyone see you meet the Tánaiste?"

"I dunno. Maybe. The Tánaiste had a room so he must have checked in. I came to visit. Maybe some of the staff saw me. I dunno."

"What was your meeting about?"

"Hah! Manning was pissed off at me! Mad that we hadn't found Rainey's documents."

"What did he tell you to do?"

"He was sure that Burke had them. And he was pissed off that Burke wasn't in jail, charged with killing his wife. So he wanted the documents and he wanted Burke dead. Must hate that fella real bad."

"So you sent Tucker to Burke's apartment."

"To find the documents. Yeah."

"And kill Burke."

"No. I didn't send him to kill Burke."

"So he just killed a cleaning lady instead!"

"Listen, that had nothin' to do with me. Tucker went crazy. If Burke hadn't attacked him, nothin' would've happened. It's that fucker's fault!"

"Mr. McGinnis, do you think I'm naive? Manning wanted to get rid of Burke and you told Tucker to kill him. Didn't you?"

"No, I only told him to get the documents!"

"And did you?"

"We found nothin'. I don't think there's any fecking documents!"

"Look, Mr. McGinnis, you're telling us nothing here."

"I'm telling you what I know. Alright!"

"Let's start at the beginning. We know that Tucker killed David Manning's wife, Pia. We have his DNA to prove it. Who gave the orders?"

230

"Commissioner, you know who.   Manning, that's who. He wanted rid of that slut and he hoped he could pin it on Burke. Get rid of that fucker at the same time."

"Mr. McGinnis, do you have any proof of these charges against David Manning?"

"You mean hidden recordings, stuff like that?"

"Yes, or emails, something in writing, photos … you know, everybody's got a camera on their phone these days."

"No. You only have my word. I'm telling you the truth. You know that."

"I'm surprised that a man like you didn't take out some kind of insurance in case something went wrong."

"Yeah, I fucked up, didn't I?   But how could anything go wrong when my orders came from the Tánaiste, the second most powerful man in the government?"

"Who believes he's the most powerful man in the country, Mr. McGinnis!"

The interview ended as unceremoniously as it had begun. The Beetle was taken back into custody and his lawyer, James Doherty, was advised that the actions on the Criminal Assets Bureau would be suspended until further decisions were taken.

62

"You had me worried. But you're just lying around doing nothing. Faking it!" The gurgling laughter broke through Ed Burke's headphones. He pushed the Siemens TV up on its arm, removed the headphones, and turned to see Maria Lane.

"Oh, my God! You caught me!" Ed pushed the button that controlled the bed and sat up, "Maria, thanks for coming. It's wonderful to see you."

"Can you go for a walk?"

"Absolutely! I'm fine. They'll probably discharge me this evening. At least I hope they will. My doctor, Dr. Casey, will see me about 8 this evening. He'll make the decision. I can't see any reason for keeping me here any longer. And I've got things to do."

"So, let's go for a coffee."

Ed Burke swung his legs out of bed, slid his feet into his slippers, and put on his robe. They walked past the nurses' station, down the corridor, through the double doors and up the staircase to the restaurant. Perched on a balcony, it overlooked the magnificent three storey atrium that gave a sense of grandeur to the entrance lobby and admissions desk. A grand piano sat regally on a circular blue Celtic carpet in the centre.

Ed had not seen this before, "Magnificent! Looks better than the interior of a Hyatt Hotel. I've never seen a hospital as good looking as this in the States!"

"This is the future. The new private clinics. But they charge a fortune. And there are plenty of customers willing to pay for it."

At 3 pm the restaurant was almost empty. They took their coffees to a table near the railing that overlooked the grand piano down below.

"Who told you I was here?" asked Ed.

"Who told me? You're joking! The whole world knows you're here. You've been on the front pages in the papers and the top story on TV news. Reporters are all over Omey Island re-enacting the attempt on your life. The Taoiseach faced questions on the matter in today's session of the Oireachtas. A number of the opposition TDs asked some very tough questions. They wanted to know if the attempt on your life was connected to the murder of the Tanaiste's wife. They also asked questions about the Ansbacher accounts and the Tribunal into that and zoning corruption. They made a good attempt to tie all the knots together. Looked like the work of Tom Flanagan and his colleagues. They're putting the heat on. I never saw the Taoiseach lost for words before. His normal speech hesitancy turned into splutters at times. It looked embarrassing. And guilty! I'll bet Tánaiste David Manning is looking over his shoulder tonight!"

A dreamy distant look had come over Ed. Maria put her hand across the table and, touching his fingers, said, "Tell me about Pia."

Ed flinched. She could feel it in his fingers. He had been taken totally unawares and seemed to be looking for the words to answer.

233

"Have you talked with anyone about her since she died?

Finally Ed said, "No."

"Don't you think you should?"

"Too painful, Maria. I haven't even let myself deal with it. And, even if I'd wanted to, there's been no-one to talk with."

"You can talk to me. You know that, don't you? You need to talk about her. Did you love her?"

"Love? Love, yes, yes. Infatuated, always. That's what comes to mind first. When we met at Trinity, she was like a magnet for me. A magnet that fired all my passion. And, when we met again after twenty years, nothing had changed. The magnet hadn't lost any of its power. It was easy to light that fire again. The embers still glowed. And the fire was even stronger this time. Yes, I loved her."

His eyes swam in tears that hadn't fallen, "He killed her. I'm sure of it!"

"You can't be sure. You have no proof."

"Oh, I'm sure. We know that Brendan Tucker was the executioner. But he was only following orders. I believe those orders came from the Tánaiste himself!"

"How much do you know about David Manning?"

"Enough! He's ruthless, power-hungry, clever. And very dangerous!"

"His success inspires. Many people look up to him. They use him as a role model for their kids."

"That's exactly why he's dangerous! He has the voters behind him. Poor orphan becomes Taoiseach! I can see the headlines. In America, it would go down well. The Horatio Alger, rags to riches, story. He'll become an icon. And he'll use that iconic power to subvert the European Union for

234

his own greedy purposes. And the purposes of your TP McGrady and gang!"

"But the public see none of that. They only see how an abandoned young boy, mistreated in a horrible orphanage, went on to be an A level student and win scholarships to the best schools. They only see hard work and achievement and struggle overcoming adversity. That's what the public see when they look at David Manning."

"Well, we have to start educating the public about the Tánaiste. That's where I hope we'll get lucky with Begley's Ryder Cup DVD. Give us some dirt we can use."

63

Ed Burke and Sean Coyne set up a daily schedule to download TP McGrady's captured emails from the Islamabad sever. On the sixth day they intercepted an email from McGrady to Murphy at his Dublin law firm. Seeing Murphy's name on the email raised it to a high alert for Burke. The email was cryptic, but it wasn't difficult to read between the lines. McGrady was a prime bidder in the €500 million redevelopment of a Dublin shopping centre. Murphy sat on the local council committee charged with assessing the sealed bids and selecting the winning bid. He knew the assessment criteria. Lowest bid was not the only factor. Key strengths in other areas were also essential.

McGrady had already submitted a sealed bid. Only one other development company had the capability of meeting the objectives set out in the council's initial request for proposal. Their bid had been opened first so Murphy was aware of how well they met the proposal objectives. Murphy had then told McGrady the details of that competing bid so that MCGrady could immediately modify key elements of his own bid, ensuring that it would then win. The email alerted Murphy that the modified pages were ready and confirming that Murphy would replace those pages in the bid, reseal it, and present it to the council committee early next morning.

"Gotcha!" yelled Burke.

"The balls of it!" shouted Coyne, "can you believe 'the balls of it'?"

"How do you think he is where he is? Twenty-five years ago he was an IRA hunger striker in Long Kesh prison. Today he's the power behind the scene in this country. And it was ill-gotten IRA money that funded him. Does he owe them? That's scary, don't you think?"

"What're you going to do?"

"It's not what I am going to do, it's what we are going to do."

"Right! You're right."

"I'm going to turn this email over to Flanagan and co. They'll find out who the losing bidder is. And set them straight. That should start a major court battle. Tie McGrady up in the courts. And Murphy too! It would be a bonus to strip him of his right to practice law."

"How about this headline: *Ex-IRA hunger striker in major development battle.* Always good to remind the world that McGrady was IRA. He thinks we've forgotten. Well, I'll remind everybody!"

Pleased with themselves, Ed left to contact Flanagan and see Maria Lane. She deserved an advance warning of what was about to descend on her boss. Sean Coyne felt that he should apprise McDevitt at *The Irish Daily News* as well.

64

"Great, Ed! This is good stuff. We'll tie McGrady up in knots. I'll find out who lost the bid for this shopping centre. There's no doubt that they'll go to court, tie McGrady up. Can Sean Coyne give this front page and keep it there for a few days?"

"Sean is talking with McDevitt at *The News* as we speak. That's exactly what he wants to do."

"Perfect! The news will upset the entire community. They're depending on this centre for jobs, better quality of life. The LUAS were even planning to put a station there to support the new apartment buildings. This court case will set that back for months."

"And it'll get the voters upset. That might be even more important."

"Yes, yes! If Coyne can slant the story to impugn the Tánaiste and his handling of his ministry ... that's it..."

"Exactly! We need to sow the seeds of corruption right into Manning's office. Tarnish him, make him lose his standing in the next opinion polls. "

The phone intercom buzzed on Tom Flanagan's desk. He answered and then looked at Ed, "We'll pursue this at another time, Ed. You have a young lady waiting for you."

Maria Lane sat in the *FlanAir* reception area browsing the latest *Image Interiors* magazine.

"Planning a make-over?"

She looked up at Ed and laughed, a throaty hearty laugh, "I love this stuff. I think if I had millions I'd have a house or an apartment everywhere. Dublin, New York, somewhere in the sun. Ah, fantasies!"

"Well, in the meantime, would you settle for lunch?"

They found a cosy corner nook in a small French bistro nearby and Maria said, "You said you had something important to tell me?"

"Yes, I didn't want you to be blindsided. It's about McGrady."

Ed told her about the fraudulent development bid, starting with the email they'd retrieved from McGrady's system to the collusion between McGrady and Murphy in the bid rigging, and ending with Tom Flanagan's intent to locate the losing bidder and set a major court battle in motion.

"But McGrady's very shrewd. They won't get anywhere. And he has influence with the media. They'll bury this on the back page!"

"No, they won't! Sean Coyne plans to make this front page news and keep it there. The *Times* and the *Examiner* will get on the bandwagon. Believe me! "

"I hope you're right."

"You can help. Before this hits the fan. See if there's anything, anything at all, in McGrady's files that we can use against him on this deal. Will you do that?"

"I'd be surprised if there is. But I'll do it."

They changed the subject then, went back to apartment makeovers and fantasies about living in exotic places.

Ed said, "There's only one place where I have an apartment. And it's a place I love."

"I know. New York!"

"Good guess!"

"Not really. Part of you is still there you know."

"Yeah, I miss Kevin. I'd love to be able to pop across town and take him out for the weekend."

"He's coming over this summer, isn't he?"

"Yes, he is. I can't wait. But, listen, even if Kevin didn't exist, I'd still want my apartment in New York. It's up on the Westside, around 75th and Broadway. A short walk from Lincoln Center, Central Park, the Museum of Natural History which I love, great pubs, terrific people, and the buzz. It's all about the buzz! There's a buzz here now too, better one in Galway I think, but nothing compares to the New York buzz!"

"I've never been there."

"We'll have to remedy that. When this is all over, I'll take you there."

After lunch Ed Burke went back to his apartment in Ballsbridge. Sean Coyne called to say that McDevitt loved it and gave him the go for the front page on the McGrady bidding scandal. Said he'd stop by and spend some time on Begley's system, maybe get lucky again.

"An outward sense of normality and an underbelly of threat!"

As Sean sat at the terminal, Ed repeated this a couple of times, seeking more resonance each time. Sean looked at him in amazement.

"Are you changing careers? Going into the acting business?"

"Funny, funny!"

240

"Seriously, sounds like you're rehearsing for a play."

"I heard this on the radio this morning and it stuck in my mind ever since."

"OK, so ..."

"Wait a minute! Don't you think it describes what's going on here? You don't have to watch foreign news at six o'clock to get that feeling. Don't you think so?"

"I suppose. The country's running around like it's mad. That's the way we are now. We're workaholics! Just like the Americans. Yeah, that's our new *outward sense of normality*. And the Tanaiste and McGrath are *the underbelly of threat*. Is that it?"

"I couldn't have put it better myself."

65

Three days after *The Beetle's* interview with Commissioner Clooney, Justice Minister Brian Cosgrove walked into the Taoiseach's office with a DVD of the interview in his hand.

The Taoiseach expected him, "Is that it, Brian?"

"Yes, Taoiseach, I'll set it up."

"You have an hour. I've asked for all calls to be put on hold."

Brian Cosgrove inserted the DVD in the player that sat in the corner of the Taoiseach's large office and pressed play. For the next forty minutes the Taoiseach sat transfixed as he listened to *The Beetle.* Commissioner Clooney had already shown him the video that Billy Nee had made in the interview with Ed Burke.

Minutes after the DVD had ended, both men simply sat there. Waiting. Neither wanted to speak first. Finally the Justice Minister said:

"If David Manning ever went on trial, this testimony would have to be strong enough to convince a jury. And strong enough to withstand cross-examination by the best lawyers in the business."

"This is not good enough to present to the DPP," said the Taoiseach.

" You're right, Taoiseach."

"If we ever charged David Manning and all we had was this testimony, we'd start a political crisis in this country that's never been seen since the Civil War."

The Justice Minister nodded in agreement and the Taoiseach continued, "We can't put Manning on trial. You know that, don't you?"

"But we cannot do a cover up!"

"Imagine, our Tánaiste on trial! The damage to our reputation would be irreparable. The *Industrial Development Authority* might as well pack its bags and shut up shop. They'd never be able to attract another major multi-national company to this country."

"Manning knows this, doesn't he?"

"Manning holds this government to ransom. He's the leader of his party and he brought them into the present coalition government. Many of them didn't want to be in government with us. But he convinced them. All he wanted was the deputy leadership. To become Tánaiste!"

"But we can't go along as though this never happened, Taoiseach."

"We won't. The man is a murderer. And he's a clever bastard. I know he has a lot of powerful friends in this country who depend on him for their sweet deals."

"We think they're depending on him for much more than that. They want him in your job. And they have plans to change policy at the EU level to suit them. He's just the man to push it through. When Ed Burke first came to me with this theory I dismissed it as paranoia on his part. An attempt to get Manning one way or another for the death of his wife."

"Burke's at the centre of this, isn't he?"

"Yes, Taoiseach. McGinnis's man Tucker tried to kill him in Connemara."

"On Omey Island?"

"Yes, Taoiseach."

"Oh, I know all about it. The opposition tried to make points about it in the Dail. They wanted to know if the attempt on Burke's life was connected to the murder of Manning's wife. They also asked questions about the Ansbacher accounts and the Tribunal that's looking into that as well as the zoning corruption. Somebody's feeding them!"

"Burke. It has to be him."

"It's bigger than Burke. He might have lit the match but somebody else is fuelling the fire!"

The Justice Minister then briefed the Taoiseach on Ed Burke, from his return to Ireland to work on the Barton Tribunal to his affair with Manning's wife, to her death, to the killing of Johnny Fox. During it all he voiced Burke's strong feelings about a conspiracy involving Manning, that he'd be the next Taoiseach, and that he'd be President of the European Union a few months after the election.

"That's exactly where he and his powerful friends want him. At the heart of the EU."

"Where they can influence the direction of the union."

"Not just influence it. They see it under the control of bureaucrats, socialists, and communists. They will buy, bribe, coerce, induce, and push the EU into policies that will result in Europe being governed by their cabal. In a way, they'd be as great a threat as the Nazis!"

"He has to be stopped."

"How, Taoiseach?"

"Manning is a vain man. That's his Achilles heel. And his vanity will blind him. Tell Ed Burke I want to see him."

66

"Ed, may I call you Ed... are you well again?"   The Taoiseach took Ed Burke's hand in his own and held his elbow as he guided him to a chair in his office.

The Taoiseach's private and public image stamped him as Prime Minister.   In his fifties, he stood erect as one would expect from his former military career.   His suits said Saville Row and his ties were the envy of every man, and woman too.   A full head of dark hair, razor cut by the best Italian barber in Dublin, contrasted well with his handsome but rugged features.   But that image belied the Taoiseach's real strength, his people skills.   He disarmed people immediately and they never failed to see the sharp and shrewd mind behind the central casting image.

"Yes, Taoiseach, I'm fine.   They took good care of me in the Galway Clinic."

"You know why you're here, don't you?"

"Yes, Taoiseach, the Justice Minister briefed me."

"Are you behind the questions in the Dail from the opposition?"

"Yes, you could say that I know about it.   I started out completely alone after Manning's wife, Pia, was killed.   I was a suspect in her murder and I didn't have a friend in this country.   But there were other people out there who knew.   Knew what the Tánaiste was up to.   Knew the powerful men behind

him. Knew about the planning corruption. Knew
about the abuse of power. They wanted him stopped.
They are behind the Dail questioning. And, I'm
sorry, Taoiseach, they've only just begun. They want
to make this country too hot for Manning and his
backers."

"And his backers? The men who are pulling
the strings. You know who they are?"

"Yes, I do."

"I'd like their names. If I'm going to fight this,
I need to know who my enemies are."

"Well, you won't believe me when I tell you."

"Try me."

"OK. TP McGrady, Jack Simpson, Shane
Braddock and George O'Hara."

"I don't believe you!"

"I said you wouldn't, Taoiseach."

"These men are Ireland!   They are our
strength.   They're well   known and respected
internationally. We couldn't buy the great PR they
generate for this country."

"You're right! But they are totally corrupt and
they are dictators. And the more powerful dictators
become, the more corrupt and dangerous they
become."

"But surely not George O'Hara. He's a good
friend and a great benefactor. He gives millions to
every charity in the country."

"Yes, again you're right. Who would suspect a
man like O'Hara? No-one! That's his strength. He
looks as pure as the driven snow. But that's all going
to end soon. I'll warn you – Sean Coyne of *The Irish
Daily News* is about to run a story on him. Seems
that he has left this country with a collection of
illegal toxic dumps. A real big one across the border
in Northern Ireland. That won't help you with Ian
Paisley! Or Tony Blair!"

"Ah...dammit!"

"And the Archbishop of Dublin thinks he's a saint! Next week he'll be right up there with their paedophile priests. Another nail in the coffin of the Catholic Church."

"Now, now, now ... we don't need to get them into this ... it's a big enough mess without them."

"As I said, the good news is that we're going after the whole bunch."

"We? You and who else?"

"Well, you'll find out eventually.   Tom Flanagan of *FlanAir* and a number of his friends are fed up with it all. Flanagan especially – because of Manning's dirty fingers in the Dublin Airport development plans."

"What do you mean?"

"Well, I wouldn't expect you to know but the Tanaiste owns part of the land where he is urging the government to build the new terminal.   It's all very well hidden.   His name doesn't appear on a thing. But we know.   Just like we know that he stashed money in the Cayman Islands in Ansbacher. But you won't find his name on anything there either!"

"Not surprising!"

"And there's not enough solid evidence to bring any of these people before the Barton Tribunal. So we have to destroy them in public. Destroy their credibility.   Destroy their integrity.   Ruin their reputation."

"But we might ruin Ireland's reputation as well."

"That's a risk, Taoiseach.   But we'll damage Ireland for ever if we let these men use their wealth and power and use Ireland as a platform to manipulate the EU.   And if they succeed, what next? The world? I'm not scaremongering but the prospect is frightening!"

"But we can't wait for all that. The election is coming up. Manning could become the next Taoiseach!"

"You're right. We have to stop him."

"Yes, but you know that Manning is the head of his party. He brought them into coalition with us. We couldn't have formed a government without him. Since he became Tanaiste I believe his power with the voters has doubled. Have you seen the latest polls? He's out ahead of all of us. He takes the credit for the success of this government although he's had nothing to do with it. And I take the blame for our failures."

"That means that we have to destroy him. Undermine him with the voters."

"We can't put him on trial. You see that, don't you? With the circumstantial evidence we have, they'd laugh us out of court. He'd accuse us of a plot against him. The people would believe him. I'd hate to think what'd happen then. A coup d'etat! The unimaginable! Well, think the unimaginable this time!"

"But we have to destroy him, Taoiseach!"

"I know. Do you really think he had his wife killed?"

"I was in love with Pia. I'm sure you've been told. Some think my desire for revenge is getting in the way of my cold legal reasoning. I assure you, it's not. Yes, I believe he gave the orders to kill his wife. We know that Tucker killed her. We know that Tucker worked for Joe McGinnis, *The Beetle.* We now know that McGinnis worked for Mortimer and for David Manning. Yes, it's all circumstantial. And McGinnis has no credibility. But I believe that David Manning ordered the murder of his wife. And tried to pin it on me!"

"I've seen Nee's affidavit and I've seen McGinnis's interview and I am convinced. The Tánaiste is a dangerous man. And a damned clever one!"

"The Minister of Justice says that you won't turn all this over to the DPP. He says you won't charge him. You'll be accused of a cover-up if this hits the newspapers. And it will. Sean Coyne of *The News* has been working very closely with me on all of this. He believes strongly in the freedom of the press."

"Sean will get his story. David Manning is finished. But we've got to do it my way. "

"What way is that, Taoiseach?"

"I want to destroy him! Destroy his reputation. Show the country how corrupt he is. What can you and Flanagan do to help me?"

"We've already started, as you know from the Dail questioning. We are attacking and undermining his backers. We're sending a strong message to them. This is war. We're also interfering with business deals they are working on. In general, making things hot for them. We also want to undermine Manning in their eyes. If they believe he's no longer any use to them, they'll drop him. Throw him to the wolves."

"Good!"

"But we need to move fast. Before the election campaigning begins."

"So do whatever you need to get Manning for me. And do it now. I'll keep an open line here for you."

The meeting was over. The Taoiseach shook Ed Burke's hand and ushered him out of his office.

67

David Manning never suspected a thing. He met the Taoiseach at ten am for his regular bi-weekly meeting. Usually an event of little substance that gave the Taoiseach the chance to put the arm on him to support some pet project or something. But this morning everything looked amiss. No coffee and croissants sat waiting. The Taoiseach wasn't in his usual friendly manner. He looked grim.

"David, sit down. You must know by now that we arrested Joe McGinnis, *The Beetle*. What you don't know is that he made a confession. I'm going to show you a video."

The Tánaiste knew that *The Beetle* had been arrested but his sources inside Justice never told him that *The Beetle* had made a confession. He showed no emotion, gave nothing away, as the DVD ended.

The Taoiseach, angered as much by Manning's cool, imperturbable manner, as by the DVD, said, "You have used your office to undermine my government, David. Well, you're not going to get away with it!"

"Taoiseach, this is absolute nonsense! You're not going to believe a lying criminal like McGinnis?"

"Yes I am!"

"Then you've taken leave of your senses!"

"Have I now? *The Beetle's* confession is only the opener. And all the murders. Marty Rainey,

Johnny Fox, Martha Cooke, your own wife! Nothing's too high a price for you!"

"Are you mad?   Are you saying that I killed my own wife?"

"Don't fecking play smart with me!   I'm saying exactly that.   Tucker killed her; The Beetle gave the orders, The Beetle worked for you!"

"I know where you got that ridiculous nonsense from. Burke, isn't that who? Well, I think he was in collusion with Tucker. I think he killed Pia. He hated me.   And I think that Pia was probably blackmailing him over something. He's clever. And experienced at that kind of thing. Did he tell you that many of his clients in New York were mafia. I'm sure he learned a lot there!"

"That's wild-eyed shite! And you know it!"

"And your shite about me is just as wild-eyed!"

"No!   I believe it to be the truth. And, as terrible as these crimes are, I believe your biggest crime is your attempt to undermine this state!"

"Taoiseach, now you're speaking in riddles. Are you sure you're feeling OK. The pressure getting to you. Why don't you relax in your last couple of months."

"You'd like that, wouldn't you?   Then you could walk into my shoes and run this country for you and your power mad friends!"

"Taoiseach, I'm sure I don't know what you're talking about."

"Don't be coy! I know that McGrady, Simpson, Braddock, and O'Hara are pulling your strings. They want you in my job and they want you to coerce the EU in the same way that you've coerced those in this government. Change the EU policies going forward."

"You're mad, Taoiseach! You're mad!   If anyone hears you they'll have you locked up. And then I won't need to spend any money to get the

251

voters to give me your job at the next election. And you know they're going to give it to me, don't you. And there isn't a thing you can do about it, is there? You wouldn't even be sitting there as Taoiseach if I hadn't brought my party into government with you."

"I want your resignation! And I want it now. We can release a statement saying you're leaving because of your health. And that will be true. It will be because of your health."

"This is a joke? Right? You know I am not going to resign. And you know you can't use that DVD for anything. Nobody will believe it. It'll make a laughing stock out of you. Do you want to be remembered in that way?"

He stood up and turned to leave.

"Taoiseach, you can't intimidate me."

"I'll give you a week to reconsider. I'd advise you to take my offer. I will bury you. Discredit you with the voters. You'll lose the next election. But I'll do even worse than that. I'll make you a liability for your powerful backers. They'll dump you. Maybe even in one of O'Hara's toxic dumps."

"You're a sick man, Taoiseach!"

"I'll give you a week. You don't want to be remembered as the Jimmy Hoffa of Ireland. Buried, never to be found!"

The Taoiseach's threats unnerved the Tánaiste as he hastily fled the office.

68

TP McGrady met David Manning in the courtyard of Collins Barracks in the early afternoon. A neutral place, well away from their offices and minders. Manning had called for the meeting. McGrady sensed the urgency in his voice.

David Manning arrived first. Standing in the magnificent central square, surrounded by the large blocks of the barracks, a sense of awe overcame him. Blue skies overhead perfected his feeling of being in an enormous room. Now part of the *National Museum of Ireland*, it once housed the British armed forces and was handed over to Michael Collins in 1922 after Ireland had won its independence. Now it proudly bears his name.

The square was empty of tourists, almost as though they knew that it was reserved today. As Manning waited his mind wandered to Neil Jordan's recent *Michael Collins* film and he saw, in his mind's eye, the re-enactment of the British handover to Collins after 700 years. *Over eighty years ago,* he mused, *time to hand the nation over to a new generation ...* His musing was rudely interrupted.

"Inspiring place, David."

"Yes, TP, always, always..."

"Let's walk. You needed to see me."

"Yes, indeed. We have a war on our hands. I came from a meeting with the Taoiseach. Let me fill you in."

For the next fifteen minutes, David Manning brought TP up to-date on his meeting with the Taoiseach and the final ignominy, the request for his resignation.

"David, you've brought this on yourself."

"Now wait a minute, TP. I am not going to get it from you as well!"

"I'll be blunt. People are saying that you had your wife killed. I'm not one of them. But this fellow Burke and his colleagues in the press are doing a smear job on you. All I'm saying is that you must have created enough smoke to help them light the fire."

"Burke is out to get me. He's behind most of this."

"Don't get paranoid on us. You can't be the leader we want you to be if you let the bastards grind you down."

"But the Taoiseach is out to get me."

"He can't touch you. You have more power with the voters than he does. Don't you read the polls? You're the most popular politician in the country. Even if he tries to get you, it's only a couple of months till the election. He might convince a couple of percent of the voters by then but most of them won't believe a word of it."

"What about you?"

"What do you mean?"

"He knows. Somehow he knows that we are connected. That you and your colleagues are the strength behind me. That I intend to push your agenda, your policies here and in the EU when I become Taoiseach."

"That's a bluff. He knows nothing. He's just fishing. Looking for a crack in your defences."

"Don't underestimate the Taoiseach.   He's shrewd. He's going to start a war. I know it. We have to fight back. No, no. We have to strike first. Don't you see that?   He's got some skeletons in his closet. They're not much but you and your friends can blow them out of proportion. Give him enough headaches between now and the election to keep him off balance."

"But that could backfire on us. Give him the sympathy vote. Don't forget, half the women in this country want to mother him and, believe it or not, the other half want to sleep with him."

"So you're going to leave me to hang out there."

"Listen, if you can't handle this ... if you make the wrong moves... how the hell can we expect you to act when a real crisis occurs on your watch ... consider this a test, David."

With that, TP McGrady turned and walked away.   David Manning stood and watched him, incredulous.

The consortium met in TP McGrady's house in Dalkey that same evening. The meeting was a formality.   They knew that David Manning had turned out to be a bad investment. Only one choice remained.   A write-off!   TP assured Braddock that two specialists from his American office would arrive next week to write-off their investment.   Shane Braddock would meet and brief them.

69

In New York, Sal Migliore walked down 7th Ave. to Bleecker Street. The evening was mild and filled with anticipation, one of the emotions that made Manhattan his favourite place. And this evening he was going to dine in one of his favourite establishments, the New York Rifle Club, known to Italians as *Tiro a Segno,* the oldest private Italian-American club in the country. It had been founded in 1888 by Giuseppi Garibaldi. His signature is on the original charter on display in the lobby. *Tiro a Segno* means "shoot the target," but most members go there for the food, not for the small shooting gallery in the cellar with three wood-paneled ranges and a choice of shooting targets.

At Bleecker Street he made a left and, when he reached MacDougal Street, he made a right. He stayed on the right hand of the street until he saw the burgundy canopy outside number 77. The small 'speak-easy' window in the door of the Rifle Club slid open to reveal two eyes under thick black bushy eyebrows. The eyes examined the man outside and, seconds later, the door opened to let him enter.

"Sal, we have your table. Can I take your coat?"

"Grazie, Nick. Is Mike here?"

"No, Sal. Not yet. But you know Mike. Never been early for anything. But I'm sure he'll be here soon. Why don't I show you to the table and we'll get you a drink while you wait."

Sal was ushered between the tables of the very busy dining room, acknowledging a nod here and a smile there. Well known faces punctuated the room, from prominent labour leaders to captains of industry as well as a couple of movie stars.

Waiting for Mike, he settled for a campari and soda and the menu, and reminisced about the first time he'd met Mike Stiglianese. He'd invited his attorney Ed Burke, an Irishman, to dine here at the club and Ed had asked if he could bring a close friend. Turned out that that friend was Mike Stiglianese, another club member. They'd never crossed paths before but they'd become good friends in the years since then. *How many years*, mused Sal, *must be ten at least.* As Sal got to know Mike better he learned of the affection Mike had for Burke. And the debt Mike felt could never be repaid. Mike's export/import business had been raided by the Feds and Mike had been charged with shipping technology to China, technology that could be used in that country's nuclear development program, technology banned from export by the US government. Mike claimed that he was being framed, being set up by an 'Elliot Ness' fed who wanted to make a big name for himself in Washington, who had targeted Mike Stiglianese because he was related to one of the New York families, and who thought he could penetrate the family if he targeted a vulnerable member. If convicted, Mike would surely have spent the rest of his life in prison. Or he would have been forced to cut

257

a deal with 'Elliot Ness'.   Exactly where the fed wanted him.   Ed Burke had defended him with the force of an F. Lee Bailey, exposed the fed conspiracy, destroyed 'Elliot Ness', and obtained dismissal of all charges against Mike. Mike felt he owed Ed his life.

"So what's good, Sal?"

Sal looked up to see Mike hovering over him with a big grin on his face. A large overweight friendly man, Sal always thought of a teddy bear when he saw him.

"You're late. I'm ready to order, Mike. What kept you?"

"Agh, you don't wanna know," and sitting down, he asked again, "So what's good, Sal?"

Sal handed him the menu and replied, "I'm goin' for the *Barilla Lasagnette al Ragù di Carne,* the barilla Lasagna with the braised meat sauce. Can't get pasta anywhere else like it.   Unless you go to Italy."

"Looks good. Think I'll have the same."

Sal laughed to himself. Ever since they'd been coming here, Mike had always waited to see what Sal ordered and often copied him. Sal felt flattered in a strange way.

Halfway through their meal and a good bottle of Barolo, Sal ventured the topic that had made him invite Mike to dinner.

"Ed Burke. He went back to Ireland last year, didn't he?"

"Yeah."

"Do you keep in touch?"

"No, you know how things are? You mean to, but ..."

"But you know where he lives, don't you?"

"Sure. He gave me his address and his phone number when he left. What's this all about? Why all these questions about Ed?"

Sal paused, sipped his wine, looked furtively at the tables nearby, and said in low tones, "You know Big Tony, don't you? Big Tony Purelli?"

"Yeah. What about him?"

"You know Big Tony's an independent *contractor*?"

"I hear what I hear. That's all. I got nothin' to do with the business."

"I know that. Well, I know of a contract that Big Tony got a couple of days ago. Outta the country."

"So whatta I care?"

"The contract's in Ireland. Some government guy over there. And a bonus for a lawyer named Burke."

"Fuck! You're shittin' me, right!"

"Mike, would I fuck around with you on somethin' like this?"

Mike's easy going face had now changed into something sombre, like a summer sky that had been invaded by thunder clouds.

"Jesus, I'd better warn Ed."

"That's exactly why I told you."

"Do you know who's doin' the job?"

"No, but I can nose around. See who's headin' outta town. Give you some names. Couple o'days, OK?"

They finished the Barolo, skipped dessert, and settled for two espressos. This wasn't a time to linger over the sambucca.

Three days later, Mike got a call from Sal giving him two names and the expected date of departure. Mike got on the phone immediately to Ed Burke in Dublin. After the call Burke found himself in a quandary. Two hit men on their way to Dublin to whack the

259

Tanaiste - and himself as well if he happened to get in the way.

Whack the Tanaiste! Burke's mind flitted through the possibilities. *Maybe that's the kind of justice he deserves. Let's face it, he killed the woman I loved and I'll never be able to prove it. Never see him stand in a courtroom for a single day. The Taoiseach, as conniving and devious as Machiavelli, won't permit it. He wants him shunted to the side, ostracised and barred from political life. Yeah, the Taoiseach will settle for the Tanaiste's resignation. On the grounds of health. Manning will never resign. I know he won't. And he won't be brought to justice either. So this is the justice he deserves. Isn't it?*

He went to the drinks cabinet, poured himself a jigger of Black Bush, and took it back to his chair in the living room. According to Mike, the two *contractors* were due in Dublin in three days time. Plenty of time to head back to Connemara and let them execute their summary justice. As he sipped the whiskey, he contemplated that position. But it didn't sit well with him. *Too long working for my mob clients in New York,* he thought, *it's so easy to see their world as the real world, the world of the eye for an eye and a tooth for a tooth. In a way I came back here to get away from that world. And now it's following me here. No, no! I can't do this! I've got to stop it. I can't turn a blind eye to this.*

He finished the whiskey, then picked up the phone and called Brian Cosgrave, the Minister of Justice. Cosgrave wasn't in his office so he left an urgent message. Next he called Tom Buckley and Tom agreed to meet him within the hour. Finally he dialled Sean Coyne and got no answer until he remembered that Sean had moved back in with his mother. He searched through his wallet and found the telephone number that Sean had given him a few days earlier. Scratched on a piece of torn envelope, he hadn't had time to transfer it to his address book. He dialled the number.

70

At thirty-four Sean Coyne had buried his father and moved back into the family home to take care of his sixty-five year old mother in the early stages of Alzheimers.

Married at nineteen, separated at twenty-one, and divorced in 2003 when Ireland finally made divorce legal. Sean had led a hedonist lifestyle for the past ten years. Gifted with boundless energy, his big open face acted as a magnet for many young ladies. But as soon as any relationship turned serious, Sean moved on. He feared commitment, fearing failure itself. But his lifestyle had worn thin in the past three years and had turned into too many hung-over mornings that were beginning to affect his career. Only his talent had saved him but he knew that that wouldn't last. So, in a sense, his father's death and the need to care for his mother saved him.

He was in the kitchen preparing tea and toast for his mother when he heard the phone ring. She answered it and he could tell from her voice and her questions that she felt uncomfortable. *Probably another damn sales call*, he thought.

He walked through to the hallway and found his mother standing there with the phone in her hand, looking bewildered, "I don't know who this is. But he says he wants to speak to you, Sean."

Sean took the phone from his mother and said, "Hello."

"Sean, I need to see you right away. Can you leave there soon?"

"What happened?"

"I can't explain over the phone. I'll just say this – we've got big trouble!"

"OK! I'll get there as soon as I can."

71

An hour later Sean Coyne arrived at Ed Burke's apartment in Ballsbridge. When Ed opened the door, Sean could see the anxious look in his eyes.

"Ed, what's happening?"

"Sean, thanks for coming.   I asked Tom Buckley to join us. He should be here any minute. Can I hold it till he arrives. Let me get you a coffee."

"Coffee! Jeez, you look like you need something a little stronger!"

"You're right! But I'm afraid I'll have to take a rain check on that."

Sean sat down and flipped on Sky news as Ed went off to the kitchen to make the coffee. The usual daily headlines greeted him: dozens killed by a suicide bomber in Iraq,   British police arrest five suspected terrorists in Halifax and Birmingham. Same deadly daily dose. Switched to Fox, America's *fair and balanced* news. Amazing! Totally biased right wing news commentary promoting itself as fair and balanced, hosted by a chatting group of presenters who thought their humour and repartee was captivating. Looked like somebody had spiked their coffee. Disgusted, Sean turned off the TV as Ed returned with a large pot of coffee.

"Ed, when you see the madness in the world, our problems seem to pale in comparison."

264

"One damn good thing, we've stopped the killing. We're not bombing Harrod's in London or blowing up the British Prime Minister in Brighton any more. But don't let that delude you. There's more than one way to take away people's freedom and democracy. And the Tanaiste has found it."

The doorbell rang and Ed opened it for Tom Buckley.

"Tom, Sean Coyne. Don't believe you've met."

"Sean, see your face in the papers all the time. It's almost as though I do know you."

"Yeah, Tom. It's hard for me to stay anonymous."

Tom joined them and accepted a coffee. Then he looked at Ed.

"Sounded serious when you called. What's up?"

"OK. A few hours ago I received a phone call from an old friend in New York. Someone close to the mob. I'll repeat what he told me."

Ed then talked about Mike Stiglianese, how he trusted him and what he'd told him about the two hit men on their way to kill the Tanaiste. For a while, both Tom and Ed sat there incredulous. Then they almost drowned each other out in their haste to talk. Both had the same thought.

"Tom, you go first."

"Damn it, stupid of me but my first thoughts were that this was great. Manning deserves it. Save the taxpayer the costs of a trial. Nice and simple."

"Those are the first crazy thoughts that entered my mind too."

Ed looked at both of them and agreed. Then he teased out the matter with them, as he had in his own mind earlier. Reluctantly they all agreed that they'd have to stop it. At that moment the phone rang.

"Ed Burke."

"Brian Cosgrave.You called. Sounded urgent."

"It's critical. I can't talk over the phone. Can I come to your office now."

"OK, get here as soon as you can."

Ed put down the phone and explained, "That was the Minister of Justice. I have to see him now. I'll call you as soon as I can."

72

Brian Cosgrave looked stunned after he'd heard what Ed Burke had to say and his language departed from the usual, " Damnit! The balls of it! To think they can send hired killers into this country to take out a government minister. Who the fuck do they think they are?"

"Brian, these guys are getting half a million. It's just another job for them."

"Well, it might be just another job in the States but they've got to think again if they're going to try that here."

"We've lost our innocence! We're no longer a provincial little backwater where things like this only happen in foreign countries. Besides, if my friend Mike hadn't called me this would have gone down without us knowing a damn thing about it. And we would be having a state funeral. And the nation would get another martyr. Jesus, we don't need any more martyrs. I'd vomit if Manning was elevated to martyrdom."

"So who's behind this?"

"I've thought about that as well. Stiglianese said the contract came from a big player on the business scene. *Another countryman of yours*, he said to me. He didn't know the name but he was sure that the guy was into real estate and banking. And he thought he owned a lot of those designer Irish pubs that you find everywhere these days, from Moscow to Timbuktu."

"You named him. You know that, don't you?"

"Yes. TP McGrady."

"Once an IRA man, always an IRA man. They never change their stripes, you know."

"Yeah, killing was a skill he learned before any other, wasn't it? But, think about it, this hit was ordered by us!"

"Have you taken leave of your senses!"

"No, no, think about it. We set out to undermine the Tanaiste with his backers. Smear him in the papers. Destroy his credibility, plant rumours about him. Spook McGrady and his gang behind him, make life too hot for them, get them to abandon Manning. We were too successful. We never thought this through. We never considered that they'd kill Manning!"

"I never even considered that possibility. Neither did the Taoiseach."

"Well, you'd better brief him on what's going down."

"You know when these killers are coming here?"

"Three days from now. Mike gave me their description and even the flight they've booked. Aer Lingus, arrives in Dublin around seven thirty in the morning."

"But what about guns, weapons?"

"I'm sure they're picking those little items up when they get here. These guys are professionals. And they operate internationally. Besides, I'll bet McGrady's old buddies didn't decommission every weapon they had. Nobody really believes they did, do they?"

Brian Cosgrave stood up and stretched his body, as though that would clear his mind. He walked over to the window and looked out on Dublin. He knew that no matter what he did the opposition would roast him in the *Dail* over his handling of this. That is, if the truth ever reached the public. Turning around, he squared his shoulders, the body language of a man who'd made up his mind.

"I'm going to set up a meeting with the Garda Commissioner. No later than the morning. Stand by for my call."

"Tell Commissioner Clooney that I want Detective Buckley to attend. He's been involved in all of this since Manning's wife was killed. And he knows about this. I sought his opinion before I saw you."

"Well, I don't know what the Commissioner will think about that. But I'll tell him. He likes to make his own assignments."

"Can you find out the Tanaiste's schedule over the next three days?"

"Right. That is important. I'll have that with me when we meet again."

73

At nine the next morning, Ed Burke and Tom Buckley joined the Minister of Justice in Garda Commissioner Clooney's office.   The Commissioner looked at Tom Buckley.

"Detective Buckley, this is highly irregular. You're here because Mr. Burke asked my permission. I know you're a key member of my homicide team but a matter of this magnitude wouldn't normally be discussed in your presence.   So I've made an exception.   From this minute consider yourself assigned to this."

"Thank you, Commissioner."

"Let's hope you'll still want to thank me when this is all over. If it will ever be over.   Mr. Burke, Brian has filled me in on this dirty business. Is there anything more I should know?"

"No, Commissioner."

"Anything to add?"

"Only that I briefed the Taoiseach last night and he will give us his full support. He plans to call you and discuss extra security. And I have the Tanaiste's itinerary over the coming week.   I have a copy for each of you."

Brian Cosgrave handed out a one page schedule of commitments for David Manning for each of the next eight days.

The Commissioner asked, "When are these killers planning to be here, Mr. Burke?"

"Day after tomorrow. They arrive at Dublin airport around seven thirty in the morning. Aer Lingus, New York to Dublin."

"So it's the Tanaiste's whereabouts on that day and the subsequent days that we should focus on. Right?"

"Right. But I believe that they won't prolong the assignment. These killers, as you call them, are experts. They'll want to be in and out of the country in a couple of days. So I'd suggest that we focus on the Tanaiste's whereabouts on the day they arrive and the two following days," said Ed Burke.

"I've already considered that," said Brian Cosgrave, "and I examined this schedule closely as soon as I got my hands on it. You'll see that Manning is tied up in Government Buildings all day on the day of their arrival. Meetings of the Dail followed by various committee meetings. A day filled with bureaucracy. I think they'll want to get at him somewhere else, don't you think?"

"Yes, I'm looking at this. The next day would be perfect. In the morning, he's opening a new hotel in Smithfield, right in the heart of the city. But it's the afternoon that's attractive. He's attending a GAA event in County Roscommon. And they've taken over the dining room in Strokestown Castle for a reception later in the day. Perfect location. Open spaces, little chance of collateral damage."

"I'm not so sure," said Commissioner Clooney, "you have to consider the getaway. It's easier to disappear in the city. But out in Roscommon they'd have to get back to Dublin or at least to Shannon. You don't have a time and date for their flight out again, do you?"

"No, I wasn't able to get that.   I asked my source in New York but he drew a blank on it."

"OK. I'll assign someone to it. I'll have them check all the airlines, every manifest over the next month."

"Can you check on the planned flights of private commercial planes? "

"You don't think ..."

"I don't know.   I'm sure that the Justice Minister has discussed our suspicion about who might have ordered this.   If we're right, that man has a couple of Gulfstreams at his availability at all times."

"I'll check that out as well.   Now, let's get down to business.   Here's what I propose," said the Commissioner, as he stood up, came around his desk and faced them all in his usual presentation stance. With no pointer and no whiteboard, he had to rely on his hands for emphasis.

"I'm going to assign a special three man team to this case. And, Tom, I want you to head the team. I want you to meet these thugs when they land at the airport and I want you to stick to them like glue. We won't detain them for questioning. I want to see who meets them and where they go because I have two objectives here, the protection of the Tanaiste and the unmasking of the man who funded this. And I think the latter may be more important than the former.   I want to keep it low profile without raising the eyebrows of Charlie Crowe of RTE. All we need is him on our heels in the middle of this. He's like a terrier when he smells something afoot. Sinks his teeth in right away.   I do not want the media anywhere near this. I understand that you're pretty chummy with that crime reporter Sean Coyne. Keep him well away from this!"

Ed Burke didn't answer. He was not going to keep Sean Coyne away. Too many years in America instilled in him the first amendment rights and the freedom of the press. He wanted a record of this and he trusted Sean Coyne to give an accurate one. It wouldn't be a whitewash from anonymous government sources.

"And, Mr. Burke, after you point out these hit men to my team, I want you out of it. Do you understand?"

"Commissioner, I can't make that promise."

"It's for your own good. You're on their hit list too. That's what you've told us, haven't you?"

"So I understand. But what do you want me to do? Run away and hide somewhere."

"It's only common sense. I know you're not a coward. But it's only natural to have some fears."

"Yes, I'm afraid. I sure as hell am! But I want to be around when these guys make their play. I have faith in Tom and his team. Besides, these gangsters don't know that their cover's been blown. And I want to see the end of David Manning!"

"If you wanted him dead, why did you tell us about this at all?"

"Commissioner, I thought pretty hard about that. Believe me, I was tempted."

"So I don't understand. You're going to save his life now. Why hang around and take the risk."

"This is the end of Manning whether he lives or dies. It's the end of him. And I want to look him in the eye!"

"Mr. Burke, it's your life. Don't say I didn't warn you?"

74

Ed Burke's alarm went off at five thirty am, too early. He hadn't slept very well, waking up frequently with snatches of bizarre, nightmarish dreams lingering in his mind. *It's the day that's in it*, he said to himself, as he stepped under the warm shower.

Outside at six am, dressed and cupping a warm traveller mug of strong coffee in his right hand, he opened the rear side door of Tom Buckley's unmarked garda car.

"Right on time, Tom."

"Traffic'd be murder on the M1 north to the airport if we left any later.   Gerry, say hello to Ed Burke."

The plainclothes garda in the driver's seat glanced back and said, "Good, morning, Mr. Burke. At least it's not raining."

"Mornin' Gerry.   Call me, Ed.   OK?"

"They're due to land at seven-thirty. I'd like to get there no later than seven, in case they have the wind at their back and make it in a little earlier. But you can't get anyone in the airlines to talk to you these days.   The people have been replaced by machines!"

They got lucky and reached the airport at a quarter to seven.   Gerry pulled the car into the kerb outside the arrivals building and Ed and Tom got out and walked into the terminal.   They checked the arrival times on the video screens and saw that the flight was due in from New York at seven twenty. So they got two more coffees, the morning papers and relaxed in the waiting area. They chose seats off to the side with an unobstructed view of the doors through which their targets would arrive. Mike Stiglianese had given Ed the names and a fair description. One tall Sylvester Stallone type, heavier and paunchier looking, and one Al Pacino type, slicker and meaner looking. Ed decided to refer to them as Sly and Al.

At ten minutes past seven, 'landed' began to flash on the flight info on the screen overhead.

"Looks like they had a wind at their back after all," said Tom.

"Good. I hate hanging around airports," said Ed.

At exactly seven twenty-five Sly and Al walked through the arrival doors with a weekender bag each. They were unmistakeable.   Travelling light.   They stood in the middle of the exit area, blocking other passengers who were pushing their way through to be greeted by waiting family and friends.   Soon a limousine driver spotted them and waved. *Must have had the same description as me*, thought Ed. They walked up to him and he led them out of the area. Ed and Tom followed at a discreet distance.

Outside, the driver guided them to a waiting limousine. Ed and Tom re-joined Gerry in the garda car and waited.   The limousine pulled out and they followed.

The morning rush hour traffic was building now and travel into the city much slower. Forty-five minutes later, the limousine dropped Sly and Al at the front entrance to Bewley's Hotel in Ballsbridge. A tourist hotel in the right neighbourhood. Perfect location.

275

Tom and Ed hopped out of their car and entered the hotel, taking seats off to the side in the large spacious lobby. Sitting behind their newspapers, they watched Sly and Al checking in. There was only one other person at the reception desk, a business type and he was checking out. As he stepped away, Sly and Al were greeted by the young lady in reception. *Sounds foreign,* thought Tom to himself, *probably Polish or something. No Irish in these jobs any more.*

Check-in completed, they didn't take the elevator to their rooms. Instead, they took the central stairs under the glass canopy down to the lower level towards the lounge and O'Connell's restaurant. Ed and Tom waited till their heads were out of view and then followed. When they reached the bottom of the stairs they didn't see them. The dimly lit lounge sprawled large and wide, making it easy to lose someone. Then they heard the voice, unmistakeably Brooklyn. Staying out of view, they could still see a man sitting in a recessed area beneath the stairway. It was Shane Braddock. Sly and Al stood facing him.

Braddock had waited in the large sprawling lounge one floor beneath the reception foyer. Dim lit, with seating well spread out behind pillars, it suited his purpose well. No need to attract attention. As arranged he wore a red apple in his lapel. The Big Apple, the sign of New York.

He didn't have to wait long.

"Mr. Braddock. I believe you're expecting us."

Shane Braddock looked up, and up again, into the face of a towering beefy six-footer. A younger, slimmer man stood beside him.

"Yes, I am. Won't you join me."

After these unnecessary civilities, mainly for public consumption, Braddock said:

"You know why you're here and I know why as well.   I'm led to believe that you are specialists at this type of investment write-off. And that you will ensure that the write-off does not lead to any excitement in the market. So let's make this brief. I do not want to be here a minute longer than necessary."

He took a package from his jacket and, sitting between both men, carefully introduced them to its contents which included photographs and an itinerary. A smaller envelope contained only one photo and an address. They were advised that this was not their main objective but, if the opportunity presented itself, then they would earn a nice bonus. He also gave them a number to call where a man would arrange to provide them with the tools of their trade.

They were a quick study and Braddock rose to leave. The meeting had taken fifteen minutes.

Even though they did not hear the details, Ed Burke and Tom Buckley knew that they'd seen the contract specs being delivered. They waited until Braddock was gone and then they left.

75

Tom Buckley thought he would be early for the hotel opening in Smithfield. He didn't want to be the first there. His team had told them that Sly and Al were on the move, most probably headed there.

"Ed, let me drop you off in Ballsbridge. You shouldn't be here!"

"Goddamit, Tom, ever since I woke up and saw Pia dead in that room in St. Cleran's the only thing I wanted was the end of this Tanaiste. Are you going to deny me that?"

"You know we can't guarantee your safety. You know that, don't you?"

"Yeah, yeah, I know, I know!"

That was the end of it. Tom Buckley had made his pitch. He hadn't expected success and he was worried. He felt responsible for Ed Burke but he knew that the protection of the Tanaiste was his principal responsibility. He glanced across and saw Ed sitting there, looking straight ahead, his jaw firmly set. Neither of them thought that the hit men would try anything at this open event. They probably wanted to get an up-close look at their assignment.

Gerry, the driver, parked their car on a side street beside a Chinese emporium, a market that sold every knick knack made in China. A young Chinese man, standing in the doorway, smiled at them. Eager for business, hoping to make sales to many of the people who would congregate for the hotel opening.

At ten am Smithfield was already filled with people crowding the open square in front of the new hotel. Dwarfed by the tall space-age lights that guarded the space, Burke had the surreal feeling that he was attending a Star Trek convention. The opening ceremony was scheduled for eleven am. Time for them to reconnoitre, to try and locate Sly and Al. They decided to split up, agreeing to meet in thirty minutes at a spot where they could observe the ceremony. Tom Buckley went clockwise, Ed Burke anticlockwise, and Gerry went right into the middle. Ed stuck close to the buildings, taking his time, waiting till he had a clear view before moving on. Fifteen minutes later he saw them and he saw Tom Buckley at the same time. He waited until Tom joined him.

"They're not hiding, are they?"

"No. They probably think that they'll pass as another couple of American tourists. Thick on the ground in Dublin these days."

"Well, they've positioned themselves well. They can't be more than twenty-five yards from the event. Any closer and they'll be looking down the Tanaiste's throat!"

"I have a bad feeling."

"You don't think they'll attempt it here, right in front of all these people!"

"No, my common sense tells me no ... but I still have a bad feeling about this. And you shouldn't fucking be here. You know that, don't you?"

279

Ed gave him a pained look and asked, "Where's the extra security?"

"Must be well hidden. I only see a couple of traffic cops keeping an eye on the crowd. They're here to keep order if necessary. Unlikely at an event like this."

"Well, I don't see anyone that looks like security."

"Probably well hidden. Easy in this crowd, you know."

Gerry emerged from the crowd. The two other members of Tom Buckley's team were with him. They decided to move as close to Sly and Al as they could without raising suspicion. Tom ordered Ed to stay where he was. Microphones were being set up and a red carpet rolled out. A ribbon had already been tied across the front entrance to the new hotel. A shining brass plaque embedded in the marble pillar memorialised the event, stating that the hotel had been officially opened by David Manning, Tanaiste and Minister for Trade and Industry.

Ed checked his watch. Ten minutes to eleven. The mayor appeared, chatting affably with two dowager looking ladies. He was soon followed by the hotel owner and major property developer, Harry Mulholland, accompanied by his minders, two young men in well-tailored business suits. Then the key hotel staff appeared, the manager, concierge, the head chef, sommelier, head waiters, receptionists. Conversation had lulled to a constant buzz as people strained to get a better view

At exactly three minutes past eleven, the Tanaiste arrived with a staff aide and a garda clearing a way through the people congregated behind the temporary barrier. Smiling and waving to the crowd, he greeted the mayor and gripped Harry

Mulholland by the hand and held it for the longest time.

Finally the opening ceremony got underway. The mayor welcomed everyone, praised the architects, and everyone involved, and then invited Harry Mulholland to speak. A man as economic with words as he was with his wallet, he introduced the Tanaiste and left the microphone. That's when the oratory of the morning began. The Tanaiste looked like he was here to make a major political speech. He was already campaigning for Taoiseach. It was so obvious. Five minutes into the speech, Ed found himself shifting his stance from leg to leg, not out of tiredness but out of impatience and boredom. He'd been observing Sly and Al as the proceedings commenced but the Tanaiste had distracted him. Now he looked and they were gone.

A loud bang somewhere ahead shook the ground beneath him and a cloud of dense smoke enveloped the crowd like a thick fog. People started screaming. Panic set in and the crowd tried to flee, pushing and shoving and bashing into each other. Ed had only one thought. Get to the Tanaiste.

That's when he heard the gunfire and his worst fears took shape. Pushing his way through the fleeing crowd, oblivious to his own safety, he elbowed his way towards the Tanaiste. The smoke irritated his throat and he took out a handkerchief he always carried and held it over his mouth and nose. He kept moving until he tripped and fell flat on his side. Stunned and hurt, he struggled to his feet as the smoke began to clear. He felt a hand supporting him and looked into the face of Tom Buckley. The people had fled and he could see Gerry and another garda on Tom's team stand looking down at a body on the

281

ground.   Even at that angle, Sly was instantly recognizable to Tom.

"Is he ...?"

"Yeah, he's dead. We got him but his partner got away. He won't get far. We have every garda on full alert, and the area is cordoned off. He doesn't know this town. We'll get him!"

"What about the Tanaiste?"

"They got him. He's still alive, but barely. The ambulance is on its way."

The smoke had now cleared, the crowd gone, and a few of the hotel staff crowded around the Tanaiste as he lay on the ground near the microphone where he'd been in full flow only minutes earlier.

Where's the extra security the Taoiseach promised, thought Ed and just as quickly it hit him, *conniving and devious, that's what he is ...never intended to provide extra security, probably never told the Tanaiste that he was under any threat whatsoever...oh, yeah, conniving and devious...*

He walked to the Tanaiste and knelt down beside him. Blood oozed out of the Tanaiste's mouth and his eyes stared wide and scared. He tried to speak but only choked in his own blood. Ed Burke could not resist looking him in the eye, just as he'd hoped to do. He said nothing but he didn't have to. David Manning knew a face filled with revenge, even this close to death.

Tom Buckley reached down and pulled Ed to his feet.

"It's over. Let it go!"

Sirens blocked out all other sounds as four gardai on motorcycles ran the vanguard for an ambulance with flashing red lights. In seconds, it seemed, they applied pressure bandages to the Tanaiste's wounds, cleared his airway, placed him on a stretcher, loaded him into the ambulance, turned around and screamed out of Smithfield, on their way to the nearby Mater Hospital.

76

The Mater Hospital was on high alert as the ambulance carrying the Tanaiste rolled up to the front door of A&E, the Accident and Emergency department. A full trauma team waited inside.

News travelled fast. Curiosity seekers as well as concerned citizens stood in small groups speaking in hushed tones outside. Gardaí had already cordoned off the hospital. RTE television were establishing a base on the opposite side of the street where their cameras could capture every coming and going. Charlie Crowe was expected on site at any moment.

Inside the hospital, the trauma surgeon, Dr. Alan Carson, moved around the stretcher as nurses cut the clothing from the body. The Tanaiste was unconscious. Dr. Carson checked the airway to ensure the Tanaiste was breathing. He checked the pulse and checked for any major haemorrhage. The pressure bandages applied by the paramedics had temporarily clotted the wounds. He checked for head and spinal cord damage and probed for any other hidden injuries. Then he had the nurses insert two large IVs, one in either arm, and start administering IV solution as fast as possible. He drew blood for lab tests and to cross and type for blood transfusion. He placed a Foley catheter in the bladder and inserted special lines to measure blood pressure and heart function.

But even now Dr. Carson could see the abdomen swelling, a sure sign of massive internal bleeding. He'd have to operate immediately.

Ed Burke and Tom Buckey arrived at the Mater Hospital at about the same time as Dr. Alan Carson started to operate to save the life of the Tanaiste. Stepping out of the car, they were immediately spotted by the RTE News crew. Charlie Crowe almost ran towards them, sticking a microphone in Ed Burke's face.

"Mr. Burke, can you tell me what happened? Is it true that the Tanaiste's been shot."

Tom Buckley stepped between Ed and Charlie Crowe, "No comment. The Commissioner will be issuing a statement later."

But Charlie Crowe persisted, "Mr. Burke, has the attempt on the Tanaiste's life got anything to do with the recent murder of his wife? You were there at that time too. What have you got to do with this, Mr. Burke?"

But Ed Burke didn't answer. He followed Tom Buckley across the street where the guards on duty let them enter the hospital. They were met inside the door by a hospital spokesman who was handling all communication regarding the Tanaiste.

Answering their questions, he said, "No, the Tanaiste's in surgery as I speak. No, I don't know his condition. No, it'll be at least two or three hours before we know anything. And then you will probably hear it from Dr. Alan Carson himself. He's the trauma surgeon who's treating the Tanaiste. May I offer you a room where you can wait or use the phone in the meantime?"

They thanked him and accepted the room. Once inside, Ed collapsed on a chair.

"There's a coffee machine in the hallway. Can I get you a cup," asked Tom.

"Yeah, and put a good shot of brandy in it!"

"Damn right. You need it. We both do but that'll have to wait for a while."

When Tom left the room Ed reached for the phone and called Sean Coyne, "Sean, I want you to have the exclusive on all of this. Charlie Crowe's outside prancing around like a cat on a hot griddle but I could tell by his questions that he knows nothing. Nothing at all. So, can you make the first page in the evening edition? You can, good. OK, here goes. Here's a first person account of today's events. You know enough to add as much speculation and innuendo that you think McDevitt will go with. Enough to keep you short of a lawsuit. OK?"

Tom arrived back with the two coffees as Ed was relaying the morning's events to Sean Coyne. Hanging up, he said, "I wanted to get the story out there. Sean should have first crack at it."

"Did I say anything?"

"No, you did not."

"Well, you should know me well enough by this time. I've taken big risks over the last few weeks. It's about time the people knew what's goin' on."

Gulping half his coffee, he grimaced. *At least it's wet*, he thought, but that's all he could say about it, s*ure isn't Starbucks.*

Picking up the phone once more, he made another call. To Maria Lane.

"Oh, I was so worried. I heard about the shooting of the Tanaiste and I knew you'd be in the middle of it."

"I'm OK, honest I am. I couldn't tell you anything in advance. I didn't know until two days ago and I've been on the run ever since."

286

"Where are you now?"

"I'm in the Mater. The Tanaiste is being operated on. We won't know the outcome for a couple of hours. I want to stay close till then."

"Call me when you can."

"I will. Is your boss around?"

"Funny you should mention that. When the news came in of this shooting he made one phone call to Shane Braddock and got out of here real fast. As though he was leaving a sinking ship. Does this have anything to do with him?"

"What are you doing this evening?"

"I'm waiting for a call from you."

"Well, keep the evening open. I want to see you and I'll tell you all about it then."

He hung up the phone and gulped down the rest of the coffee. Somehow it didn't seem so bad this time.

At four pm, Ed was slightly dozing from fatigue and Tom was sunk in the daily paper when a weary looking doctor entered their room unannounced.

"Gentleman, I am Dr. Alan Carson and I understand that you are the Gardai involved in this case. I was asked by our hospital administrator to brief you before I speak to the media."

"Thank you, Doctor," answered Tom, considering it unnecessary to enlighten the good doctor that Ed was not a member of the Gardaí.

"How is the Tanaiste, Dr. Carson?" asked Ed.

"Not good I'm afraid. He's regained consciousness but he's under sedation and I doubt if he'll be able to see anyone for a day or two."

"Will he make a full recovery, Doctor?" asked Tom.

287

"No, I'm afraid that he won't. His spinal cord was damaged by one of the bullets. Irreparably I think. It's unlikely that he'll ever walk again. And he has some bruising to the lung so we have him on a ventilator. But his vital signs are strong and I see no reason to believe that he won't make it. That's my prognosis at present."

That was it. Brief and brutal. Dr. Carson left. The assembled media waited outside for him. The doctor would be an instant star on the evening news, not just RTE, but SKY and the BBC, and CNN would pick the story up as well.

77

Ed Burke sat in the Jacuzzi soaking the evening away when the doorbell rang. His watch on the cabinet top nearby said eight pm. *Aw, hell! I forgot about the time!* Jumping out of the Jacuzzi he towelled himself quickly, pulled on a sweater and sports trousers, and ran towards the door.

"You're dripping wet!" Laughter convulsed Maria Lane as she stood at his front door, a carrier bag in each hand.

"Can you believe it? I was in the Jacuzzi and forgot about the time," said Ed sheepishly as he kissed Maria on the cheek and ushered her through the door.

"For medicinal purposes," she said, placing a carrier bag on the table and opening it to reveal a bottle of fine wine and a Drambuie.

"Drambuie! The yellow dram. My favourite nightcap."

She headed towards the kitchen with the second carrier bag, saying, "I hope you have a wok."

"What are you doing?"

"I'm going to cook dinner."

"But I've made a reservation."

"Well, cancel it! You need some TLC tonight. And I want to hear what happened from the horse's mouth. So make yourself useful. Open the wine."

The steam rose from the stir fried chicken, prawns, Chinese vegetables and noodles that sat in the wok in the centre of the table. Maria filled their bowls for the second time and Ed replenished their glasses. He raised his glass and clinked Maria's.

"Slainte!"

"You are very talented. This is delicious."

"Thank you. Now, tell me what happened today before you get all mushy."

Ed started with the phone call from Mike Stiglianese three days ago and ended with the briefing he'd received four hours ago from Dr. Alan Carson in the Mater Hospital.

"So he's going to live."

"Well, that's what the doctor said. But he'll never walk again."

"I want him to live. He's got to live. I want him to testify against McGrady. I know it's Manning you hate but, for my money, the real evil is McGrady. He destroyed my brother and he's been using and destroying people ever since. The Tánaiste's been his creation. He's the Frankenstein here. God, how I want to see him put away for the rest of his life!"

The tears were rolling down Maria's cheeks and Ed reached over and took her out of the chair. They stood up and he took her in his arms. She cried on his shoulders as he caressed her hair. Taking her face in his hands he kissed the salty tears from her eyes, the tip of her nose, and then her lips. Gently at first and then with a ferocity that surprised them both. Maria blew out the candle on the table and Ed led her by the hand to the bedroom.

78

Next day Ed Burke tracked TP McGrady down at his members club at the Royal Dublin Society. Maria Lane had arranged the meeting and TP McGrady was expecting him. Not far from his apartment, the taxi dropped him off in a few minutes outside the Members Club in the RDS on Merrion Road in Ballsbridge. Dublin 4, the only address worth having for a man like TP.

Ed stood in the middle of the magnificent reception hall, stunned by the oil paintings, the crystal chandeliers and the regal high ceilings. A place of power and majesty, designed to convey precisely that. A sweeping mahogany staircase led up to the private rooms on the next level.

The Members Club lay to the left of the reception hall. Ed followed the long corridor with the sandstone walls and art everywhere. He passed the library and sneaked a peak at its skylights and illuminated glass panels. At the end of the corridor he found the burgundy red bar with its cream pillars and wooden floor. TP McGrady sat sipping a scotch.

"Ah, Mr. Burke, good to see you. What can I get you?"

"Oh, something simple. Just a beer I think. Carlsberg."

"Let's go to a table. They'll bring your beer."

TP chose a corner table. They were early, eleven thirty, and members who lunched there hadn't arrived yet. As they sat down, the waiter arrived with Ed's beer.

"I only agreed to see you Mr. Burke out of a sense of curiosity."

"And what makes you curious?"

"Simple. I wanted to know how a fellow countryman like yourself with the great privilege of a Trinity law degree and a successful New York law career could end up so fucked up. If you know what I mean."

"Are you trying to bait me? Because if you are, it won't work."

"Bait you, Mr. Burke? You surely can't be serious. You are a fool. You left this country and you should have stayed away."

"You'd have liked that, wouldn't you?"

"What do you know? Pretending to take the high moral ground. You left. We stayed. I fought to free this country. From its past as much as from its colonial rulers. You didn't stay and fight. You're a coward. You took the easy way out. So you have not earned the right to come back here and criticise!"

"Criticise! That's rich! You're not building a nation here, McGrady. You're raping it. You're not a democrat. You never were. As far as I'm concerned, with people like you running the country, we've simply exchanged colonial despots for our own home grown variety!"

"You know nothing. You'd have us live in poverty. Do you know how many new jobs we're creating year on year? Do you know how many millionaires were created in this country every single month during the past year? Do you know that? It takes power and the guts to exercise it ? That's how we do it. Do you think that your simple minded ideas of democracy of the people for the people could accomplish that?   Even your US of America knows those noble sounding words are a load of shite. That's the country you emulate, the country you chose over this one. So don't come in here to lecture me."

"That's not why I came to see you. I came here to tell you that I know you have blood on your hands!"

"Now you've gone too far!"

"I thought you were curious."

"But I don't have to sit here and have you slander me."

"Mr. McGrady, the Tánaiste is your creation. David Manning is the puppet of you and your corrupt little circle. A circle that led to the murder of my friend Marty Rainey and the killing of the Tánaiste's own wife. He ordered it. I know that and you know that. The delusion of power that you saddled him with led him to believe he was invincible. That he could get away with anything. Even the murder of his own wife. So he became too hot for you. That's why you imported those two thugs to take care of him, isn't it? Still operating in the gutter, TP!"

"What a fantasy! You're a deranged man, Burke. Nobody in their right mind would believe a word of that. You'd better leave. You've exhausted my curiosity."

"The Tánaiste will survive. And survive to testify against you. You're finished. It's only a matter of time!"

"Get out! Get out right now!"

"Oh, I'd be happy to, McGrady!"

As TP McGrady got redder in the face, Ed Burke walked out with a lightness in his step.

But the Tanaiste did not make it.   That same
afternoon, the nation was informed of his death.
Normal programming was interrupted on RTE and
news   anchors   hurriedly   arranged   special
programmes, with guests from the world of politics,
academia, and commerce.   Previous programmes
were dissected to create a collage of David Manning's
rise to prominence from an abandoned orphan to the
second most powerful man in the land.   And now to
martyrdom, a strange accomplishment in a land at
peace.

79

A State funeral was held for the Tánaiste.

Ed Burke and Sean Coyne attended, Sean as a journalist and Ed out of a sense of disbelief. He still couldn't come to grips with David Manning's death. Sean picked Ed up in Ballsbridge at 10.00 am. The funeral mass was scheduled for 12 noon and they wanted to see who attended.

On the way to the funeral, Sean couldn't resist, "You seem to be in mourning. I didn't know you cared!"

"This funeral should not be taking place."

"Ed, it was a joke, ease up! What do you mean? You think he shouldn't get a State funeral?"

"No, I think he shouldn't be dead at all."

"Whoa! Give me that again!"

"Don't you think it's a bit convenient for him to die. McGrady and gang get off the hook. The Taoiseach averts a national crisis. It seems to me that both of them must be happy today."

"You're not suggesting ..."

295

"Yeah, maybe I am. When that young doctor, what's his name, Alan Carson saw Tom Buckley and me in the hospital he was pretty convincing. He said that Manning would be paralyzed. But he said that he'd live. I believed him. And I still do."

"So you think that someone hastened the Tánaiste on his way?"

"I do. But we'll never prove it."

"You think McGrady did it?"

"I dunno. I met him at the RDS and he didn't seem to be intimidated by the attempted murder of the Tánaiste. He showed no fear when I told him that the Tánaiste would talk. Maybe he knew something I didn't know. Maybe the Tánaiste would have too much to lose if he talked. Millions stashed away somewhere that McGrady was protecting for him. When you're paralyzed millions can buy you a lot of care. A home in the sun in the Bahamas. Private nurses in attendance. If all that was at risk, then McGrady would have nothing to worry about. The Tánaiste would never talk. And that's why McGrady showed no fear."

"But, if Manning was knocked off and it wasn't McGrady, then who ..."

And seeing the look on Ed Burke's face, Sean almost lost control of the car, "No! No! Jesus Christ! You're not thinking what I think you're thinking! The Taoiseach! But that's crazy! Tell me you're not thinking that!"

"Sean, you better keep your eye on the road."

They'd arrived. Large crowds surrounded the church. Sean used his press card to get one of the last parking places left. They squeezed into the back of the church and waited and watched.

Mourners, including VIP guests, members of the political parties and members of the Oireachtas, began arriving at the church. They packed the large church for the two-hour service. The Taoiseach, accompanied by his aide-de-camp, arrived at 11.45am, followed shortly afterwards by the Lord Mayor of Dublin. It seemed to Ed Burke that a smile of satisfaction lingered on the Taoiseach's face as he acknowledged Ed in passing.   Hundreds of politicians, members of the Council of State, MEPs, church leaders, judges, diplomats, local authority members, senior gardaí and representatives of national organisations were present.

Ed Burke and Sean Coyne left after the requiem mass.   They did not follow the cortege to the cemetery.

80

Ed Burke bit his lower lip as construction slowed the traffic to a crawl in Ennis. *When are they going to complete the damn bypass,* he swore to himself, *they'd better wake up around here!*

Thirty minutes later, out of Ennis at last, he put his foot to the floor and flew the rest of the way to Shannon on the new highway.

He felt excited as he walked from the car park to the Arrivals building at Shannon Airport. Ducking between two taxis, he negotiated the swivel door and marvelled at the throng of people: people arriving, people waiting, people hugging and kissing, people looking lost.

Looking at the screen mounted high, he watched the flight information scroll down. *There, there it is,* he said to himself, *E113, Aer Lingus from New York, arriving 7:20 a.m., landed.* His watch read 7:35 a.m. *He'll be here any second now.*

Clusters of people waited expectantly outside the Arrivals doors. A trickle of people emerged, some striding purposefully, others searching anxiously for a face they'd recognize, yet others running and hugging their waiting family and friends.

Ed felt nervous. And couldn't explain the feeling to himself. He had butterflies in his stomach.

298

Then he saw him and his nervous feeling changed to one of pride. Eleven years old, head up, confident, heading towards him, a smile on his face.

"Kevin! Kevin!"

Kevin heard his name and saw his dad waving. He ran towards him. They hugged for ages. So tightly their bodies felt as one. Ed's eyes were wet with tears, happy tears.

He looked over Kevin's shoulder just in time to see a man dodging the clusters of people as he rushed towards them.

AL ...!   Ed had only enough time to push Kevin to the ground before Al stopped, raised a gun, and fired. People scattered in all directions and Ed Burke fell beside his son, blood beginning to stain the front of his shirt.

The private Gulfstream IV jet, cleared for take-off twenty minutes later, lifted into the clear blue skies over Shannon. The lone passenger watched the flashing lights on the police and emergency vehicles clustered around the departures building. He watched the ascent, seeing the patchwork quilt of green below disappear. Levelling off at thirty-one thousand feet, he reached for the phone, dialled a number and sent a two word text: *contract filled.*

LAST DAYS of the TIGER   Pat Mullan

LAST DAYS of the TIGER   Pat Mullan

Pat Mullan was born in Ireland and has lived in England, Canada and the USA. He now lives in Ireland. He has published articles, poetry and short stories in magazines such as *Crannóg, Buffalo Spree, Tales of the Talisman, Writers Post Journal.* His short story, *Galway Girl,* was short-listed for the WOW Awards and was published in the new WOW Magazine in Galway in April 2010.

Recent work has appeared in the anthologies, DUBLIN NOIR (published in the USA by *Akashic Books* and in Ireland and the UK by *Brandon Books)* ,*City-Pick DUBLIN* (published by *Oxygen Books* in 2010 to mark Dublin being chosen as UNESCO'S City of Culture for 2010), and *NOIR by NOIR West* (from Arlen House) in 2014.

His first novel, *The Circle of Sodom,* received two nominations, one for Best First Novel and one for Best Suspense Thriller, at the 2005 *Love Is Murder* conference in Chicago. His second novel, *Blood Red Square*, was published in the US in 2005 and a new edition, published in 2011, is now available on-line as a paperback and as an ebook. His latest novels, *Last Days of the Tiger* and *Creatures of Habit* are now available on-line as ebooks on Amazon Kindle, Barnes & Noble's Nook, Kobo, and elsewhere; they are also available in paperback.

He is a member of *International Thriller Writers, Inc.* and *Mystery Writers of America.*

Visit him at: **www.patmullan.com**

LAST DAYS of the TIGER   Pat Mullan

LAST DAYS of the TIGER   Pat Mullan